Fortune's Hostage

JULIA HARDY

First printed in this edition 2018

Published by Stanfred Publishing 2018.

ISBN: 978-0-9934830-5-9

DEDICATION

For Grant,
My love, my life, my happiness
Thank you for your patience, understanding and
unconditional support

Books written as Julia Hardy

Fortune's Hostage (2018)

Books written as Kelly Clayton

The Jack Le Claire Mystery Series:-

Blood In The Sand (2015)

Blood Ties (2016)

Blood On The Rock (2017)

Coming Winter 2018

CyberSisters – 4 women. Online crime. What do you do when you've lost everything – even your self-respect?

ACKNOWLEDGMENTS

There are many people who have helped me with this novel and been so incredibly supportive.

Jennifer Quinlan (Jenny Q of Historical Editorial) is, as always, my first set of "eyes" and her keen sense of story development keeps me firmly on track and opens up new possibilities. Jenny is also a fabulous copy-editor and always goes the extra mile in everything she does. Jenny has many talents and designed my fabulous cover.

To Suzie Cross and Liz Campbell, many sincere thanks for taking the time to read, to comment and to help me shape and improve Fortune's Hostage.

Heartfelt thanks to Liz Campbell and Kath Middleton for proof-reading. Any remaining mistakes are, as always, my own!

To my fellow Blonde Plotters, Gwyn GB and Deborah Carr, fine writers and great friends. Thank you for your continued support.

Without doubt, my deepest gratitude belongs to my husband, Grant, who is my biggest champion.

CHAPTER ONE

London, England
June 1813

Having arrived late for the Countess of Trent's annual ball, Benedict Warrington, Earl of Rothsea, stood inside the entrance hall and cynically surveyed the elegant but frenzied mob before him. Most of them were in pursuit of spouses, lovers or greater mischief. As was usual at such events, the unmarried misses would keep to the ballroom, tracked by the watchful gazes of their careful chaperones and ambitious mothers, all under the speculative glances of interested suitors and dissolute fortune hunters.

No doubt there were others who had more honourable reasons for attending these damned balls, but, as one who had done his best to avoid them for years, Benedict couldn't think of a single one. He had timed his arrival so that the major-domo would have relaxed his position and would no longer be standing to attention, ready to announce the names of new arrivals to those guests already assembled. He had no wish to overly advertise his presence in London, not until he had accomplished the task in hand.

With a glance, he noted a few gentlemen escaping through a pair of large doors at the far end of the ballroom—no doubt a gambling or smoking room set aside for the men to congregate, and the perfect place for him to find who he was looking for. In addition, the card room would have the added attraction of the complete absence of simpering, blushing misses and their marriage-minded mothers.

Ignoring the gazes of his fellow guests, Benedict entered a spacious room where he was met with the shuffling of cards, the smell of fine brandy and a mass of evening-clad males, hoping to find the one face he sought. Within seconds, a tall, dark-haired man excused himself from the group with whom he had been conversing and came swiftly across to greet Benedict, a rare smile lighting his stark, forbidding features.

Richard Pembroke, Duke of Westbury, clapped Benedict on the shoulder in a gesture of welcome. "Rothsea, it is a pleasure to see you, my old friend. I could scarce believe my eyes when I read your letter that you were coming to Town. I understood you had family business to attend to?"

Benedict returned his friend's smile, although he feared it wouldn't reach his eyes. "That is why I am now in Town, but that sorry tale can wait. Right now I'm more interested in why you're attending the countess's annual marriage mart? We used to avoid such events like the plague. I was astonished when your household advised I could find you here. Anything you want to tell me?"

Benedict teased, though in truth he couldn't imagine the Duke of Westbury contemplating marriage by actually looking for a bride himself. He would probably have his man of business draw up a shortlist of cool, icy beauties suitable to bear the mantle of the Duchess of Westbury. There would be but little to choose between them in looks or personality, and the duke wouldn't have a care for either their individuality or their wishes. He would choose a perfectly proper duchess, not a wife. For that was the way of aristocratic unions.

Westbury smiled. "Actually, I am part of this year's social whirl to keep an eye on my late sister's daughter. She is my ward and recently out of mourning for her parents. My aunt, Lady Bentley, is staying with us as her chaperone."

"Well, I shan't keep you from your watchdog duties. Rather you than me. I am for White's tonight—I hoped to see you and let you know I have arrived in Town. I have some business to attend to but would like to catch up. I may need to call upon your wisdom."

* * *

Eloise Camarthon stood by the edge of the dance floor. She was surrounded by fellow debutantes but held herself slightly apart as she surveyed the dancing couples. After the seclusion of the last few years, she was enjoying the distraction of the Season, determined to take pleasure in every new experience that came her way. When the unmistakable strains of a waltz broke across the chattering in the room, Eloise felt movement at her elbow as Sir Frederick Richards possessively claimed her arm "My dear Miss Camarthon, I believe this is my dance?"

Eloise inwardly sighed as her hopes were completely dashed—she had forgotten that she was promised to Sir Frederick for this set. "Why yes, my lord, indeed it is." Although handsome enough, with his neatly trimmed brown hair and even features, there was something about Sir Frederick's pale blue eyes that Eloise did not like. There was, it always seemed to her, a look of calculation, of weighing the situation and working out where his advantage lay.

Sir Frederick held her a fraction too close as they moved into the opening position. As they whirled around the dance floor, Eloise discreetly pulled herself back to a respectable distance. She glanced at her dancing partner and inwardly recoiled at the smug, self-satisfied look on his face.

Eloise knew she was reckoned to be an attractive and well-connected girl, and, by those with intelligence enough to consider personality and wit an advantage, she was probably considered a catch in her own right. Whilst not classed a beauty, especially as this year's vogue was for blond hair, blue eyes and slender figures, she passed for handsome enough. Her tawny curls were piled atop her head; her green eyes were surely of a pleasant shade. Perhaps her figure was more buxom than the vogue, but her gentle curves drew more than one admiring glance. But at almost twenty-one, she was no fool. Her main attribute was her wealth.

She was roused from her musings as the waltz ended and Sir Frederick spoke. "I don't know about you, my dear, but I'm overwhelmed by the crush and need some air." They had stopped by an open door and he swiftly propelled Eloise unseen out onto the balcony and into the cool night air.

Before she could summon the wits to protest, Eloise was swept to the farthest part of the wide terrace, which overlooked the tiered gardens. The area was dotted with tall potted plants, which created private screened areas, making any assignation relatively unseen, and it was into that hidden darkness that she was forced.

Her throat constricted with a rising panic as she swiftly assessed the situation. She kept alarm from her voice, was direct and polite. "My lord, I must ask you to unhand me immediately. I wish to return to the ballroom. It is not appropriate for us to be here."

He pulled her deeper into the shadows. "Come on, my pet, when our betrothal is announced, no one will care if we were a little indiscreet tonight."

Betrothal? My pet? Had he run to madness?

"My lord, this is outrageous. I insist that you act like the gentleman you supposedly are and leave me alone." Eloise tried to pull back, but he was too strong for her. She frantically struggled to release her wrists, which were trapped by his hands. His grasp was not gentle and rough fingers pressed into her very bones. Just as she opened her mouth and drew in a ragged breath to scream, a deep voice broke into the silence of the night.

"Richards, let the young lady go." Startled, Eloise

sensed a rumble of menace in the man's tone.

Sir Frederick immediately released his hold but kept his arm around her waist as he turned to face the man who had interrupted him. "I'll have you know you are talking about my affianced bride, sir."

Eloise moved, shaking his arm away. Emboldened by the presence of her rescuer she didn't hold back. "You should be ashamed of yourself for telling such a falsehood. We are most certainly not engaged. You forced me out here with ill intent."

The wind shifted, and the light from half a dozen lanterns briefly illuminated the man's face. Sir Frederick's eyes widened in seeming recognition, and he made a choking sound. His hand left Eloise's waist at lightning speed. Wiping his brow, he bowed to her and apologised in a slightly thickened tone. "Forgive me, my dear. I see I was mistaken in that I believed our regard to be mutual."

After a nod to the gentleman, he mumbled, "My lord, no harm has been done." With that, he bolted into the gardens.

CHAPTER TWO

Eloise took a breath to calm her pounding heart and acknowledged her saviour with a nod of her head. "Well," she murmured, "that was well done. He is a mere puppy, but I did not care to be found out here with him." For all her bravado, Eloise was shaken, but she was determined not to let it show. She needed nothing more than to escape back into the lights, noise and comfort of the ballroom.

The deep voice was mocking. "I know Sir Frederick of old. He is a fop, and his pockets are rumoured to be empty. If I gauge the scene correctly, he obviously thought it easier to compromise a girl rather than court her by conventional means. The diamond pins scattered through your hair would settle his account at White's many times over."

"I have no intention of being trapped into being any man's wife." Her voice was a snap.

Her rescuer stepped out from the shadows, and Eloise

shivered. She may consider Sir Frederick a puppy, but this man—well, he was certainly a wolf. Eloise could not tell the colour of his eyes, as the light came from the room behind him, masking finer detail and shadowing his features, but he was handsome from what she could see. A part of her brain managed to register that she should be unconcerned with her saviour's looks and simply be grateful that rescue had come. His hair, dark blond with streaks of lighter and darker tones, fell unrestrained, untamed, and her fingers tingled, itched to feel its softness, to wrap a silken wave around her finger and . . .

His dry rejoinder broke into her thoughts. "In that case, I would avoid being coerced into escaping onto dimly lit terraces with any of your other suitors. Not unless you wish to speed along the nuptials. Or was that the intention?"

The lift of an eyebrow that accompanied this inflammatory comment made Eloise's hackles rise. "I was not coerced or persuaded to take the air, sir. I did not willingly place myself in this situation. I was directed here without my agreement and despite my protests."

He dipped his head in acknowledgement of her words. "I am grateful I was able to be of assistance. For I can assure you that had someone other than I come upon you, the seal would be set upon your fate."

She had to admit that he was right. She needed to keep her wits about her in future and avoid compromising situations. Like this one, for example. For she was still alone on the balcony with a gentleman, albeit a different one!

"My thanks are most sincere. Had I been seen by

another, the situation may indeed have been irredeemable. For although nothing untoward occurred, we are both surely aware that it is perception, rumours and appearances that rule our world and not something as simple as the facts."

With a nod of dismissal, Eloise turned to sweep past her rescuer and suddenly found herself hauled back and trapped against a large and firm chest. She stumbled, instinctively threw out her hands, and found herself grasping smooth material; to steady herself, she appeared to have clutched his coat—a midnight-blue superfine, she noted, surprised that she still had the wits to notice what he was wearing, especially when that garment was far, far too close to her own person. Surely, she should be thinking—and worrying—about something else entirely?

Aghast, Eloise lowered her hands to her sides and made to move back; however, two large hands clamped firmly around her waist and pulled her tight against a long, hard body. Being held by this stranger was very different from her experience of a few moments ago with Sir Frederick. This seemed so much more natural—safer but, in contradiction, infinitely more dangerous. Warmth radiated between them and the hands at her waist branded her with their searing heat, even though the fingertips barely grazed the silken material of her dress. They were close enough for her to smell him; a male musk that was not at all unpleasant and infinitely preferable to the cologne drenched dancing-partners she had endured for weeks.

Deep blue eyes stared into hers and his voice was a rumble of disdain. "So you'd have sorted out Sir Frederick yourself and no harm done? Let us see your independent spirit get yourself out of this little pickle."

He pulled her closer, but his grasp was not rough. "Not so easy now, is it? You have to understand that you cannot defend yourself against sheer brutality."

She should be horrified, shocked to her core that this man dare place his hands upon her, yet she sensed no real threat.

"I have younger sisters and have warned them of the dangers of men and how awareness of their situation must be their friend. Almost all men could physically overpower a woman—especially a well-bred and innocent young lady—and some have no scruples when it comes to how they catch a wife."

So he was trying to teach a lesson to what he deemed a foolish girl. Her cheeks burned in shame at what he must think of her. He was—Eloise tensed in shock. She had absolutely no idea who this man was!

Reality swept over her as she laid her hands against his chest and firmly pushed. Her uncle would be enraged if he ever found out she had dallied on the balcony with this man, and the tabbies of the ton would never let her live it down.

She broke free, although, in truth, he had simply removed his hands and let her go, and fled into the ballroom without a backward glance.

* * *

Benedict watched her go and raked a hand through his hair. To his surprise, he trembled a little and his heart was racing. He drew his thumb over the pads of his fingertips, surprised that all seemed as usual. His skin had blazed with fire as his fingers grazed along her rib-cage and rested on her waist. The fine material of her gown a tantalising barrier between burning flesh. He shook his head, but the thoughts would not leave him.

He had been on his way to collect his cape when he saw the couple move onto the balcony. Sir Frederick Richards's hand had forcibly pushed the girl ahead. He had taken a moment to check that all was in order and walked into a scene that was patently not acceptable; certainly not to the girl, and absolutely not to himself.

Then he had acted as bad as that fool Richards. What had compelled him to draw her closer, lay hands on her? She was an attractive girl and there was something in her steady green eyes that had drawn him in. She also showed strength in that she hadn't resorted to a fit of the vapours given the situation. None of that excused, or explained, his actions. Christ, he was lucky that no one saw them or he would be the one facing an irate family. He should leave. Time was running out.

* * *

The streets of London took on an altogether different hue as the sun disappeared for another day. Bartholomew Jones was not a man to lose himself in indulgence. He did not live above his means, nor spend his coin on women or debauchery; he did not drink to excess, bar occasionally, and he most certainly did not gamble. But he made his living, a good one at that, off those who did. He carefully made his way across the muddied street towards the inviting lanterns of the chophouse. The man he was meeting tonight had always been an excellent connection. Perhaps the best he had ever made. He was reeling him in tight, and Bartholomew was looking forward to his payday, which he hoped wouldn't be too far away.

Yet again he thanked the foresight of his late father-in-law. London was a prosperous city, but he made his living from those who needed that rarest of commodities—cold, hard coins. Moneylenders would never be treated as equals by the ruling classes, but Bartholomew had been well-educated under the largesse of his father's master. The countryside had held little allure for him, and upon arrival in the city he was lucky enough to have met his future wife—and her father. Bartholomew had married the girl and taken over the family business. Once his wife's father had passed, he brought in a partner, or rather had been forced to, and life was sweet.

A clatter of hooves on the cobbles brought his attention to the present moment and he hurried into the tavern, nodding at the innkeeper as he headed to the private room he had reserved. His guest was already waiting for him in the snugly furnished dining parlour.

"You are late, Jones. Sit, I have little time." The voice was one that did not brook disobedience. Bartholomew suppressed a grimace as he noted that his guest had already ordered a pitcher of wine. From the looks of the man, it must be nearly empty already.

Bartholomew was happy to dispense with any pleasantries. "Let us get to the point. I need more money."

"I know, I know, but I will get it to you. I always do."

This was accompanied by a dismissive hand wave.

"I cannot wait for your hand to turn at the tables or whatever it is you do to get additional funding."

The laugh was shallow. "I have high expectations. You need not concern yourself."

"But I am concerned. I have obligations. I do not know if I can entirely rely upon you."

The man's face darkened, and his words were choked out. "Careful. Do not speak to me this way."

"Just make sure I have the agreed funds within the month. I travel to Huntley and will be gone several weeks."

A hand shot out and grabbed his coat. "What business have you at the Huntley Estate at this time?"

He pointedly looked at the fingers on his arm and was pleased to see them removed. "I have not seen my Papa for almost half a year, and he gets no younger. He works tirelessly as the Duke of Westbury's private secretary and I find we have grown apart a little. I mean to remedy that. As you well know, I have other friends in the area."

"Then I bid you safe travels and a pleasant stay. Your words are noted and you will get your due."

Bartholomew shrugged into his coat and headed through the tavern. The evening was fine, and it would not take long to walk home. Cooking smells perfumed the air and his tongue flicked out and wetted his lips. Abigail was a good wife and kept a bountiful table. Cook had promised a beef-and-ale pie, and there would be mashed potatoes and beer. He quickened his steps.

The road narrowed and veered off into the twisting lanes that crisscrossed the heart of London. He turned into a narrow alley and halted as he heard hurrying feet coming closer. He glanced over his shoulder and saw, with surprise, that his guest had followed him.

"You wish to speak further?"

The laugh was a snarl as the man bore down on him; his face unsmiling and his eyes hooded. Bartholomew backed away, moving deeper into the shadows.

"You've said enough tonight, my friend. Enough to sign your death warrant."

Bartholomew froze. No doubt drink was running his tongue. "I do not comprehend your meaning, my lord. Let us speak another day. You do not seem yourself."

He turned to leave and stumbled as a gloved hand grabbed at his throat. He fell to the ground as the dark figure loomed over him, raised his walking stick and, holding it high, brought it towards him with vicious force. As the stick made contact with his skull, pain blinded him. He groped the ground, trying to gain passage and raise himself, but he was weakened and disoriented.

The words were a whispered curse in his ear. "I can't let you live. You must see that. Westbury must never know of my true circumstances."

The second blow took his strength; the last stole his will. His eyes closed, and he welcomed the blessed darkness where pain did not exist.

CHAPTER THREE

Eloise awoke to the familiar, gentle chatter of her maid, Anna. "Miss Eloise, I've brought you a nice cup of tea. Here it is, lovely and milky, just as you like it. Come on; sit up like a good miss."

Eloise's eyes slowly fluttered open, her vision shadowed by lingering sleep. She idly glanced at the open door to her dressing room. Instead of the usual calm and order, chaos reigned; all of her travelling trunks, dress robes and hatboxes lay open with her belongings spilling out of them.

Obviously noting her mistress's horrified expression, Anna quickly interjected, "Sorry, miss, I've nearly finished. All your lovely new pieces have been packed, and His Grace said as he'd sent a note to Madam Veronique to have the rest of your last order delivered direct to Huntley."

Eloise closed her eyes and sighed. "Anna, tell me, quickly and simply, whatever is going on?"

Anna placed her clasped hands in front of her and, clearly concentrating, replied, "When you all got back from the ball last night, His Grace went into an awful snit, so he did, bellowing for Mr Higgins. Seems we're all repairing to Huntley today. Mr Higgins sent word that I was to have you ready to go soon as, miss."

Anger bubbled beneath the surface. Was she such a child that her uncle could order her about like a piece in a game of chess? She was sure she had never been awake at such an unnatural hour in her entire life, and why on earth were they going to the country estate? They weren't due to travel there for several weeks. Something was afoot, and she had a feeling she wasn't going to like it, not one little bit

* * *

His head was pounding as he rooted through the pile of morning mail. He'd left the body of Bartholomew Jones lying in the narrow alley and headed home on foot. He was glad of his dictate that the staff not await his return. It had been born of a desire to keep his wider peccadillos from being gossip fodder for the servants, but it had served him well the previous night, for there was no one to see his sullied cape or bloodstained cane. He'd fed the cape to the fire in his bedroom and used his washing water to carefully wipe clean the dark red spots from his walking stick.

He'd slept without disturbance for the first time in many a night. Bartholomew Jones had been no fool and would surely not have exposed his business contacts too readily. He expected that his home would hold his notebooks and records, but Jones had long confirmed that these were annotated in code. Knowledge of his involvement with the moneylender would have died with the man. This bought him time. Time to work out how to achieve his aim. He had to have her, but how did he get her? He flicked through his mail; stiffened card invitations, perhaps a personal missive or two and undoubtedly a load of final demands from his more crude creditors who had no respect for his position and cash flow concerns. He always paid them eventually.

He had ways of obtaining information on a certain household, and perhaps there would be news. One letter in particular made him smile. His plans were falling neatly into place.

* * *

Anna helped Eloise into a deep blue travelling dress as she quickly finished her toast and tea. She briefly glanced at her pale-faced reflection in the mirror and, with a resigned shrug, set off to find her uncle. He wasn't in the breakfast parlour; therefore Eloise tried his study next. She entered with a sharp rap on the wood-panelled door.

Her uncle turned from his stance by the window. "Do please enter, Eloise. Oh, I see you already have."

She perched on the nearest chair, back straight, knees and ankles pressed together and, to complete the picture of calm, her hands rested lightly in her lap. This vision of tranquillity was ruined the second she opened her mouth. "Uncle Richard, what on earth is going on? Surely we cannot in truth be decamping to Huntley, not whilst the

Season still has weeks to run?"

He crossed the room, bent down and gently lifted her chin until her gaze was level with his. "We are indeed leaving immediately for Huntley. I sent a messenger ahead at first light to warn we are on our way and the estate is to be readied for us."

Eloise fought the tears that threatened to spill from her eyes. Had she done something wrong? This impulsive action was quite unlike the Duke of Westbury. "But why? Am I being punished for something?" A horrible thought suddenly crossed her mind and made her pale. What if he knew about her being out on the balcony last night? Unbidden memories of the night before came crashing into her mind with vivid imagery. Her cheeks burned, and she prayed the colour didn't betray her.

He drew back and looked at her suspiciously. "I sincerely hope you haven't done anything that merits such punishment, my girl." At Eloise's carefully innocent look, he carried on, "It is for your own protection. I want you out of Town. I am afraid that this year is worse than last. I only turned down three offers for your hand last Season. I have turned down five so far this year."

Eloise was puzzled. "But I wasn't even out last year, how could that be? They couldn't have met me elsewhere. We have been well secluded at Huntley these last years."

As Eloise looked at her uncle's steady, concerned gaze, realisation dawned, and she drew back in disgust. "Sight unseen! Good God, they offered sight unseen! They didn't care what I looked like or sounded like, what I thought, who I was! The money was all they wanted. Have I at least met this year's proposers?" Her voice shook, the hurt evident.

The omnipotent Duke of Westbury momentarily closed his eyes. "In the past weeks, I have refused offers from Sir Giles Mountjoy, Viscount Arandale, Lord William Carrington, the Earl of Stephanage and Lord Hereford. Avoid them in the future. Your wealth is a powerful inducement to any man, Eloise, elevating one with a meagre fortune and making an already rich man a force to be reckoned with in this country. I don't want to see some rogue turn desperate and try to place you in a compromising situation. It wouldn't be the first time a fortune's been got by ruining a young girl."

Eloise reflected on the previous night. No doubt that was exactly what Sir Frederick had intended. "So Sir Frederick Richards was not one of the five who offered for me?"

Her uncle's eyes narrowed and he glared for a moment before shaking his head. "No, but he was one of the three from last year. The other two have both married. Has Richards been bothering you?" There was a fierce look in his eye that she most certainly did not want to enflame.

"Not exactly, no." Eloise didn't want to take their discussion down that path. In reality, the stranger had bothered her much more than Sir Frederick.

"Did something happen last night that I should know about?" His voice had an accusatory tone that made her want to scream.

Collecting herself and assuming her most innocent expression, Eloise replied, "Not at all, Uncle Richard. There is nothing you should be aware of." And that, she thought, was certainly not a lie as her uncle most definitely did not need to know about the events of the previous evening—ever!

CHAPTER FOUR

Benedict held his tongue and tried to count to ten. He got as far as three before exploding. "With Bartholomew Jones dead, we have no hope of discovering who was funding him. Where were your men?"

Sir George Evans, the junior government minister who sat opposite him drew back, his nostrils flaring as he cast a superior look down the length of his aristocratic nose. "The Crown wishes to apprehend the money, and the man, behind Jones' lending business as much as anyone, but we had not the resources to place a permanent tail on him. It is unfortunate that he was set upon by ruffians, but that is Whitechapel for you."

The excessively cultured tones of the minister grated on him, but he remained calm. "I do not have intimate knowledge of the rougher boroughs of London, but I do know that Bartholomew Jones was directly responsible for the death of my cousin's husband."

The other man's sigh was an affectation. "We are aware of that, and it is thanks to you we have become aware of Mr Jones' activities. However, his untimely demise does mean that we have come to the end of the path."

He fought the desire to lay blame on the Crown. They hadn't followed the man, and that was that. "What about his widow? Have your men spoken to her?"

"Yes, she is a simple woman who believes her husband honestly carried on her late father's moneylending business. They lived well, but of their class, and there is no sign of the kind of coin that was loaned to men such as your late cousin."

Was that it? He'd be damned if he gave up now. "He needed a backer. Jones loaned money and threatened ruin and disgrace on behalf of someone else. My cousin was being blackmailed, and the trail leads back to Bartholomew Jones. Now he is dead, and we are stuck."

"Perhaps not. According to his widow, Bartholomew Jones was planning a visit to his father. It is the only lead we have and may come to nothing. We shall have to send someone to Huntley Rise, the estate of the Duke of Westbury."

He snapped to attention. Perhaps he could indeed kill two birds with one stone.

* * *

Eloise and her uncle travelled half a day before the carriage eventually turned onto a private road. The road home.

Although not marked as such, it led only to the Huntley Estate and the jewel in its crown, the manor known as Huntley Rise.

The magnificent pale sandstone mansion was comprised of the original long building, which rose three storeys high with attics atop, flanked on either side by matching two-storey wings. The main house had been built a hundred years before, and the simple elegance of its clean lines had been replicated in the east and west wings, which had been added half a century later. The polished stone gleamed as banks of long multi-paned windows reflected the watery light.

To Eloise, it was simply home, the place where she had found comfort and succour after her parents' deaths.

The senior staff were waiting with smiles of welcome, and Eloise returned them with pleasure before making her way to her room to refresh herself and change into a simple muslin gown. She headed to the orangery, the latest addition to Huntley. As the weather was cool, the glass-walled structure was a comfortable place to sit and reflect—and to while away the time until she had to face her uncle across the dinner table. She was still trying to accept that she had been ceremoniously bundled from Town and did not trust herself to have a civil conversation with her bullying relative. His actions had been high-handed to say the least. A booted step on the tiled floor caught her attention. Her musings must have magicked him, for her uncle walked into the conservatory.

"Ah, Eloise, my dear—there you are." He dropped a light kiss on the top of her head before he sat down opposite her in one of the comfortably upholstered wing chairs. His smile seemed a little forced, and he looked distracted. "Is aught wrong, uncle?"

"I have this minute been speaking to Gareth Jones."

Eloise had long warmed to her uncle's private secretary. "And how is he? I have not spoken to Mr Jones since early in the spring."

"Not at all good. He has just left for London. A rider arrived this morning with some disturbing news. I am afraid it is an indelicate subject, but his son, Bartholomew, has been found dead."

Eloise knew her uncle only wished to protect her, but surely it was rather more indelicate for poor Mr Bartholomew Jones to be dead than for her to be hearing of it.

He cleared his throat, as if the words he had to say were choking him. "My dear, it may have seemed very precipitous of me to insist we leave Town, but I found myself with no option. You have one of the largest fortunes the marriage mart has seen in some years, which makes you a prize to be obtained at almost any cost."

Eloise couldn't mask her frown, but her uncle was apparently unconcerned and continued, "Not that you wouldn't be sought after for your own fine attributes, but, and let us be frank, your fortune is your biggest attraction."

She let that pass. There was no point arguing with a patent fact.

He paused, looked directly into her eyes, held them in an unflinching gaze, and then continued, "I have therefore decided that you must marry quickly. I'm sorry, my dear, but if you do not choose an appropriate husband before summer has ended, I shall have to choose one for you."

Eloise shook her head. The words buzzed around her, through her, broke apart into fragments, before the whole message became clear—and unmistakable. "Please, you cannot mean this!"

He stood, taut lines marring his brow. "There is no alternative. Your father allowed for me to marry you to whomsoever I please before you are twenty-one. I will not have you marry some fortune hunter who will make you miserable."

"But it shall be all right as long as the man making me miserable is fine and upstanding! Uncle, please don't do this," she begged. "You promised! You have always said I could take my time and marry as I pleased, even if my pleasure was not to marry at all."

Halting, he glanced back, the only indication of emotion the tic working at the side of his mouth. "I wanted to give you time; allow you to find a man you could admire and respect, even have some affection for. Circumstances have changed. I underestimated the pull of your fortune. But I now appreciate that you are not safe, and will not be so, until you are married and your fortune is in your husband's hands. I will not have a scandal. You shall be married and to my satisfaction."

"But, Uncle . . ."

He held up a hand, and that, coupled with the harshness of his face, stopped Eloise from saying anything further. Her uncle was not a man one could easily defy. And certainly not when he was in this mood.

"You, more than anyone, know I have done much to protect this family's name and that of your father. I will not see it ripped asunder because some fool seeks to compromise you. And it will happen. It's the easiest way to obtain a wealthy wife. I shall not hear another word. I have made arrangements, and we are to have a house party. I sent out invitations before dawn. Amongst our guests will be several eligible gentlemen, and you shall marry one of them before summer's end—that is final!"

He held out his hand and passed across a piece of paper; she took it and stared at her shaking hand before looking at the page itself. Careful marks were made next to the names of certain gentlemen. "These men whose names I have marked are all upstanding and from fine families, with wealth of their own, good prospects and better reputations. The others are my friends, some married already, and also some guests of our aunt. I would not embarrass you by only inviting those eligible. I shall see you later." With a nod as imperious as his latest pronouncement, he turned and left Eloise alone.

She picked up the list again and looked at the marked names, none of which meant a great deal to her. Some she knew socially, others only by sight. Some she knew not at all, and yet supposedly one of them would be her husband before summer's warmth gave way to autumn winds. The very idea chilled her.

* * *

The stillness of the lazy country afternoon was broken by the rhythmic, thundering hooves of the magnificent midnight-black stallion, its entire being intent on the exhilaration of the road ahead.

Benedict bent low over the animal's back, urging the beast faster and faster still. Man and horse in perfect accord, flying through the hedgerow-lined country lanes, not another soul in sight.

Spotting an open gate into some fallow fields, he urged his horse off the lane. "Come on, boy, let fly. I'm sure Westbury won't begrudge us a wild gallop across his land."

Nostrils flaring, the black horse elegantly, and seemingly effortlessly, charged across the wildflower-strewn meadows. Benedict's thigh muscles bunched, and his experienced hands kept the prime animal in check. All he could hear was the thrumming of the wind as it sped past his ears, accompanied by the rhythmic chant of hooves pounding earth.

He urged his mount onwards, his attention entirely focussed in the moment; in the melding of man and beast as his horse's raw power and his tight control fused together. It was as if they could read each other's minds, and in that moment each had the gift of freedom. To become more than they were as separate beings.

Immersed in this euphoria, he was a second too late to hear the loud report that came from the woods to his right. He jerked around as an object sped past his arm, knocking against him. Suddenly, the world tilted upside-down, and he came crashing to the ground. All went black.

* * *

Eloise joined her aunt and uncle in greeting their guests. Three large coaches arrived at almost the same time, and a gentleman alighted from each one. Eloise knew only one of them.

Lord Bellingham approached, bowed to her uncle and bent over her aunt's hand. "My dear Lady Bentley, you look excessively well. Thank you for your hospitality."

"Thank you, my lord." She turned to Eloise. "You remember my great-niece, Miss Camarthon?"

"Of course. It is a great pleasure to see you again. I have not been to Huntley in some time and would relish a turn around the gardens at some point. I hope it would not be an imposition if I were to ask you to accompany me?"

Eloise dipped into a curtsey. He was handsome enough, rich, a politician and unmarried. He was not a particular friend of her uncle's, and his name had been ticked on the eligible bachelor list. "It would be my pleasure, my lord."

Westbury turned. "Aunt, may I present Lord Gooding and the Earl of Everton to you. Gentlemen, may I introduce my aunt, Lady Bentley, and my niece, Miss Camarthon."

The taller of the two also seemed the elder by a few years. He was well-built, perhaps in his late-twenties and had pleasant features. He bowed. "I am Everton, and it is a pleasure to join you." His eyes held Eloise's for a fraction longer than was appropriate. The younger stepped forward. He had even features and could perhaps be considered handsome. In fact, both men could. Eloise caught herself. She was acting as if she were examining a new horse.

"Ladies, it is indeed a pleasure. I am Lord Gooding. Miss Camarthon, I believe you know my cousin, Lady Arabella Whitley?"

"Why yes, I do. It is a small world." Lady Arabella was a firm favourite with Eloise. Did Gooding curry favour in this way?

"My cousin informs me you are a fine horsewoman. Perhaps we could ride out?"

"I look forward to it."

Higgins discreetly coughed behind them, and her aunt suggested the gentlemen be shown to their chambers. As they moved away, Eloise recognised the keen interest of all three men. Was this a foretaste of how the next week would be conducted?

Her uncle said, "We await one more guest. I am sure he will be here soon."

She was about to enquire who they were waiting for when a jet-black stallion came thundering along the drive, a fine carriage travelling more sedately behind it. The horse reared on its hind legs as its owner halted outside the wide front steps, and the rider effortlessly jumped to the ground. Passing the reins to a waiting groom, his voice filled the air. "Apologies for my tardiness, Westbury. There was an incident whilst travelling through the north edge of the estate. Please excuse my disarray."

Her uncle descended the wide front stairs to welcome his guest, concern written over his face. "Are you hurt?"

"Nought that can't be mended."

Her uncle beckoned the man to ascend the steps. "Ladies, may I present the Earl of Rothsea. Rothsea, my aunt, Lady Bentley, whom you know, of course, and my niece and ward, Miss Eloise Camarthon."

Her aunt moved forward. "My dear boy, it has been an age. How are you?"

Eloise's eyes met Rothsea's, and her breath caught. It took all she had to maintain her composure. Dear Lord, it was him. The man from the balcony. Her heart pounded in an irregular beat, and her skin heated as her mind whirled.

He bent low in a deep bow, and when he rose, his mouth lifted in a smile that did not reach his eyes. His deep voice betrayed no recognition, "Lady Bentley, Miss Camarthon, it is all my pleasure."

Her uncle was uncharacteristically grinning. He obviously knew the earl well and liked him in equal measure. "Go and get settled, and after you have changed for dinner, please join me for a drink before we meet with the other guests. You can tell me all about this mishap of yours."

Eloise hadn't uttered one word, and as Rothsea moved away, without glancing in her direction again, she allowed herself to exhale—a long, slow breath that came out as a fractured sigh. Aunt Harriet looked at her in concern. "Are you all right, my dear? It has been a tiring day."

"I am fine. I'm anxious to make sure that all is in order for our guests. As everyone has now arrived, I shall take this opportunity to rest a little before dinner. Please excuse me."

Taking flight to her suite of rooms, she threw herself onto the ivory brocade-covered daybed that lay alongside her balcony. The doors were open, and the long muslin curtains gently ruffled in the whispering breeze. She could not believe it! What awful, dreadful luck that he was here and that he seemed to know her uncle so well. What if he told him about their meeting? And that he had found her there with Sir Frederick? Eloise felt nauseous as she considered what her uncle would do. He would—actually, she had no idea what her uncle would do, and she most definitely did not want to find out.

Her best solution would be to avoid the earl as much as possible, which would be absolutely no hardship at all. She had to pray that he could—and would—keep his silence.

CHAPTER FIVE

Tucked away in the east wing, Benedict nursed a balloon of brandy, which he slowly sipped as he sat in contemplative silence. He glanced around his lavish chamber. Whoever had organised the necessaries had certainly seen to their guests' comfort. Lady Bentley was known as an accomplished hostess. Or had she delegated these tasks to Eloise Camarthon? He was still in shock that the girl on the balcony was his friend's niece, but he had greater issues to contend with, and Westbury's invitation to join the Huntley house party had been fortuitous indeed. Benedict downed his brandy and headed to the back of the house, where Westbury maintained his private rooms.

He strolled past the painted gazes of long-dead ancestors who seemed to stare down their refined noses with a ducal family's habitual disdain. In front of him was the closed door of Westbury's study, but before he could move towards it, his attention was drawn to a large, superbly executed portrait of a handsome couple with two small children. The woman was seated on a chaise longue, a baby on her lap and a pretty little girl leaning against her legs. The man stood proudly behind his wife, one hand possessively laid upon her shoulder. Benedict recognised them as the late Viscount Barchester and his wife, Catherine, who had been Westbury's older sister. The little girl had to be Eloise and the baby her younger brother, James, the current viscount. He grew sombre as he considered their likenesses—a fine family, rent asunder by the tragic deaths of their parents.

Firm footsteps on the wooden floor alerted Benedict that he was no longer alone. Turning, he greeted Westbury, whose eyes, shadowed and clouded, stared at the portrait.

"It was a carriage accident, was it not?"

Westbury's eyes were hooded and his expression closed. "Yes. It is a blessing they passed together. I do not believe Catherine, or for that matter Barchester, could have lived without the other.

Benedict was surprised. Raising an eyebrow, he asked, "They were a love match?"

"I was only a boy when Catherine met David, but even I could see that they had a powerful connection. They were simply meant to be together. Catherine had barely turned seventeen, and our parents were hosting a house party as a way of easing her into society before the formal Season began. Fate, in the form of Barchester, stepped in. Our fathers were friends, and I guess that smoothed the way. Catherine was engaged before she even had her come-out. David was only twenty-three, well-set, courtesy of the extensive Barchester estates, and already on his way to amassing another personal fortune—and it is that fortune which leads me to my current predicament. James is spending the summer with his Barchester relatives and learning how to manage his estates. It is his sister who exercises my mind at present."

Benedict's throat tightened. He had no wish to speak of Miss Camarthon, at least not yet. Westbury gestured for him to sit in one of the comfortable club chairs placed in front of the unlit hearth. Benedict accepted a glass of claret as Westbury poured himself a drink as well and said, "First things first. I believe you sought to play down the incident that occurred on my land. What happened to you?"

"I took a nasty tumble, although thankfully the only real damage was to my clothing and, of course, my pride." Benedict sipped his wine and continued. "I have a new stallion. Gilgamesh is a fine beast. I decided to try him out, gave him his head and veered off the lanes to go across your fields. I heard a noise; something hit my arm and the next thing I knew I was flat on my back, staring at the sky, with Gil giving my face fat, slobbery licks. That was more than sufficient to get me to my feet."

"A noise? And you were hit?"

"Yes and yes." Benedict read the question in his friend's eyes. "It was from a gun. Luckily, the bullet only grazed me, but it was a shock at the time. My man was following behind me with the carriage and came riding out to find me. He dressed my wound, but truly it is a graze, nothing more."

"Damn. I am sorry this happened to you, and on my land. I'll alert my head groundsman. I don't mind the locals venturing forth to take a few brace of birds here and there, but to endanger a person is unthinkable. Would you ride out with some of my men in the morning to show them exactly where this happened? I do not wish to jump to conclusions, but we have had Gypsies on the meadows by the northern boundary. I would like to make sure all is as it should be. "

"Of course."

"That is settled, then. Tell me, how is the family?"

"My sisters are indeed a trial. My father treated them more like boys; they love riding, and he even taught them to shoot. Now my mother must try and turn them into ladies. She has time on her side with Madeleine, who is only thirteen, but Beth is seventeen and has no use for gentler pursuits. My mother still grieves for my father, and my sisters do not have her full attention. Action is required. I'm getting married."

Westbury spluttered and choked.

* * *

Eloise had given Anna a long overdue day off to visit her parents, who lived several miles from the village of Huntley. This meant that it was another of the household maids, Sarah, who assisted her in dressing for dinner. She let Sarah prattle away as her hair was arranged. Her mind was a chaotic jumble. What bad luck that Rothsea was the man from the balcony and her uncle's friend. Did she not have enough to contend with?

The maid's husky voice broke into her musings. "There, Miss Eloise, doesn't that look pretty?"

Eloise raised her eyes and looked into her dressing

mirror. Her hair was pulled away from her face, the thick locks gathered into a mass of tumbling curls, a few of which had been loosened to frame her features. "That is lovely, thank you."

She caught Sarah's gaze in the mirror and took in the saucy look that was quickly suppressed, leaving only a knowing glint.

"Begging your pardon, miss, but you'll be fighting all those fine gentlemen off. All those eligible gents. Makes you wonder why they're all here and the London Season not even ended yet."

The staff gossiped, but few were as brazen as Sarah. "That's enough. Please do not speculate about the duke's whims."

There was a ripeness, an earthiness about Sarah that disturbed Eloise. The maid was only slightly older than her, and yet there was an age of difference in their experiences of life. Sarah's eyes were downcast, and she bobbed in recognition of the rebuke. Eloise wasn't fooled for a second, and Sarah's next jaunty words belied her supposedly subdued demeanour.

"Right, stand up and have a proper look, miss. You look right fancy."

Her dress was new, pale ice-blue spotted voile laid over a satin underdress of a slightly darker hue. Caught at the shoulders by tiny capped sleeves, the neckline decorated with delicate blue satin rosebuds.

Pearl-tipped pins were scattered throughout her hair, and in her hands she held her late mother's pearl necklace. The clasp was too tight for her or Sarah to fasten on their own. She would seek her uncle's assistance.

"Thank you, Sarah, that will be all."

Sarah bobbed and, as she made for the door, looked over her shoulder and said, "Mind you have a good evening, miss."

Eloise laughed to herself as Sarah sashayed out the room. Sarah's family had worked the Huntley estate for generations. The pert and pretty maid, with her chestnut curls, was popular and well-liked—even if her ways were a touch forward sometimes.

Eloise headed towards her uncle's study and was about to knock on the closed study door when she heard voices within—her uncle had company. As everyone would soon be assembling for pre-dinner drinks, she concluded he wouldn't be long and decided to wait in her private sitting room, which was next door. She would catch him on his way to the drawing room.

The small private space was decorated in pale green and lemon, with comfortable furnishings. Two small sofas sat at right angles to each other, facing a wide fireplace, which was currently filled with a vase of delicate, creamy roses. A portrait of her parents, commissioned to commemorate their betrothal, was displayed above the mantel. The evening was mild and the room stifling. Eloise opened the windows wide and heard her uncle speak—the doors to his study must be open as well—but it was the deep timbre of the voice replying that made her halt as shivering pinpricks caused her skin to chill. She did the unforgivable. She listened.

The Earl of Rothsea said, "I simply cannot afford to let Beth have her come-out at the moment. It is a price I cannot pay, and it is my own fault. Maybe I need to find a rich wife who can help bear the burden."

Eloise immediately walked away, and the voices faded. Pensively, she quit the room. She'd ask someone else to help her with the necklace. Higgins, perhaps. Her mind strayed back to the conversation she had overheard. What had the earl meant? She knew she should not have eavesdropped, nor should she be unduly concerning herself with affairs that were not her own. But it sounded like Rothsea was in financial difficulties. What else could he have meant? Not that it was any business of hers.

* * *

Westbury had taken a sip of wine at the pronouncement of such marital plans. He fell into a choking fit which only subsided when Benedict leaned over and smacked him hard on the ducal back. Westbury's voice was hoarse. "What do you mean you're getting married? To whom?"

As Benedict settled back into his chair, he said calmly, "No need to take on so. I haven't actually found anyone yet but I will. The girls need a firm, ladylike hand. Mother is still too submerged in grief, and Aunt Gertrude is simply an aging hoyden herself. The only solution is for me to find a wife. I was jesting about the rich part."

Westbury stilled; his gaze direct and penetrating. "Does that mean all is now well?"

Benedict sobered. Westbury was one of the few people who knew the extent of his late father's debts. "I thank you for your discretion. I have cleared every one of Papa's notes. Some men incur credit through vices, gambling and women; others let greed blind them—but not my father.

He borrowed money to make vast improvements to the estate. The problem was that he didn't live long enough for some of his longer-term investments to bear fruit."

"Your actions are laudable. I suppose it is indeed time you married. You have the succession to consider."

This was a touch ironic coming from Westbury, a man who could have been betrothed a dozen times over the last few years to the catch of each season, should he have wished. "Indeed. I have it in mind to marry a good woman who can take over finishing Beth and ensure that Maddie doesn't spend all day with her nose stuck in a book. I need a woman of good lineage, who can tend my houses and give me an heir. In fact, that solves another of my problems." Benedict paused to take another drink.

"My family has been light on males over the years. We've been strong on the direct line, but not on spares. I set my man to find my heir. If I never have a son, I do want to know the man who will take over my responsibilities and bear the fruit of my ancestors' hard work."

"And is he worthy of the title, should the worst happen?"

"My heir is the Earl of Strathleven—a Scottish title. He is younger than me, it seems, albeit not by much. However, that is immaterial; Strathleven has no interest in opening discussions with his English relatives and sent my man away with a flea in his ear. Therefore I shall need to provide my own heir. This takes me back to finding a wife."

"Where will you find this paragon?"

Benedict laughed and drained his glass. "That, my

friend, is the problem. I fear I have no real idea how to go about finding a bride."

Westbury sighed. "Well, it is coincidence that you raise this topic. Marriage is actually very much on my mind at the moment."

Benedict's mouth gaped open, and he quickly snapped it shut. "Really? I had no idea you too were thinking that way."

"I'm not. I mean Eloise's marriage."

Benedict stiffened in surprise and carefully schooled his features. "I hadn't realised that congratulations were in order. Who is the lucky man?"

"I don't know, and nor does Eloise. Neither she nor I have actually picked him yet. I am tired, disgusted and appalled by the fortune hunters and rakes who have circled ever closer since her debut, so I've invited some of the ton's most eligible bachelors to this gathering. One of them is bound to suit, and I aim to have her married within six weeks."

Benedict's response was automatic. "You've invited me. Do I take it that I am included?"

Westbury's laughter echoed through the room. "Heavens, no. Don't worry; you're definitely not on the list. You're here as my friend, to keep me sane in all this madness. I would also appreciate any information you may have on the potential suitors—first impressions or general opinions. I want to make sure I get this right. I care very much for Eloise, and I am only trying to protect her."

"Are these potential suitors aware of the opportunity in front of them?"

Westbury shrugged. "I would imagine some are.

Rumours have surely been circulating." His tone was dry and resigned. "And what an opportunity it is. My late brother-in-law had some pretty outlandish ideas, chief of which was that Eloise deserved to be as financially well-off as her brother. From the unentailed estate at least.

Rothsea smiled. "A laudable attitude, perhaps, but the second a lady marries, her fortune becomes her husband's to do with as he will."

"I know. Barchester's will was written when he first married my sister. He stated that all his children should inherit an equal share of the assets not entailed to the viscountency. He cannot have foreseen how much money he was going to make and that they would only leave two heirs."

Benedict paused. "Perhaps that is what lies at the heart of your issue with Barchester's will. He died far too young."

Westbury's sigh reverberated through the room. "I know, but I cannot change the terms of the will now. So back to your initial question; I have not made it explicit to the single gentlemen that I am offering my niece in marriage. However, I believe my inviting several eligible gentlemen, and in the midst of the Season, must make my intentions clear—and for that I do apologise."

Benedict took in Westbury's grimace but couldn't understand his meaning. "And why apologise to me?"

"My dear friend, I simply wanted your company and support, and now you will be classed amongst the suitors, I am afraid. There has been a little talk. No one knows enough to say anything outright, but there have been whispers of Rothsea debts."

Benedict tensed. "But nothing substantiated—otherwise I would not be welcomed as I am."

"That's because you've dealt with the issue and paid off any debts that were there. You are well-liked, and there are many who will swiftly quieten these gossipmongers."

Acrid bile rose in his throat. "Apparently that won't prevent me from being seen as desperately chasing your niece's fortune."

"Best you stay away from her, then."

He couldn't help the unbidden laughter. "Westbury, that sounds like a warning! Am I not good enough?"

"I jest. Eloise is far too young to aid you in bringing up your sisters."

Westbury rose and laughingly patted Benedict on the back.

"You have title and wealth, and the ladies flock around you, but you have an eye for those ladies in return. You are also used to getting your own way." Suddenly serious, he continued, "I may want Eloise married, but I do want her to be happy in a quiet and settled life."

Benedict was silent for a moment. He didn't know what to think of this and sipped at his wine before changing the subject. "I have a confession to make. I was delighted to receive your invitation, but I also have another reason to visit Huntley."

Westbury's face betrayed no surprise at this comment apart from an almost imperceptible narrowing of his eyes. "What is your meaning?"

"My cousin's husband got into trouble. He was mixing with a less than salubrious crowd and racked up gambling debts. The poor fool apparently couldn't bear to approach his family for help and turned to a moneylender. He killed himself three weeks ago."

Westbury's face was solemn. "This is indeed a tragedy and I grieve with your family in their loss. Without being indelicate, may I ask how this relates to Huntley?"

"We found letters amongst his possessions. The moneylender was a Mr Bartholomew Jones. He has recently been found dead."

Westbury drew back and his brows knitted together in a dark frown. "My secretary's son? His father left for London as soon as he heard of his death. I had no idea that was his business. His father told me Bartholomew had taken a position with a wealthy lord. Although that was a few years ago."

"Do you know which lord?"

"No, I cannot recall. I wonder if I ever even knew. I have received word that the father returns tomorrow. We can speak with him then."

"Thank you. I have been working with Whitehall to try and find evidence that proves Jones was a blackmailer. The wheels of government move slowly, and their ineptitude means we have no idea who killed Jones, nor whether it was an attack by footpads or a deliberate action by someone known to him. I am actively investigating this matter with the blessing of the authorities. May I speak to the staff? See if anyone has any useful information?"

"Of course. I shall instruct Higgins that you are to be given all cooperation. We'll see what Jones Snr. has to say tomorrow."

He nodded his thanks, but his mind was whirring; seeking possibilities and discounting options. If only they knew who Jones had been working for; at least there would be another path to explore. He brought his mind back to the moment. "I am sure it should not need to be said but may I ask that you allow the manner of my relation's death to remain between us. It is widely believed that he was killed whilst trying out some new pistols. You obviously appreciate what the issues would be were the truth known."

The unspoken word hung in the air, reeking of social outcast. Suicide.

Westbury's face was unreadable and his voice brusque. "Of course. It would be unthinkable for the truth to come out."

CHAPTER SIX

The majority of the house guests had gathered for drinks in the spacious drawing room. Eloise glanced around and saw someone whom she could not delay in greeting; Lady Maria Fitzgibbons was attending the house party primarily as a guest of her aunt. She was past fifty—that being the age she admitted to, although the lines adorning her face suggested she was indeed past it by more than a decade, perhaps even more. Eloise approached the group of ladies with whom Lady Fitzgibbons sat and dipped an elegant, deep curtsey. "My ladies, you look very fine this evening."

Her words were met with regal head dips of acknowledgement, but it was Lady Fitzgibbons who spoke, "Thank you, child. Now do tell. Which of these chaps will you choose as husband? Eh?"

Eloise gasped but quickly recovered, sure that only her burning cheeks betrayed her shock at such directness. "Why, my lady, you jest. His Grace simply desired a respite from Town and a few days of convivial frivolities."

A "humph" was Lady Fitzgibbons' only response. As her ladyship's beady-eyed stare alerted Eloise that more of the same was on the way, she turned to the other ladies to try and engage them in conversation but was arrested by Lady Fitzgibbons' hand, which caught her wrist in a claw-like vice. "Come and sit down and have a chat with me."

A dark shadow fell over them, and Eloise happily turned to greet whoever had saved her from further interrogation. However, her heart sank, and her stomach rolled, as she saw who her saviour was.

The Earl of Rothsea addressed the gathered ladies. "A pleasure, as always." He bowed extravagantly, causing the aged doyennes of society to titter amongst themselves. He bent low and bestowed a light kiss on Lady Fitzgibbons' gloved hand before turning and repeating the gesture with the others.

He acknowledged Eloise with a murmured, "Good evening, Miss Camarthon."

Her quiet "my lord" was lost as the drawing room doors were opened by the footmen and Higgins announced dinner.

Her uncle offered his arm to the elderly Lady Dumbarton and, slightly raising his voice, addressed the room. "We find ourselves very informal this evening. Gentlemen, please lead the ladies to dinner."

Lady Fitzgibbons rapped Rothsea across the arm with her fan. "On you go," she commanded. "Take her in boy. Dolt! The chaps weren't as slow in my day."

He turned and set Eloise's arm on his sleeve. He didn't look particularly enamoured of the situation. "Miss

Camarthon, it would be my pleasure."

She stiffened for a moment and dipped her head in acknowledgement as they moved with the others towards the dining room. Her steps were heavy and a bolt of tension knotted her shoulder blades. She'd have to brazen it out. There was no other option. "Thank you, my lord, that is most kind of you. It is a pleasure to make your acquaintance. I trust you are well after the incident that occurred on the way here?"

"I am, thank you for your consideration." He bent towards her and spoke sotto voce. "But let us acknowledge that we are not exactly strangers. I assume Westbury has no idea of your tendency to wander onto darkly lit balconies with strange men?"

She gritted her teeth and her reply was a whispered hiss. "You are indeed correct that my uncle has no knowledge of that regrettable event."

He raised a brow but simply said, "Take care in future; otherwise, you'll be betrothed before you know it."

She cursed her snapped reaction. "My lord, forgive my tongue. I beg you not to reveal a word of those unfortunate circumstances."

"Please be reassured. I am not a bounder, and, more importantly, for he is my friend, I do not wish to incur Westbury's wrath."

He appeared to be in earnest and she had no other option than to take him at his word. As they settled into their seats, she smoothed her skirts, and fussed with her table setting, moving her dessert fork to align with the rest of her cutlery. Then she moved it back for it had been perfect in the original placement. There was nothing else left to delay the moment. She asked, "Lord Rothsea, is your estate near here?" Her tone was completely correct, proper and very, very distant.

She was having some difficulty in keeping her wits in order. A palpable tension had her on alert. All she had to do was keep the conversation general and she'd be absolutely fine. She took another steadying breath. She would be fine.

His deep voice caused an unusual tumbling sensation in the pit of her stomach, as he answered her question. "No, my principal estate, Cranham Chase, is a journey of several days from here."

"What a lovely name. You have family there?"

"Yes. My two younger sisters are Lady Elizabeth, known as Beth, and Lady Madeleine, who will only answer to Maddie. They are, respectively, seventeen and thirteen years old."

"How lovely." With that, the next course was served, and she turned to the gentleman on her other side, but her quickened heartbeat and heightened senses kept her very aware of Rothsea.

* * *

At her aunt's direction, the flock of ladies converged in the drawing room after dinner, leaving the men to enjoy their port. Aunt Harriet had managed to wrestle the tea trolley from Lady Fitzgibbons, who loved to be in the thick of things, although not without a tussle, and the esteemed dowager was now comfortably settled with her cronies, sipping tea and dispensing undoubtedly frank comments about the rest of the ladies present, who had settled themselves into small groups.

Eloise did her duty and moved amongst their guests, ensuring they were enjoying themselves and trying to keep her mind from Rothsea. However, this was not to be. As she neared three young matrons sitting on chairs by the open terrace doors, a murmured name caught her attention.

"Rothsea? I hadn't seen him in some time, and yet he has been all around Town this past week. Why, I do believe he's ready to set his nursery up." As her avid listeners gasped, the pretty young matron giggled behind her gloved hand before continuing, "It's a pity he hadn't the same inclination when I made my come-out!"

As the three laughed in delight, the other two expressing similarly bold sentiments, Eloise gave them a wide smile and sailed past. That was one conversation she most definitely did not want to join.

The crescendo of voices coming from the direction of the hall announced the arrival of the gentlemen. Eloise moved towards her aunt and took station next to her as their guests mingled.

"Lady Bentley, Miss Camarthon, it is a pleasure to be invited to Huntley," Lord Bellingham addressed them. Eloise bobbed a curtsey as her aunt inclined her head. Bellingham, if rumour proved right, would one day make a senior government position. He was known to be dedicated and committed, laudable indeed when he could spend his days simply tending his estates, which were said to be substantial.

Her aunt replied, "It is our pleasure, my lord. I hope

you enjoy your stay in this county. Do you know it?"

"Not at all. I am looking forward to appreciating all the beauties of this area."

"As am I." This last came from Lord Everton. Yet again, his dark-eyed gaze held Eloise's for a little longer than was sociable, and she was left in no uncertainty that he admired her and classed her amongst the attractions. Eloise felt a little light-headed with dread as she considered this, and her mind was muddled. Her uncle's ultimatum weighed heavy. A smooth voice saved her from having to reply.

Rothsea murmured, "Miss Camarthon," as he bowed over Eloise's hand, before addressing her aunt. "Lady Bentley, you run a fine table, and the arrangements have been delightful. May I offer my sincere thanks on behalf of your grateful guests?"

Aunt Harriet visibly preened. Dear heavens, Eloise could virtually see her pinken with pleasure. "Why, thank you, although I must not take all the credit. The duke's staff is exceptional, and my own dear niece is always a great help." The last was accompanied with a smile towards Eloise, who was trying to smile prettily whilst concealing her gritted teeth. She had hoped to avoid Rothsea in the crowd.

"I am sure you are blessed in Miss Camarthon's company," Rothsea said and further entreated, "I came to enquire if you would have any objection to Miss Camarthon taking a stroll on the terrace with me. After the . . . exertions . . . of the day, I find I am in need of a little fresh air."

Eloise couldn't believe the effrontery of the man. Why,

the cunning brute. In this short discourse, he had curried favour with Aunt Harriet and then neatly reminded everyone that he had a nasty accident only earlier that day, and all in the same breath.

Eloise waited for her aunt to politely deny the request, as she took her chaperoning duties seriously.

Aunt Harriet smiled. "My lord, what a delightful suggestion." Turning to her niece she said, "Eloise, my dear, I insist you take a gentle stroll with Lord Rothsea. The air will do him good."

Rothsea bowed and, turning, drew Eloise's arm into his as he navigated them both through the groups of guests towards the open balcony doors.

Eloise was bemused. What on earth was wrong with her aunt? Unless, she suddenly thought, perhaps Aunt Harriet was truly worried about Rothsea's constitution after his accident. Stealing a glance out of the corner of her eye, Eloise's look was caught by his strong, steady gaze. He didn't appear to be ailing; in fact, he seemed anything but. She quickly turned away—then almost faltered when Rothsea lightly pressed his palm against the small of her back to guide her out to the terrace. She tried but couldn't quite suppress a shiver as his hand burned through the layers of her clothes, into her very skin. Her cheeks flamed and Eloise adjusted her position so that there was a gap between them as they walked out onto the wide stone-paved terrace. The tension between them was still palpable, so raw, that Eloise almost believed she could run a shaking finger over it and touch the nascent power. Giving herself a mental shake, she pushed these fanciful, but disturbing, thoughts aside.

The long, wide terrace was dotted with intimate groupings of wrought-iron tables and chairs with well-padded seat cushions. Each small round table bore lighted candles, protected from the night breeze by pottery dome coverings that let filtered light shine through cut-outs in the clay, the holes shaped into stars and slivers of moon. Areas of the terrace were made even more private with screens of carefully tended potted ferns and flowers and a smattering of life-sized stone statues.

As Rothsea steered her away from the few couples already enjoying the night air, Eloise recalled where she was and exactly who she was with. Her field of potential husbands had dramatically shrunk to the few gentlemen picked out by her uncle. She most certainly did not wish even the meagre control she had taken out of her grasp due to an indiscretion. She had escaped unscathed with her reputation intact from their last encounter. It would be best not to push her luck. Eloise knew she must return to the others in plain sight.

"My lord, I trust that the air has refreshed you."

"Indeed, but there is something I wished to speak to you about. Westbury has advised me of the purpose of this house party in relation to your marriage plans."

Her chest tightened with taut coils of shame and she briefly closed her eyes, but the words hung in the air and could not be ignored. "Forgive me; I did not expect my uncle to be open about his purpose. You find me at a loss."

"I do not mean to embarrass you. It is simply that I would urge caution on your part. Many men may show one face to a potential wife and conceal the one he more commonly shows to his friends. It is just that, well, your fortune is a draw."

She drew her brows together and didn't give a damn if she'd get lines on her face. "I am fully aware of that as, apparently, is most of the ton. I thank you for your words, but do not be concerned. I am wary of anyone's motive in wishing to gain my favour."

She indicated numerous guests enjoying the cooling breeze. "I see some of the others have had a similar notion to take some air. Perhaps you would care to join them? I am afraid I must take my leave of you and assist my aunt with the other guests."

"I commend you for trying to rid yourself of me; however, I have more to say, so I would ask you do me the courtesy of listening. I have to admit that I was shocked to find that the forward miss from my balcony encounter was my friend's ward and a supposedly respectable young lady." His smile, and the accompanying glint in his eye, betrayed his amusement.

Forward! "Yes, well," Eloise continued in a rush, forging ahead to finish saying her piece, then she could leave the blasted man alone. "I would be eternally grateful if you would forget our initial meeting and," here Eloise's voice caught a little, "beg you not to say a word to anyone of my folly." She could only hope that he would act as a gentleman.

Rothsea's eyes were a deep blue, and she found herself in danger of drowning. She simply could not move away. Rothsea gently placed a finger under her chin and tilted her face towards him.

Coolly, he held her gaze. "You have my word that I

shall not discuss the subject with anyone but yourself."

Eloise slowly backed away, with the knowledge that this would likely be the only concession she would get in this matter. "Thank you, my lord. I sincerely appreciate your discretion; let us mention the unfortunate situation no more." With a small smile, she turned on her heels and escaped inside. Rothsea did not follow.

* * *

As he watched her re-enter the house, Benedict had a strange desire to make sure they shared another "unfortunate situation" and see if she regretted that!

Mentally shaking himself back to reality, he reassured himself as to his current course of action. Eloise had made it clear that she had no expectations of him and would prefer to pretend the incident had never happened. He was sure they hadn't been observed during their first meeting, and so all was well. There was no need for him to offer for her simply to save face, for the circumstances would not please Westbury.

He stifled a yawn; it had been a long day and he was ready for bed. He went in search of his host and found him in conversation with Higgins. He slowly approached them, stopping a little way off and deferentially waited for Westbury to finish his discussion, but he immediately turned to him.

"Your timing is impeccable. I have instructed Higgins to see that the area of your accident is searched at sunrise. It is a damned shame that the light was fading by the time you arrived here."

"I know. We can but hope that there will still be some recognisable signs of whoever was there. As agreed, I shall ride alongside the men. I can easily pinpoint the area."

"Higgins will organise everything." With a brief bow, the butler disappeared, and Westbury turned to him. "I have heard from the estate manager. He has no knowledge of any poachers in that area. There have been sightings of the Gypsies though. They have long had permission to hold their summer camp on the edge of the estate. We have never had trouble from them before, but you never know."

"I have always found that they usually want to be left alone. Apart from petty pilfering, they are no real harm. In any event, why shoot at me?"

Westbury shrugged. "Have you annoyed anyone recently?"

"Most certainly. But probably not enough for them to have me killed."

Westbury's face wore a dark scowl. "You were riding across an open field, and your attacker was hidden by the trees. This sounds like more than a poacher's shot to me. I don't like this on my land, especially not when I have a house full of guests."

"Don't worry. I am sure it was nothing."

And with that, he sought his bed, rest and the hopes that his sleep would remain undisturbed by dreams of his host's niece.

CHAPTER SEVEN

After a restless night, Eloise woke to Sarah's low voice. She wearily opened her eyes; her body was listless and heavy. She was discomfited by the Earl of Rothsea's presence and had to face a day of smiling and trying to choose a husband, for that was what it boiled down to. Hopefully, it would be raining to match her mood, for she did not fancy traipsing around in the sunshine with a false smile upon her face and a dark cloud over her heart.

Sarah opened the heavy curtains with a brisk swoosh, and brilliant sunshine streamed into the room. "Well, that put paid to that hope," Eloise muttered.

Sarah quickly turned around. "Begging your pardon, miss, I didn't hear you right."

"Nothing of importance. Never mind me. Come, I must ready myself for the day."

She stiffened her resolve. She had to find a husband, or her uncle would do the job for her. She thought of

Rothsea. He was here as her uncle's friend, but did he have any interest in throwing his hat into the ring as a suitor? He certainly drew her in like a moth flitting about a flame. The question was: Would she get burned?

She had to take control and try to learn a little more about the gentlemen her uncle found eligible. No one had stirred her interest, made her consider a second look; apart from one, and he was perhaps more than she could handle in a husband. Not that he had shown the slightest inclination in that direction.

She watched as Sarah carefully finished styling her hair, smoothing it into a braided chignon at the base of her neck. The young maid's eyes sparkled, and a vivacious energy radiated from her. Eloise went to speak and hesitated until she found the rights words. "Do you have a young man, Sarah?"

Sarah's eyes flicked to hers, an amused glint all too apparent before she looked away. "Well, miss, can't say as I do and can't say as I don't have a young man. But I do have a gentleman friend who keeps me company from time to time." There was a wealth of suggestion in her words.

"And what is he like?"

"He's a man, miss. A real man, not some below-stairs boy. Educated and talks nice too. A proper gent."

Eloise imagined that Sarah would easily catch the eye of a farmer or a prosperous tradesman. The pretty maid had little schooling herself, and would undoubtedly look up to anyone who attended lessons.

"Well, your secret is safe with me, and I hope everything works out and you'll be very happy."

Sarah would be looking for a way to obtain a better life, but what else did she want in a husband? And what about herself? What did she want?

* * *

Benedict decided to start with the one person who would no doubt know most of everything about the Huntley Rise estate: Higgins.

The butler stood ramrod straight and fixed him with a direct gaze. "His Grace has asked that I accord you all assistance I can. Bartholomew Jones must've been around ten when first he came to Huntley. His mother had passed the year before, and his father looked to give them both a fresh start. Gareth Jones was from the gentry, but a younger son. His education stood him in good stead, and he took position as His Grace's secretary—not that my master was the present duke, for his own father was still alive. The Jones boy had his learning from his father and ran wild the rest of the time." His voice was rigid with disapproval.

Benedict couldn't help but question if the butler was jealous of Gareth Jones' higher standing in the household. God only knew why but the servants had a more rigid hierarchy than the aristocracy.

"You said he ran wild. What did he do?"

"He had few responsibilities and less inclination to obtain any. Any time not spent at lessons you'd find him roaming the estate. Initially, he played with local youngsters and haunted the woods; later he frequented the hedge taverns and inns."

That was a surprise. "The hedge taverns are a rough place for a gently bred boy."

"Don't worry. He could hold his own."

"When did you last see him?"

"About six months ago. He came to see his father. Didn't stay long."

"Did he have any particular friends or acquaintances?"

"He was always friendly with one of the maids here. I don't think there was ever an inappropriate relationship, but they were thick as thieves even before Sarah first took up her position here."

"Would you please arrange for me to speak to the girl?"

* * *

"You said he could stay?" Westbury thundered as he stood facing his aunt. He couldn't help the tightening of his features, the tic that worked away beneath his eye or the furious tone that had accompanied his bellow.

His aunt pursed her lips. He could almost hear the unspoken tutting. "Don't pretend to be an ogre. I am aware that Sir Frederick is a nuisance, but his carriage will be fixed in a day or two at the most, and, frankly, what else could we do? He is known to us in society, and his accident happened on his way past the estate." Her smile was gentle. "They lost a wheel and had no way of obtaining other sanctuary. We could not, in all conscience, have done otherwise than to offer our home."

His anger deflated at his aunt's genteel rebuke; they were indeed stuck with Sir Frederick Richards until his carriage had its broken wheel fixed. The bounder had better behave for he knew more about that one than he cared to mention.

* * *

Eloise smiled at the patently nervous Sarah in what she hoped was a comforting matter. "Do not be afraid. The earl simply has a few questions. Is that not correct, my lord?"

The quick look she flashed Rothsea would surely betray her annoyance. She certainly wished it to. Eloise had come upon a distressed Sarah being led by Higgins to one of the parlours and, upon hearing that she was to be questioned, had insisted that she accompany her. Especially as she had no idea what on earth Rothsea could possibly have to question the poor maid about.

"Yes indeed." The inquisitor moved to stand in front of Sarah. "Please sit."

Eloise understood Sarah's panicked look. "Sarah, it would please me if you would sit next to me."

Sarah wiped her hands along the back of her skirt and perched on the end of the sofa, back ramrod straight, knees together and hands clasped. Eloise reached over and patted her hand and, turning to Rothsea, announced, "You may commence."

Her tone must have been leaning towards the imperious, for his brows drew together in a frown before he began. "Good. Sarah, please do not be frightened. I simply wish to ask you about a young man who came to live at Huntley as a boy, Bartholomew Jones. You knew him?"

Sarah coughed and quickly covered her hand with her mouth. Her gulp was audible. "Yes, I did, m'lord. We were friendly. He was ten when he came here, and I was seven." She paused for a moment. "He's dead, I heard."

"That is correct. When did you last see Bartholomew?"

"Perhaps half a year or so ago. He came to the kitchens and said hello."

"Did he do that often?"

"Sometimes."

"Did he speak of his life in London?"

"No."

Eloise could almost touch the frustration that was emanating from Rothsea at Sarah's stilted responses, and his tight voice bore out his exasperation. "What did he speak of? Bartholomew Jones was murdered, and I need to ascertain who would have a reason to kill him. Do you know?"

Sarah's hand flew to her chest, and her eyes were wide-open. "Me? No, m'lord. I don't know about any of that business. Bartholomew just came to have a chat for old times' sake, that's all."

Eloise knew Sarah well, very well. She knew when the maid was play-acting, she knew when she was being evasive and she usually knew when she was lying. And it looked like Sarah was currently doing all three if this performance was anything to go by. She would need to know more of the circumstances of his investigation before she decided how to proceed. Should she speak to Rothsea, or first confront the maid and her supposed lies? Or was that too harsh? Perhaps Sarah was simply nervous.

CHAPTER EIGHT

Eloise presented herself on the terrace to await her uncle and their guests. At precisely the correct hour, for he was a man of habit and liked neither to be early nor late, her uncle appeared, ready to lead his guests from the house. Ponies and traps were waiting patiently, ready to ferry the older guests to the picnic, or even the younger ones who didn't care for the walk across the expansive lawns.

Eloise resolved to grasp the opportunity to find out a little more about her potential suitors. She shuddered at the realisation that they were more than would-be suitors. If her uncle had his way, one of these men would be her husband. A strange chill took hold of her, even though the day was fine. She would shortly be married to one of these men unless she could persuade her uncle to change his mind.

A polite voice drew her mind back to the moment. "Miss Camarthon, would you do me the honour of allowing me to escort you to the lake?"

It was Bellingham. Momentarily caught off guard, she knew her smile had faltered and quickly recovered her composure. "Thank you, my lord. I would be delighted to."

Bellingham took her arm in his as they strolled. With his dark brown hair, cut close like a thick pelt, and his even darker eyes, patrician nose and wide mouth, Bellingham was certainly handsome, and the general consensus appeared to be that he had the makings of a fine politician; a statesman even.

"So, my lord, pray tell me what keeps you busy?" Her aunt's favourite advice on social situations was being put into action. *Get them talking about themselves. People love to hear the sound of their own voices.*

"For some time, I have been of the opinion that using my vote in the House of Lords simply wasn't enough and that I wanted to devise policies, not simply pass them through to legislation. In fact, I have recently been commissioned to chair a committee on the possible demarcation of certain northern slum areas for redevelopment."

As Bellingham discoursed in greater detail, Eloise's mind drifted as she pictured a life as a politician's wife; holding dinners and teas for other party members and supporters' wives, planning fundraisers to support her husband's causes. A life, she imagined, that would be mainly spent in London supporting her husband's campaigns, perhaps helping to draft his speeches?

Eloise turned to Lord Bellingham and said, "You must find it such a chore to deal with your political life without a wife to give assistance?"

Bellingham's glance was speculative. "That is correct. My widowed sister helps me look after my homes, but it is rather a taxing job for her. It is surely time for me to address the situation." He finished with an appraising look.

Eloise earnestly forged ahead. "I fear you misunderstand me, my lord. What I meant was that a wife could surely be of valuable help in your political life, assisting you in meetings, reviewing papers . . ."

At the look of horror that crossed Bellingham's face, Eloise realised the error in her thinking. "My dear girl," he began in an annoyingly superior tone, "why, no wife should ever have to bother herself with such matters. These topics are far too serious for a gently bred lady, who would be better served in doing what she is best suited to—ensuring her husband's home runs smoothly.

"Oh, how silly of me," fluttered Eloise, who could dissemble with the best of them, as Bellingham looked suspiciously down at her. All she needed was a reputation as a bluestocking, and even her fortune wouldn't save her from gathering dust on the shelf. The thought rose unbidden. *Are you sure?* Eloise's smile wavered as she accepted the truth that she could—and would—be forgiven a great deal due to her status as an heiress. But would anyone ever simply want her for herself?

She was saved from saying anything further as Lord Everton joined them. His smile barely lifted his lips. "Miss Camarthon, Bellingham. May I join you?"

Eloise acquiesced. "Of course, my lord. I trust the day finds all well with you?"

"Indeed. Huntley is an impressive estate, and it is

always a pleasure to be here. Do you enjoy the country?"

"Yes, I do. However, I do enjoy time in London as well."

"As do I. It is important to have the correct balance. I believe you have assisted with designing the new rose gardens?"

"Yes, garden design is a passion of mine, and my uncle kindly let me have full rein."

"My estate's formal gardens have been maintained, but they could do with a redesign. I would welcome an opportunity to see your work. Perhaps you could show me later?"

"Yes, of course."

Eloise was finding hidden meanings everywhere. Was Everton showing an interest? Just because her uncle deemed someone as a suitable husband for her did not necessarily mean they would think the same.

* * *

Within a very short time, they reached the lake and joined the others, who socialised as they sipped wine or cordials and nibbled on tiny savouries fresh from the ovens.

Eloise excused herself from her escorts and walked towards her aunt, who was attempting to beckon her discreetly.

"Aunt, is something wrong?"

"Not exactly wrong, my dear, but I fear Westbury is most upset with me. We have an unexpected guest and, certainly in my nephew's eyes, an unwelcome one. Sir Frederick Richards has long been a nuisance, I know, but your uncle seems set against him."

Eloise could not conceal her dismay. "Why on earth is Sir Frederick here?"

"His carriage lost a wheel not half a mile from Huntley. Of course his man made his way here as the principal estate in the area. It will take a few days to source a replacement wheel. All I could do was ask him and his people to stay. I had no choice."

Eloise heard the tremor in her aunt's voice and cursed her uncle for his temper. "Please do not worry. You did the right thing."

At that moment, Sir Frederick sauntered across the lawn with a jaunty air, his attire foppish and his arrogance on show. Aunt Harriet started towards him. "I better head that boy off before he does anything foolish, like speak to your uncle!"

As her aunt walked away, Eloise head swam as she took in this latest development. She turned and walked towards the outer edges of the gathering. With her back to the crowd, she faced the lake and, watching the surface of the calm body of water, tried to control her emotions. She did not know how she could face Sir Frederick. Her palms were moist, and her head ached at having to meet with him again. She had acted with bravado that night, but she had to admit to being out of her depth and dreaded to consider the eventual outcome if Rothsea had not appeared.

"Are you well?" The deep voice startled her, and she spun around.

* * *

Benedict had followed behind Eloise as Bellingham and Everton escorted her to the picnic. A rage bubbled away inside him, and he struggled to understand the source of his discomfort or why he had lain awake for half the night thinking of a young woman he barely knew. He brushed these thoughts aside, reluctant to delve further.

"Why, of course, I am well, my lord—as I trust you are. It is a fine day, is it not?" Her tone was distant and formal and held him at bay.

"My apologies, you seemed a little distressed." He paused as his gaze alighted on a group to their right, then he turned back with a growl. "The impudence of that pup! What is Sir Frederick doing here? Has he upset you?"

"No. I believe he has had an unfortunate mishap with his carriage."

He listened in disbelief as Eloise laid out the circumstances that had led to Sir Frederick Richards joining the house party. "I cannot believe Westbury said he could stay."

Eloise frowned, and her voice was a whisper. "What if he tells? On the terrace at the ball. You know what I mean."

"And pray what would he say? That he was trying to compromise you into a forced marriage before I tossed him out?" Benedict said drily.

"Of course not, but he could say that he left us alone on the balcony.

"Surely, that won't matter?"

"Society matrons are sticklers; but I was more concerned about my uncle finding out . . ."

Perhaps he hadn't entirely considered Westbury, and

his feelings, in any of this at all?

". . . for I am sure that the knowledge that we had met before you came to Huntley and concealed this fact, and that we had been alone in each other's company, would result in him having a most interesting chat with you. Do you not think?"

"I am very hopeful that Sir Frederick will keep his mouth shut."

"I trust you are correct, my lord."

"So do I. I do not like a forced hand."

Before he could continue, a voice caught his attention. "Lord Rothsea, there is a visitor to see you."

One of the footmen was hovering by his side, and Westbury had joined them.

Benedict stopped in surprise. "I am not expecting anyone. Who asks for me?"

"The Earl of Strathleven, my lord."

Eloise asked, "Who is the Earl of Strathleven?"

"He is my heir, but I have never met him." What on earth was he doing here? And more to the point what was he up to?

"Excuse me," he murmured as he headed back to the house. He quickly covered the ground, questions racing through his mind; far too lost in thought to notice that he was followed by Eloise and Westbury until he heard their steps behind him on the stone terrace. He kept going until he entered the main hall, where a man stood by the open front doors. His hair was black as night and curled past his collar, framing strong features that were softened by deep blue eyes. Beneath an aristocratic nose, his mouth was wide and set in a square jaw that hinted at an uncompromising nature. He presumed this was Strathleven.

The man headed straight for Westbury. "Your Grace, I had the pleasure to meet you once at Tattersall's, perhaps two years ago. You bought a fine black stallion."

"Yes, I recognise you. You bought some excellent greys, as I recall. I was after them myself. Welcome to Huntley."

"Please forgive my interruption of your festivities, Your Grace. I wished to speak with the Earl of Rothsea and, having journeyed the long road from Scotland, did not wish to return without having accomplished the task. I dislike leaving a chore undone."

Benedict found the choice of words intriguing. So Strathleven saw meeting with him as a chore. How interesting.

"No apologies required, Strathleven. Any connection of Rothsea is welcome here."

Benedict moved forward and took the other man's hand. "Strathleven. I am Rothsea. I must say I am surprised to see you, but certainly not unpleasantly so. I look forward to getting to know you."

Strathleven looked a little uncomfortable as he glanced at Westbury to include him in their conversation. "I am sorry for the interruption and my unannounced arrival. I visited your lawyer who travelled to Scotland to meet with me some months back. He directed me here." He turned to Westbury. "Your Grace, I shall not impose upon you and will journey to the village inn after I have spoken to Rothsea."

"I have a house full of guests, and one more is no

trouble. You are welcome to stay here until your business is finished."

"Thank you, Your Grace. In that case I willingly accept."

Eloise stepped forward, and Westbury quickly introduced her. She smiled in welcome. "Let me arrange for someone to show you to your room."

Westbury said, "Please join us for lunch when you are settled."

He steered Benedict towards the terrace and lunch. "Come; let us see if my guests have left us any food. I have to say that my interest has been piqued at your heir's sudden arrival."

Benedict followed. An heir turning up unannounced usually meant only one thing: they were considering their expectations and the likelihood of them being realised. What had changed Strathleven's mind? And what was he after?

CHAPTER NINE

Benedict and Westbury had finished eating when his friend looked towards the house. "I see Strathleven is about to join us. I will leave you to it." Their table was set a little apart from the others, and Benedict welcomed the privacy for this conversation.

He knew little about Strathleven apart from his name and title—which was surprising enough—and that he hailed from Scotland. He hadn't yet had an opportunity to peruse the background details provided by his lawyer who had visited Scotland on his behalf. Now Strathleven himself would be able to fill him in.

He had several questions to put to his heir presumptive. He wanted to know why Strathleven had sought him out, especially as the report recently received from his lawyers said that his heir had emphatically stated, repeatedly, that he wanted nothing to do with his English relative and couldn't have cared less about the title. But the first question he wanted answered was the most obvious one. How was it possible that the man who was his heir, descended through the males of their family, also bore the title of earl?

* * *

Sarah knelt in the bushes, her head low as she peeped through the dense fronds of foliage. She'd carefully folded her hem back above her knees so only her stockings touched the damp ground. She'd served and curtseyed and done her job, making sure His Grace's guests were well taken care of. There was one she wanted to look after a bit better than that.

She'd seen John Coachman not five minutes before. He was hanging around the kitchens flattering Cook and enticing titbits from the rounded widow who was mistress of the kitchens. Cook didn't sleep in the attic bedrooms but had a comfortable space to the side of the kitchens. Sarah had questioned, not for the first time, if she occupied her bed alone.

The aging coachman, with his greying, lank hair and toothless smile, had cast a quick, sly glance in her direction as he mentioned that he was sure one of the gentlemen guests looked mighty similar to a man he'd spotted in the woods around here last summer. Sarah had been sure the nosey old fool had seen them coming out of the moon-dappled copse, yet he had said nothing, and she had grown complacent. If the housekeeper knew she'd been dallying like this, Sarah would be tossed out.

So now here she was. Hiding in the undergrowth to

watch him, study him, and see who he spoke to. If he so desired, she would be available for his attentions. For he was her future, and nothing was going to get in her way.

* * *

Strathleven made his way down the buffet table, a healthy appetite evidenced by the pile of food upon his plate, glancing around to see where to sit. Benedict hailed him with a wave of his hand.

As Strathleven sat, a hovering servant unfurled a white linen napkin and placed it across his knee whilst another placed a bottle of claret on the table. Benedict poured two glasses of the dark red wine, raising a toast. "To family connections, Strathleven—distant as they may be."

Strathleven lifted his own glass high. "You must be wondering . . ."

"I would ask you . . ."

Both spoke at the same time and then, their words trailing into the air, shared a brief burst of laughter. Benedict smiled and indicated that Strathleven continue; he wanted to hear what the other man had to say.

"Thank you. If I may properly introduce myself, I am Alexander Kincaid, the Earl of Strathleven. So let me answer what must be the first unasked question. My title. How can I hold a title if I am a direct connection of yours through the male line?"

"You are correct. That has been puzzling me, so please put me out of my misery and tell me how this is possible."

"My late mother was the Countess of Strathleven, having inherited the title from her father, as he had no sons. In Scotland, you see, some titles may follow the female line if there is no son to inherit. As my mother was heir to the title, my own father, who was a wealthy landowner, changed his surname to that of the Strathleven family name." Here Strathleven let a smile quirk his mouth. "And you would not be hunting down your heir were the same inheritance path followed in England, for your younger sister would succeed you should you die without issue."

Benedict considered this. A woman holding a title was ridiculous. Or was it? He'd met some women who were more capable of managing an estate than their dissolute husbands or brothers.

He took a sip of his wine, idly twisting the stem of the fine crystal glass between his fingers. This was purely a distraction whilst he marshalled his thoughts. "I fear what I am about to say may be blunt, but I do want there to be honesty between us. My lawyer advised that you refused to make contact and asked to be left alone. Now what did he report you said . . . ?" Benedict placed a hand on his chin as if trying to pull some memory from his mind, although he knew there was a mischievous gleam in his eye. "Ah, I recall. I believe the exact words were that my man should 'tell the damned Sassenach to find another heir, for I've no interest in him or his'."

Strathleven had the grace to look abashed, and colour rose under his tanned skin as he replied a little stiffly, his Scots burr becoming more pronounced. "Aye, I must admit that I did. However, I reflected on my original comment and decided I should recommence connections with this branch of the family. In truth, I may have been hasty in how strongly I worded my comments to your man. I wished to see you as soon as possible to ensure no bad blood existed between us."

To Benedict's ear, this did not sound plausible enough. Why hare all the way from Scotland simply to open communications when a letter would have done just as well? He considered his heir over the brim of his glass and decided he'd best keep an eye on him. None of this made complete sense, but the younger man had stated his reasons, and, in all politeness, Benedict could not probe into his veracity—not yet at any rate.

* * *

Eloise wandered amongst the guests, careful to avoid Sir Frederick. He may be at her home, and she would not go out of her way to publicly snub him, but nor would she treat him as a welcome guest. All the while she kept an eye out for Rothsea. Where was the dratted man? She wanted to know why he was so interested in finding the killer of Bartholomew Jones, and she had to consider what she saw as Sarah's evasiveness.

As she skirted the lake, Eloise walked towards several ladies taking advantage of a lovely shaded spot beneath the trees. Their delicate pastel dresses spread prettily around them as they half reclined on plump cushions scattered over colourful woven rugs. Eloise noted their almost-empty glasses of lemonade and beckoned a footman to refill them.

"Ladies, how delightfully cool you look. James is bringing some more lemonade."

"We may look positively cool, Miss Camarthon, but it is a wonder, truly it is, for have you not gathered here a fine array of London's most eligible?" Lady Oswald arched her over-plucked brows and pertly enquired, "Tell me, my dear, would there be an announcement in the offing? Come," she wheedled, "you can tell us; we are the souls of discretion."

Eloise quickly hid her astonishment. How amazingly gauche! If Miss Clara Witherington had been an awful, nosy little chit, her elevation to Viscountess Oswald had finally removed what little vestige of restraint and common sense may have previously existed.

Two could play at this game. "You'll have to wait and see, my lady," Eloise archly countered. Well, that wasn't a lie. No doubt there would be an announcement within the next month or so, but to whom it would relate, in addition to herself, she simply had no idea. All she had to do was pick from the field, and no doubt the chosen one would be delighted to take control of her fortune. How very tidy.

With that depressing image, Eloise, her social smile firmly in place, moved on to another group.

Her eyes alighted on her nemesis, standing alone by the buffet table as he sipped at a fruit ice. She made straight for him. "I see you are partial to Cook's iced strawberries."

Rothsea's smile, quick and natural, gave him a boyish look, and something shifted inside her, which she quickly ignored. She really must remember that the handsome earl wasn't on her uncle's list, and he certainly didn't appear to have any regrets about that.

He indicated the range of sweet treats on the table. "They are delicious. May I offer you one?"

"No, thank you. Actually, I wished to speak to you about this morning. May I enquire why you are so interested in Bartholomew Jones?"

He stared at her for a moment and then sighed and indicated that they stroll. The boyish traces of earlier had disappeared, and his face was as a mask of granite. "Bartholomew Jones was involved in some murky matters before he died, most particularly blackmail. This has touched upon people who are close to me and with tragic consequences. I aim to find out if he was working with anyone else. And bring them to account for their actions."

"I am sorry for the circumstances." She hesitated for a moment. "You should speak to Sarah again. She is harmless, but I have known her for a very long time, and she, well, Sarah can play-act sometimes. I got the impression today that she was not telling you all she knew. I could be wrong. Perhaps it was simply a silly notion of mine."

He stayed her protestations with a raised hand. "I trust your initial reaction. I will speak to her at the first opportunity."

At that, the first bell rang. "It is time for the ladies to make their way to their rooms to ready themselves for dinner. Sarah is helping those ladies who did not bring their own maid, and I fear she will be rushed for the next hour or so."

"Very well, I shall speak to her in the morning. The passage of a night won't make any difference."

CHAPTER TEN

Anna rushed into the bedroom just as Eloise had been about to ring and find out what was keeping her. Her apologies were written on her face. "I am ever so sorry for being late, miss, but Lady Dumbarton did not bring her dresser and I had to go help out. Begging my pardon, but the lady is most insistent about what she likes. I had to redo her hair twice."

"I am sorry it has been so rushed since you returned from seeing your parents. I trust they are well?"

"Indeed they are, miss."

"I am glad to hear that." Anna's earlier words made her pause. "I understood Sarah was looking after the ladies who did not attend with their own maids?"

Anna's scowl deepened. "That is what was intended, miss, but Sarah sent word that she was needed to serve drinks before dinner and would not be available. I had to go, miss."

"Do not worry. You may arrange my hair in a simple

style. There is no need for fuss."

"I'll have you ready in two ticks of the clock."

And she did.

* * *

Eloise surveyed the busy drawing room and saw Sarah, neat in her plain black dress and beribboned apron. The serving staff were usually unobtrusive, quietly going about their work. But Sarah's colour was high, her smile bright and her hips swayed as she covered the room, offering drinks from a silver salver. Eloise frowned. Sarah had taken to being in the eye of the guests far too well. There would be trouble if Higgins saw her behaviour.

Eloise crossed to where the maid stood amongst a group of gentlemen. Her intent was to draw her to the side and quietly warn her to be more circumspect when she suddenly stopped. The group around Sarah moved and opened to allow Eloise to join the gathering. The majority of the unattached gentlemen were standing together. Her stomach rolled, and she experienced a momentary urge to run. The lamb had approached the wolves' enclosure. She set her shoulders and lifted her chin a little higher.

Sarah noticed her, and a brief smile lifted the corners of her mouth. Her eyes dipped down as she bobbed a knee bend. "Begging pardon, miss, I was serving the gentlemen, seeing if they had everything they needed." Her voice, low and deferential, did not match the coquettish look in her eyes as she glanced around the group. Bellingham looked disapproving, Everton and Gooding simply smiled and Benedict stood to the side, his face unreadable.

Eloise kept her voice light and unconcerned. "Thank you, Sarah, you have provided enough assistance for this evening. You are excused. Please leave the tray on the sideboard, for we shall soon go in to dinner."

Sarah bobbed and did as she was bid. She walked tall and straight as she headed to the door, jaunty steps causing her body to slightly sway, and Eloise noticed that more than one set of male eyes followed the pretty maid.

* * *

After dinner, the gentlemen joined the ladies in the large salon, and Eloise was not quick enough to avoid Sir Frederick.

"Miss Camarthon, I have not had the opportunity to speak to you since my arrival. May I render my apologies for the recent unfortunate misunderstanding." Sir Frederick's apologies were as unwelcome as his presence.

Eloise forced a smile. "Thank you, my lord. If you will excuse me, I must attend to the guests." She emphasised the last word, but it apparently sailed straight over his head. He was not an invited guest, and she could only hope his blasted carriage would soon be fixed.

She moved away from him, and in moments Bellingham, Everton and Gooding surrounded her.

"Miss Camarthon, I would be honoured if you would show me around the estate tomorrow. Perhaps we could ride out?" Before Eloise could reply to Bellingham's request, Everton spoke up.

"Excellent idea. I shall join you."

Bellingham's brows drew together, and his expression

darkened as Gooding gleefully clapped his hands together. "Splendid. Let's all go."

Bellingham's voice was icy. "I imagine Miss Camarthon would prefer a sedate trot around some of the more bucolic areas rather than a mass excursion."

Everton disagreed. "No, we can all ride out together. That is a much better plan."

Eloise had the distinctly unpleasant image of stable dogs fighting over a bone—and she was the tasty morsel. "Gentlemen, I am afraid I shall have no time for a ride tomorrow as we have an early luncheon organised on the terrace. Perhaps another time."

Bellingham smiled, and warmth lit his features. "That is a good idea, and I am at your service."

"And I," chorused Everton and Gooding.

Eloise smiled and made her retreat. Her head was starting to ache from the attention and the weight of the decision her uncle wanted her to make.

She sought out her aunt. "I am a little wearisome after the long day. Do you object if I now retire?"

"Of course not, my dear. You do look a little flushed. I hope you aren't sickening."

Eloise craved a few minutes of solitude and, instead of retiring to her room, quietly exited the house through a side door and headed to her favourite spot in the gardens. A beaten path led through the dense orchard foliage and opened onto a small clearing, prettily moon-dappled and blanketed in wildflowers, shining white in the lunar light.

In the centre sat an ancient weeping willow, its branches sweeping to touch the ground. Carefully parting the curtain of thick foliage, Eloise ducked her head and entered the quiet, dark haven beneath its branches. A small wooden bench was tucked against the tree trunk, and Eloise gracefully sank down onto it, leaning her head back and closing her eyes. The silence was bliss. True country silence, in that the still air was only broken by the occasional hoot of an owl or the rustling of fallen twigs and leaves as the small night creatures scuttled here and there in the undergrowth.

Her chaotic thoughts were quietening, receding, leaving behind the unassailable truth. Whether she liked it or not, she would be betrothed, if not married, before summer's end. She had to accept that she would be irrevocably tied to a man that she knew little about. She shouldn't expect any more. Ton marriages weren't generally made for reasons other than wealth, advancement or strategy. There was no expectation of love or affection; that was a boon afforded to few. Perhaps there was something to be said for a comfortable marriage without the erratic highs and lows of passion and heartache.

In the stillness of the night, her jumbled mind eased as she leant farther back against the wooden slatted bench and rested her head, tipping her chin upwards as her eyes sought out shafts of moonlight filtering through the willow.

A noise—a heavy foot stepping on a tree branch, perhaps—alerted Eloise that she wasn't alone, and a tremor of fear caused her to shiver. As she sat upright, the heavy willow curtain was pushed aside by a large hand, followed by an equally large body as Rothsea stepped into the hidden space. Her heart hammered, but not with fear.

The shaded darkness, interspersed with dappled night

light, highlighted the planes of his face, giving him a satyric look. Under his appraising, predatory gaze, the very air around them crackled and came alive, becoming heavy as the space she occupied shrank, drew in. She simply couldn't tear her eyes from his.

Rothsea cleared his throat. "I saw you leave the house and followed you into the gardens. I wanted to make sure you were all right." He paused. "Are you?"

Eloise took a moment to answer, "Yes, I'm fine," she murmured as she stood to leave. "If you'll excuse me . . ."

With a swift movement, Rothsea halted her with a light touch on her arm. Although he wasn't physically restraining her in any way, the graze of his fingers, burned into her flesh, rendering her immobile with invisible coils.

"You don't seem fine to me. Is there any way I may help?"

A taut string snapped deep inside her as a geyser of emotion burst forward. "No one may help me. You know my uncle wishes me married, and before the end of summer; therefore that will happen, for my uncle is a forceful man. He is fearful that I'll become entrapped by some scoundrel who is only after money. But," she bitterly continued, all restraint gone, "how shall we ever know the difference? My fortune is so vast that it is all any man shall ever truly see in me."

Rothsea snorted. She couldn't clearly make out the look in his eyes. Was it compassion? "You don't seem to have a terribly high opinion of yourself, or," and here he grimaced, "is it that you have a very low opinion of the men you have met?"

Eloise stiffened. "I am under no false illusions. I

appreciate that being granted control of my wealth is a powerful inducement to make a gentleman contemplate marriage with me. But what if I don't want to marry yet? What if I haven't met anyone I would actually wish to marry? None of that matters. My uncle has spoken, and therefore I shall indeed soon be wed," Eloise finished bitterly, momentarily losing her composure as she turned to leave.

He tightened his hold on her arm and drew her closer until only a puff of air separated their bodies. She could smell the faint aroma of brandy, but it was not unpleasant. A light breeze swept past and ruffled her hair. She shivered, but it wasn't from the cold.

"Hush," he soothed. "Don't become upset. Westbury is a reasonable man; surely, you can make him listen to reason?"

* * *

As Eloise leant closer, seeking comfort, Benedict forgot what he was trying to say as his mouth went dry and her perfume—rosewater and something else, lavender, perhaps?—clouded his senses. A charge surged through his body as the connection between them awakened and beckoned. Time slowed, stood still. He accepted he had a powerful attraction for her.

He closed the gap between them and drew Eloise tight against his body. Moving one hand upwards, he clasped the back of her neck, subtly shifting her face towards his. Their eyes never broke contact until he lightly touched his lips to hers. Her eyelids fluttered closed, the dark lashes in stark contrast to her pale skin, pearlescent in the moon glow.

He meant to taste her just a little, the tiniest of sips, to slake the thirst which had raged in him over the days since they had first met. However, the moment her soft mouth tentatively opened to his, the reins on his control disappeared.

With his hand on the small of her back, Benedict brought Eloise closer. Startled, she pulled back, but Benedict halted her retreat, surprising himself with a ragged breath. "You have nothing to fear from me. I won't hurt you. I couldn't."

* * *

Eloise relaxed into the embrace. She was branded, the heat from their bodies searing through her clothing. Their kiss deepened, and her arms stole upwards, tentatively caressing his chest, until she reached up and held on to his broad shoulders as if to save herself from falling. But it was too late. Her mind was spinning, and she was willingly tumbling into unknown territory, experiencing sensations for the first time which she knew she would never get enough of. She knew that a door was opening, and all she had to do was walk through it and life would never be the same again.

She revelled in the touch of Rothsea's hands on her body, his mouth on hers. Although innocent and untutored, she was a quick study and matched his movements with her own. Her lips, her tongue, her body, all of her, readily responding to his. Caught up in the sensations washing through, the rising desire, Eloise gave not a thought to propriety or what would happen next. She was throwing caution to the wind and simply existing in the moment with no regard for the future.

Suddenly, Rothsea pulled away, causing Eloise to let slip a small moan of loss. Her disappointment was short-lived as he was apparently merely moving them to the next stage in their journey. She gasped.

"Do you like this?" His voice was gravelled as he pressed gentle kisses down the length of her throat. The lightest, softest, touches. Yet he left a fiery trail in his wake that threatened to consume.

Her eyes flew open and met his.

"Shall I go on?" The invitation in his eyes matched his words. "Don't be frightened. I mean you no harm."

She moved closer, an involuntary action she couldn't control. "Yes." The word was out before her mind knew what was happening.

His hand left her waist and gently stroked upwards, stopping at her ribcage, beneath her breast. Eloise's senses leapt at the unfamiliar sensation. Her breasts ached, were sensitive and tender to every touch. She gave a quick gasp of shock as quick, seeking fingers caressed her through the fine fabric of her clothing. Her insides flooded with heat as the fine material of her shift rasped against her delicate skin.

She let out a shaking breath as she pressed closer to him, wanting something she had neither name for nor understanding of.

He held her tight, and murmured, "My name is Benedict. Say my name."

Her voice was a whisper. "Benedict, I like that."

* * *

He covered her mouth with his and held her tight, his hands roaming as they wished. The darkness was alleviated by mere slivers of moonlight that insinuated their way through the delicate boughs of the willow. They were alone, cut off from everything they knew, and trapped in a world of their own making.

Eloise moaned aloud, arching her back and pushing herself towards him, as if silently begging for relief, for release, for more. Benedict stilled at the sound, awareness hitting him as he tore his mouth from hers, appalled and ashamed at his complete lack of self-control. He had pulled the top of her dress to the side, and her breast was almost uncovered. He closed his eyes in self-disgust. He held her close until her breathing slowly steadied. As he looked at her dazed and shocked expression, guilt tore into him. He should have gone slower, taken his time. This was too far, much too far, in one assignation. The word struck him—assignation—a word resonating of the illicit and hidden. He wanted more than that from her; much more.

He gently released her. "I apologise, that was unconscionable."

As Eloise moved shaking hands to resettle her clothing, he placed his hand on her forearm, simply to give some form of comfort, but she jerked away as if scalded. With shaking hands, she righted her neckline and smoothed her dress. "Please. Do not touch me."

Her words, simple as they were, slashed at him. He

stared at her. "Your hair, it needs to be fixed a little." As her trembling fingers rose, he stayed her hand.

"Here, let me." He tucked her curls back into their clips and some semblance of order. "Not perfect, but the wind could easily have ruffled it. Someone may be walking the corridors when you return to the house."

Eloise turned to leave and seemed unsteady on her feet. "Please excuse me, my lord; it is time for me to retire—way past time." Without turning round, she said, her voice trembling, "I beg your discretion, my lord. Not one word of this to anyone, ever, else I would die of shame."

His whispered, "I promise," was left hanging in the air as she swiftly moved through the willow screen, almost running out of the sheltered glade.

Benedict let her go. They weren't that far from the house, and her path was lit by the full moon. He'd follow slowly behind, keeping her in sight to make sure no mishaps befell her. They could talk tomorrow. He needed to work out what to do next, although deep down he knew he had only one option, one road to follow. Not what he had planned for his life, especially at this time, but what he would have to accept. The question was, would she?

* * *

Eloise ran to the safety of her room, grateful that the halls and corridors were empty of guests. She was shocked, embarrassed and unsure of herself and how to react. She had allowed this man the most unimaginable liberties, had virtually begged for more, and afterwards he had politely apologised like a stranger who had stepped on her gown and torn a flounce. Nausea rose, and she slowly sank into a chair.

A bitter slap of reality churned her stomach. What a fool she was. Rothsea, no Benedict – for now he would always be so to her - was a complete rake. Not only had he seduced her into behaving like a wanton, he obviously was well-practiced in dressing his paramours and coming up with excuses for dishevelled locks of hair. How she would ever look him in the face again, she had absolutely no idea.

She clutched at her stomach and gagged as foul bile choked her. She would need to compose herself before ringing for Anna and keep the hot tears of shame at bay until she was once more alone.

CHAPTER ELEVEN

He had wondered when she would show her hand, but not if. Her kind always had an eye on the main chance, and, emboldened from their passionate encounters of the spring, she had obviously found the temptation too much to resist. However, he was uneasy at her forwardness in contacting him. He had expected a sly knock on his door in the early hours of the morning once she knew he was at Huntley Rise. But not this.

He had been surprised by the message waiting for him in his room. Carefully placed on the bed was a folded scrap of cheap paper covered in a ratty scrawl of poor penmanship and atrocious spelling. Would he please meet her by the woods on the east of the estate—where they had met before?

He saw her long before she realised she was no longer alone.

She wore a plain grey outdoor dress and had removed her shawl, which lay by her side, and discarded the small cap which she habitually wore. She had readied herself for him. The pins had been removed from her hair releasing the chestnut curls that cascaded over her shoulders and down her back. She was sitting beneath an old oak, barely visible through the screen of leaves and ferns.

When she spotted him, a seductive smile flitted across her face. She slowly unbuttoned the top button of her high-necked gown, then the next and the next, until her dress gaped wide-open to the waist, exposing her thin shift. Lying back on her elbows, she bent her knees and pulled the hem of her dress upwards until her lower legs were exposed. Her shapely calves were bare above the tops of her sturdy half-boots. She shifted as she flicked the hem of her dress above her knees and around her thighs. Dappled moonlight caressed her bare flesh, and his body eagerly responded to her enticements. What harm could there be in one more time?

"Hello, lover. I've been waiting a while for you. Come and say hello."

* * *

She smothered a smug smile; she knew he wouldn't be able to resist. They had met last summer when he had been staying in the area. She recognised the introduction came with an ulterior motive, but she was looking out for herself this time. She had known her share of gentlemen, but this one had a way of making her feel as if he genuinely wanted her for herself and not only what lay between her legs.

Sarah was twenty-two years old and had been in service for ten of those years. She was grateful for her pretty looks, for surely that was what had got her out of scullery duties and into the smart uniform of a parlour maid. Getting out of the kitchen also meant she had a chance to be seen, and who knew what opportunities there were for a good-looking girl with flexible morals and an appetite to better herself?

Sarah had found out quick enough. From a viscount's son to an elderly earl, there had been more than a few who had fallen for her charms and invited her to their room. Whether the liaison lasted a day or for the duration of their stay, Sarah always made it clear that she was a poor and humble girl, and had she mentioned her sick mother who couldn't afford medicine?

Before long she had a tidy pile of coins stashed away at her parents' home. When she had her monthly half-day off, she would walk the several miles to the two-roomed cottage where she had been born and marvel at its smallness and the meanness of its decor. Now that she knew more, Sarah resented her parents for not trying to better themselves, for not trying to get more—more of everything.

Now she couldn't help but laugh that she had believed she could escape easily enough. Gentlemen were more than happy to take what she offered and to pay for it as well. But the bargain was sealed with a handful of pennies, and Sarah wanted more—a great deal more. She wasn't getting any younger. She needed to secure her future with more than a coin here and there in exchange for a tumble in the dark.

Her lover walked towards her, and Sarah smiled, her eyes shining with desire. For desire him she did. He was a good-looking man, a gentleman, and he could very well be Sarah's ticket out of here.

* * *

Sarah's voice was husky and inviting. "I've missed you. My arms have been empty since you've been gone." She was trying to gentrify her accent, and that annoyed him. She was a peasant slut. Did she think to get more from him than a quick tumble in the dark?

He snorted in disbelief. "Don't play that game with me. I'll wager you've been crawling all over any male who's stayed at Huntley this twelvemonth. We both know you're not the exclusive kind." And thank the lord for that. He neither needed nor wanted the likes of her in his life. Certainly not now—when so much was at stake. "What do you want of me?"

"Just you—the smell of you, the taste, the feel."

She patted the ground beside her and enticed him through lowered lids. Her unbuttoned dress fell open, the dark aureoles of her nipples clearly visible through the thin material of her shift. His next words would be important. He badly wanted her—the air was thick with desire. However, and this was the crux, he had to tread carefully. No word of this could get out. Not if he wanted to win all that he desired. For Sarah was too close to home for comfort.

Passion scented the air; Sarah was an earthy creature who knew how to use the talents she had been given, and she teased and enticed and drew him in.

As he moved towards her, she leaned forward, her ample breasts spilling over the top of the worn shift. He closed his eyes and stiffened his resolve as he knelt in front of her.

"Sarah, I am afraid I am neither in the mood for, nor in need of, your services."

He saw her blanch at his words and anger hardened her features, but her words were conciliatory. "Lover, don't be like that. You know what Sarah can do for you, can give you. I've been thinking, seems a shame to only have the chance to be together every now and again." He drew back as she teased her fingers across his chest. "Maybe I could move to be nearer to you—you could set me up nearby?"

The sharp bark of his laugh echoed through the trees. "You are delusional. I shall not be formalising any arrangement with you and, in fact, will not be alone with you again. Keep away from me."

He gave her one last condescending look before turning to walk away.

"Oh no, you don't. I know what you're up to. It's Miss Eloise, isn't it? We all know why you're here, what all you fine gentlemen are after." Sarah spat the words out; her eyes flashed, and fury clearly rose with her ragged breath. "Talk of the servants' hall, it is. How His Grace wants Miss Eloise married, and now here's a house full of you for her to choose from. I bet you fancy your chances—I've seen you with her.

He turned, his face contorted in rage. "Do not speak her name and sully her with your tongue."

"I'll do more than speak her name. I'll speak to her, so I will. Say as how I've been taken advantage of by one of the guests. That'll scupper your chances." Her laugh was manic, and he could see the truth of her words in her eyes. The bitch meant it.

"Don't be a fool. I'll say you were a silly little slut—always lying in wait for me, trying to entice me. No one will believe you. I'll even pay a few people to say you did the same to them—hounding them, flaunting yourself."

"You bastard!" With a roar, Sarah flew at him, grabbing, grasping, a feral look on her face as she tried to dig her nails in. He grabbed her hands and held her back, but she spat and kicked and screamed. He pushed her away with brutal force and released his hold on her arms; she stumbled and fell backward towards the massive tree trunk. Arms flailing as she tried to right herself, Sarah's head battered against the trunk, and she collapsed in an ungainly heap.

"Sarah, get up, come on." He stared, an icy coldness chilling him to the core. Time seemed to still, to slow. The commonplace sounds of the woods, leaves whispering in the breeze and scurrying nocturnal creatures, drowned out by his quickening heartbeat. Her silence infuriated him. He bent and shook her, and her lifeless body fell away from the tree, blood oozing from the gaping wound on her head.

CHAPTER TWELVE

Benedict rose early, hoping to have a private word with Eloise. However, on entering the breakfast room, he had been advised by the omnipotent Higgins that Miss Eloise was busy preparing food baskets for a visit to some of the tenant farms and would likely be gone most of the morning.

The disappointment was keen, which surprised him. He was usually a patient man, but he was far from that state at the moment. He would simply keep himself occupied until he could speak freely. He would have a discussion with Eloise, make plans and throw himself on Westbury's mercy. He strode to the stables, meeting Strathleven and Gooding along the way.

His heir's face lit with what looked like genuine pleasure as Benedict approached them. "Rothsea. Well met. I was looking for you earlier to say that I spoke to the duke last night and will stay on here for the rest of the week. It would be good to get to know you a little better."

"That is pleasing news, Strathleven." His gaze took in Gooding as well. "If you are going riding, may I join you?"

Gooding was all smiles. Of course; I promised Strathleven I would show him something of the area."

The three walked to the stables together, shortly riding out across the park, leaving clouds of dust in their wake.

* * *

Eloise was ticking items off her list as she packed the final basket. The Turner family had a smallholding to the north of the estate. Mrs Turner had recently given birth to her first child, and Eloise was tasked by her aunt to deliver good food from the kitchens: a joint of meat, some roasted chickens and fresh bread, together with ale for the new father and sweet treats for Mrs Turner.

She had hoped the domestic organisation would keep her thoughts from the previous night but it was not to be. The vivid images replayed over and over, her flesh burned with the sensation of remembered caresses, and she ached for his touch. She closed her eyes in shame. How on earth would she face Benedict when next they met?

A noise alerted her that she was no longer alone. Her aunt stood beside her. Her face was pale. "I am sorry to barge in on you, my dear. I am afraid I am not thinking properly at the moment."

Eloise moved to her side and, noticing her pallor, pressed her onto one of the straight-backed wooden chairs. "Please sit. Now what is wrong?"

"One of the housemaids is missing. Sarah Carpenter."

Eloise gasped. "What has happened?"

She sighed and rubbed her hands together. "Her bed was not slept in last night, and no one can recall seeing her after dinner."

Eloise frowned. "No one has any idea where she could be?"

"No, I am afraid not. Higgins sent a messenger to the girl's parents at first light to see if she had returned home. She isn't there."

Aunt Harriet coloured a little and looked at the ground. "Sarah is a little forward, but nothing like this has ever happened before. I have alerted your uncle, and he will arrange for enquiries to be made." She sighed. "The girl is in our employ and therefore under our care and protection. I do hope she has not fallen prey to mishap."

Eloise laid a gentle hand on her aunt's shoulder. "Do not upset yourself. I am sure all will be well, and an apologetic Sarah will return before I do. No doubt with some tall story to tell. It will be fine."

* * *

Westbury was attending to some personal correspondence when there was a loud knock on his study door. In response to his brusque command, the door slowly opened and, to his surprise, Sir Frederick Richards sauntered into the room.

His gaze was unflinching as he stayed seated behind his desk. "Sir Frederick, I trust all is well with the accommodations you have been allocated."

The fool obviously had no sense of self-preservation as he sat in front of Westbury's desk without waiting for an invitation. He sniffed as he fussily straightened his lace cuffs. "I am well pleased and would dare to assume that relations between us are cordial and you are now receptive to my desires."

"I beg your pardon. To what do you refer?"

Sir Frederick unadvisedly leant over Westbury's desk and wagged a finger in his face. "Now, now, let us be direct. Not what, but whom. My desires lie in the direction of your niece's hand in marriage, as you know full well. I am here to ask if you will now agree to a marriage between myself and Miss Camarthon."

Rage coursed through Westbury as he surged to his feet. "I have had enough of you—enough! I want you gone from this house within the hour. You're one financial disaster away from debtor's gaol and are a buffoon to boot. You will not be associated with my family—ever."

"I find that your refusal offends me, my lord. Now that I see my finer attributes are not appreciated and never will be, I can speak freely. Your niece is no better than she should be. Not only was she alone on a balcony with me, but she remained there with another—all alone."

Westbury threw himself into his chair, fists tightly clenched as he tried to keep his temper at bay. "To whom do you refer? Out with it."

"Why, I mean your dear friend, the Earl of Rothsea. I watched from the gardens. They were alone together for some time. 'Twas dark, and I could not see quite clearly. I do hope nothing untoward happened. That would be most unfortunate." He quietened as his sly words lingered in the air. "I am sure I could overlook this indiscretion in a wife, as it would be to my advantage to keep quiet."

Westbury's mind was a blank as the words slowly insinuated their way into his head. The lying little toad. If there was any man he could trust in this life, it was Rothsea. His voice was icy. "Are you blackmailing me?"

Sir Frederick smiled. "I would not say that, Your Grace. There is a way we can both get what we want. Your niece's dallying with Rothsea on the balcony will never be known, you avoid a scandal and I . . ." here he stopped and looked to the floor, but he wasn't quick enough to conceal his self-satisfied smirk,". . . and I get the wife I most want. Are we agreed?"

Westbury's gaze was direct. "I can safely say this matter will be resolved to my satisfaction by tomorrow."

Sir Frederick bowed and made to leave the room. "I wait to hear from you, my lord, and look forward to happy announcements on the morrow."

As the door closed, Westbury let out a long, slow sigh. He slumped in his chair, sharp pain piercing his temple. He knew he had no other option. There was a betrothal to arrange.

* * *

The men let loose their stallions and rode hard across the fields to the north of the estate, Gooding in the lead. After some time, Benedict hollered for them to slow down. "Let's take it easy. Gilgamesh is as yet unused to me, and I don't want to overstretch him."

The others complied, and they trotted abreast with Benedict in the middle. He turned to Gooding. "You seem familiar with this area."

"My father has ownership of a small manor not far from here. An elderly aunt lives there, and I visit her occasionally. This is fine country. However, our main estate is in Cornwall." Gooding looked to Strathleven. "And you hail from Scotland."

"Indeed. My land is on the western coast, bordered by the sea on one side and the Strathleven Loch on the other. To the north are the islands, and the south leads to the Lowlands. It is a pretty spot."

Benedict considered Gooding's words. He had not realised how much time he had spent in the area and slowed his horse even further. "I have heard that there has been a tragedy. The duke's man of business has lost his son in violent circumstances. His name was Bartholomew Jones."

Gooding let out an expletive. "Bartholomew?"

Benedict reigned in his horse. "Had you crossed paths with him?"

"No. I mean, not exactly. Sorry, I'm a little taken aback. I did not know he was dead. I knew him as a child. When we were older, we frequented some of the same local taverns. I haven't seen him in years."

Benedict asked, "Did he have any special friends, perhaps amongst the wealthy landowners or gentry?"

Gooding cocked his head to one side. "You are inquisitive. Did you know Bartholomew?"

"Not at all. It seems so awful that such tragic circumstances have touched the estate, as if the grime of London comes to tarnish this bucolic spot."

Gooding nodded, his sombre eyes locked on Benedict, and said, "We have time before lunch. Let's ride on a little farther. I need some hard exercise after hearing of Bartholomew's death. We can return by a shortcut through the woods."

Benedict looked at Strathleven, shrugged and followed suit. Gooding had been surprised at the news of his childhood friend's death; at least he had appeared to be so.

* * *

Eloise had delivered her baskets and smiled indulgently at the Turners' new-born babe. She was accompanied by one of the grooms, Seth, who squinted at the sky, his palm shading his eyes. He turned round and addressed Eloise where she sat in the trap, driven by Alfie, the youngest stable-hand.

"Miss Eloise, time is getting on. You'll be late for luncheon."

"Oh bother." She knew she had tarried too long, but the Turners' small cottage had been a comforting haven of domesticity, if not tranquillity. She quickly looked round. They were travelling along a winding country lane that she was sure doubled back on itself more than once.

"Let us venture through the woods. I recall there is a bridle path that should take the trap?"

"You're correct, miss. It will shave a good bit of time off the journey."

"Excellent, let's go."

Seth turned his horse towards the dense woods, and Alfie manoeuvred the trap through a gap in the tree line, the canopy of green deafening the sounds of the world outside the trees. The bridle path lay ahead. They could follow it all the way to the edge of the Huntley Rise lake and gardens.

The denseness of the undergrowth and the closeness of the trees stilled the air. No breeze would find its way in here. The only sound was the horses' hooves and the wheels of the trap on compacted ground as they travelled along the path. They moved in silence, as if in tribute to the majesty of nature. Eloise looked around, taking in the myriad shades of the foliage, accompanied by sudden flashes of colour from bunched together clumps of wildflowers.

"Wait—stop." Her voice seemed to boom in the quiet. She pointed to the left. "Over there, by the side of the fallen tree. It looks like clothing."

Seth dismounted. "Stay here, I'll go look. Probably rubbish thrown away by the Gypsies."

Eloise waited until he moved away before beckoning for Alfie to help her from the trap.

"I don't know, miss. Mr Seth won't like it. He said for you to stay here."

She sighed. He was so sweet but no match for her. "Alfie, I said to help me down."

He coloured and jumped to do her bidding. Once her feet hit the ground, she quickly followed Seth and soon caught up with him. He stopped, and she almost crashed into his back. He muttered what sounded like a low curse.

"Miss Eloise, go back to the trap, please."

She looked over his shoulder at the bundle of clothing on the ground. Shafts of sunlight crept through the canopy of branches and dappled shadows distorted the image in front of her. It took a moment, and then it was as if the scene rearranged itself and she could suddenly see the shape for what it was. Her knees gave way, and as she sank to the ground she screamed, a primeval outpouring of shock and heartfelt pain. Oh dear Lord, it was Sarah.

* * *

Gooding was in front as they entered the woods and carefully navigated their way through the undergrowth to join the worn pathway. The weight of silence pressed upon them, and Benedict's senses tingled. Something felt off. The silence was broken by a scream that rent the air. A woman's scream.

Benedict said, "It came from straight ahead. Keep going, Gooding."

They galloped ahead and minutes later came upon a trap with a saddled horse secured at its back. Benedict scanned the area and saw the small group in a clearing to the right. It was Eloise, and two servants.

He strode towards them. "What is going on?"

Eloise was pale and kneeling on the ground. She rose, her face stricken as she indicated a body lying at the base of a tree. "It's Sarah. She had not been seen since last night. She is . . ." She shivered and wrapped her arms around herself. "I believe she is dead."

"This is appalling—awful." Gooding's voice carried, and Benedict turned as the two men joined him. Strathleven moved towards the body. As he did, Benedict took off his jacket and wrapped it around Eloise's shoulders. She was shaking, and her eyes were blank. "She's in shock. Does anyone have any brandy on them?"

Gooding reached into his inside pocket and pulled out a monogrammed flask, which he handed across. "Here. Terrible thing, shock."

Benedict spied a fallen tree trunk. "Please sit here." He pressed lightly on Eloise's shoulder, and she dutifully sat and took a sip of brandy.

She coughed and spluttered, then pushed the flask away. "Oh, that burns. Please, no more. I am fine. Really."

Benedict joined Strathleven. The Scot looked at him with bleak eyes. "Such a beautiful young girl. What could have happened to her?"

Benedict slowly shook his head. "It is not immediately apparent. One could argue that she could have slipped." The girl was on her back, her skirts ruched around her thighs, her dress unbuttoned to the waist. "However, she is in a state of undress, so we must consider that she may not have been alone when she died." He drew his eyes away from the body and addressed Strathleven. "We must let Westbury know." He gestured towards the groom and the young lad. "Will you stay here with the body whilst we ride to the Rise?"

Their sorrowful nods indicated their agreement.

Strathleven said, "I will wait here as well. It is important to make sure the area is not disturbed, and three are better to achieve that than two."

"Yes, good idea." He turned to Eloise. "We'll be much quicker on horseback. I suggest we leave the trap here and you can ride with me."

Gooding approached, and his dull eyes lingered on the body. "What kind of monster would do this?"

"That's what I aim to find out. My horse will be slower

as it carries two, so ride on ahead and let Westbury know of this tragedy."

He mounted his horse and, leaning down, lifted Eloise in front of him. She said not a word, and her body was cold and rigid as he held her tight and galloped for the Rise.

* * *

The stable yard was pandemonium when Benedict rode in and met the pale faces and shocked whispers that awaited them. He dismounted and helped Eloise to the ground, where she was comforted by a plainly shocked Higgins who placed a warming shawl around her shoulders.

"Thank you. Has my uncle been informed of the terrible news?"

"Yes, miss. I have been waiting for you. His Grace has been informed of the situation. Lady Bentley is also aware and asked that you go see her immediately upon your return."

Eloise turned to Benedict. "Thank you for your care and attention. I must see my aunt."

He bowed. "Of course."

Higgins coughed. "My lord, His Grace awaits you in his study and asks that you attend him immediately."

"Thank you."

He quickened his step, anxious to speak to his friend. As he entered the room, Westbury rose, a grim look on his face. "Sit here. Let me fetch you a drink. You may need one. I certainly do."

Benedict accepted a large glass of straw-coloured

brandy. "Thank you. You will have been informed that we found that poor young maid. What a tragedy."

Westbury's face was solemn. "Indeed. I await Doctor Weston and Sir Jonathon Carmichael, who is the local magistrate. There is little we can do until they arrive. But if this was a deliberate action I will have justice for Sarah."

"Of course, well, I am happy to assist in any way I can."

Westbury sat behind his desk, set down his brandy glass and said, "I am glad to hear that, indeed I am. So, my friend . . . what exactly happened between you and my niece, and why did you conceal meeting in London?"

Benedict spluttered as the brandy caught in his throat, its fiery burn leaving him coughing and barely able to speak. He took a moment to gather his thoughts—and his defence.

"It is not what you may think, Westbury—there is nothing to be concerned about."

"Think! Think! I have no damned idea what to think. All I know is that snivelling toad Sir Frederick Richards is attempting to blackmail me into letting him marry Eloise by threatening to say that he saw you alone with her on a balcony, and in a compromising situation."

Benedict placed his glass on a side-table with a shaking hand. "That little good-for-nothing! It is lies."

"I knew it! You weren't alone with my niece?"

Benedict's throat constricted and he had a moment of panic. This was not going to go well. "Well, yes, I was, but it wasn't like that."

Westbury stilled, slowly leant back in his chair and raised his glass to Benedict in a parody of a toast. "Do go on. Tell me what it was like."

Benedict looked at his friend's outwardly calm and restrained manner and knew it for the lie it was. "I can assure you that Sir Frederick is twisting the facts. As I was leaving the Trent ball, I saw a young woman step outside with Sir Frederick. He seemed to be forcing her, so I followed. He was trying to kiss the girl and had her in his arms. I could see she was struggling."

"Damn it, I'll kill him."

"As soon as I spoke, he let her go. I saw him move away. He couldn't have seen anything."

Westbury sipped at his drink. "What do you mean anything? What could he have seen if he was hanging around?"

He remembered holding Eloise in his arms, as he had told himself he merely sought to teach her a lesson. There was only one option here. Denial. "There is nothing, absolutely nothing that Sir Frederick could have seen that would lead to a scandal. You must believe me."

Westbury barked out a sceptical laugh and shook his head. "What I believe is immaterial. You know how society works. It doesn't matter whether anything actually happened. It's whether something could have—and if people are talking about it. A few well-placed words are all that need to be uttered for Eloise to be on the brink of ruin. And if those censorious harpies at Almacks get wind of this, well, I'll be lucky to find a decent husband for her at all. No, there's no option. Eloise has to be betrothed, and sooner rather than later. I have no choice."

Benedict turned an astonished face to Westbury. "You cannot mean to allow Sir Frederick to marry her. That is outrageous."

"I know—that's why she won't be marrying him. She'll be marrying you."

He tensed as a chill hit at his very core. He ran a finger around his collar to loosen it, to get air. "I do not like to have my hand forced."

Westbury's retort was sharp. "Then she'll have to marry that toad. God knows but her parents will turn in their graves. No man of good family will marry soiled goods and see the consequences reverberate through his life—all the way to his children."

"You cannot, you simply cannot throw her away on that fool, goddamn it."

"Therefore you shall have to be her groom, my friend. That way if Sir Frederick dares to say anything, it will be as inconsequential as a puff of smoke. You speaking to Eloise, alone on a balcony, will be seen as romantic and charming if you are betrothed. If you aren't, it will be salacious gossip for wagging tongues. And I cannot allow that."

Benedict knew when he had no choice, and his honour could not allow him to act in any other way. He had already reconciled himself to offering for Eloise after the previous evening's events. Should it matter that the outcome would now be more by force than choice? A sense of finality settled upon him. "Very well. I will speak to Eloise as soon as possible."

Westbury's gaze was sharp. "I do not recall you being given permission to address my niece so informally—which you appear to do with ease. So perhaps it is fortuitous that these circumstances will give truth to your apparent closeness. No—do not speak. There are many questions I could ask you. The main one being why you concealed that you already knew my niece?"

Benedict squirmed. "I thought to protect Eloise."

"Ah, chivalry. Well, I expect you to speak to my niece and later advise me of the news of your betrothal. I shall forbear speaking to her until I hear from you. I expect Eloise to have a proper proposal of marriage."

"Of course. Leave it to me."

He should be feeling trapped, resigned to a fate he had not asked for—yet his heart pounded. After his actions of the previous evening, honour dictated that he must offer marriage to Eloise. Sir Frederick's meddling compelled him to take immediate action. He had no choice, but that did not dismay him. If anything, he felt relief. Eloise would have to say yes.

CHAPTER THIRTEEN

Benedict changed out of his riding clothes and set off on his mission. Upon enquiring of Higgins, he was informed that Miss Eloise was in the family quarters. Benedict took this as the dismissal it was intended to be and, with a smile, turned as if to walk towards the drawing room. After a few moments, the butler's retreating footsteps let Benedict know the coast was clear, and he retraced his steps quietly back towards Westbury's study and Eloise's private parlour. With a quick rap on her door, he opened it and went in without waiting for permission.

She sat on the sofa with an open book on her lap, though from the distracted look on her face he doubted she had been reading.

Eloise rose as Benedict entered the room, her book tumbling to the floor. A look of shocked surprise was swiftly masked. "My lord, may I help you?" she politely enquired.

Benedict closed the door behind him with a firm click.

Eloise protested. "I must insist that the door is left ajar."

Benedict advanced, shaking his head. "It is far too late for that, my dear. We need to speak, and I most definitely do not wish to be disturbed."

As he moved closer, she took a step back. "Eloise," he entreated.

She looked startled at the use of her given name. "Eloise," Benedict continued, ignoring her look of discomfort, "I am afraid there has been an unfortunate development."

She clasped a hand to her chest. "Is it about Sarah? Do you know what happened to her?"

Benedict moved forward and shook his head. "Unfortunately not. This is regarding a different matter. It is about us."

She frowned, and a tiny line appeared between her eyes. "Us? I do not understand."

"Westbury asked to speak to me earlier. Sir Frederick said that you and I had been alone together and that he could not guarantee his silence unless you married him."

She grew pale, and her eyes widened as her clenched hands flew to her chest. "My uncle would never agree to my marrying Sir Frederick—indeed, he has already refused to consider his suit. What nonsense—"

Benedict interrupted. "You are disregarding the circumstances. I am sorry, but the fact is that if Sir Frederick talks, you will be ruined or at the very least ostracized from the upper echelons, and I will have my honour in dispute. Your uncle will not bear a scandal."

"So I am to be thrown to the lions and marriage to Sir Frederick, am I? And the ducal name will be preserved, as will my reputation. There must be an alternative, surely?"

Benedict saw Eloise's beseeching look and knew, even if he had not before, that the die was cast. "You either have to marry Sir Frederick, which means he will not speak of the situation, or you marry me. By us marrying, anything Sir Frederick chooses to say will carry no weight. I suggest that the announcement be made this evening to the guests here. I shall send the notice to the papers tomorrow. We can either be married quietly at the Chase or at St George's in Town. I have no preference. You may decide."

The silence that greeted his remarks lengthened and deepened. Perhaps one had to ask a future wife's opinion? "What think you?"

Eloise exhaled on a long, low breath that resonated with fury. "What think I? I think you are an insufferable, arrogant bully who is far too used to getting his own way. So I may decide where we marry but, as is all too apparent, not if we should marry."

At Benedict's start of surprise, Eloise raised a flat palm towards him and motioned for him to stay silent, which, in shock at being so treated, he did. "You have not had the decency to make me a proposal of marriage, but have simply presented a fait accompli. However, I do wish to give a proper answer to the question that should have been asked."

Eloise raised her chin high and, looking Benedict straight in the eye, declared, "No, no, no, a thousand times no. I shall not marry you."

* * *

He said not a word, simply advanced towards her, a predatory glint in his eyes.

Eloise retreated farther into the room, Benedict stalking her step by step, his eyes never leaving hers, until she backed against the sofa and could retreat no farther. He gently pulled her into his arms. Her senses spinning, she tried to hold on to rational thought, but it fled in an intoxicating wave of desire, the intimacy of the unlit room heightening the palpable tension between them.

"My dear, if you do not marry me, and, if by some miracle, your uncle defies Sir Frederick's demands, there is every danger that our names will be bandied about in the most scandalous manner. Will you marry me? I believe we would suit well."

Her heartbeat thundered in her ears, and she simply stared, incapable of speech.

"Your silence disappoints me. I find I do not wish to be accused of something I have not done. Perhaps you need some persuasion to acknowledge that marriage to me would not be the worst thing to happen."

* * *

The rarely seen devil in him urged him on. They were as good as affianced, and a kiss would seal the arrangement. Having happily justified his actions, Benedict bent his head and covered her mouth.

He teased, nipped and tasted, all the while drawing Eloise's body closer to his, although he forced his hands to rest but lightly on her waist. His touch was controlled—no need to frighten her—but when she let out a small moan of pleasure, he deepened the kiss, running his tongue along her mouth, gently coaxing her to respond, to open herself to him. Her response was more than he could have hoped for and told him all he needed to know. She was most certainly not indifferent to him. He lost himself in the fresh, clean scent of her hair as her arms crept around his neck, pulling him closer.

The sound of slow, deliberate applause broke into their self-contained bubble and had them springing apart as Westbury's growled, "Congratulations on your engagement, my dears," slowly brought them back to earth.

* * *

Benedict protectively stood in front of Eloise. Her mind was awhirl; her lips full and bruised from his sensual assault.

Her uncle stood by the open sitting room door, a horrified Aunt Harriet by his side. His face was impassive, but the taut lines betrayed his fury. With a barely restrained snarl, he turned to Eloise, who, hair tidied, now stood by Benedict's side.

"Eloise, I see that you have most eloquently accepted Rothsea's proposal of marriage. However, I do have to say that a simple yes would have been a more than adequate response. Don't you agree?"

Benedict gently took her hand and spoke to her uncle. "Thank you, Your Grace. I am delighted to say Eloise has consented to be my wife."

Eloise knew she had little time to get herself out of this situation unscathed. "I have refused the earl's proposal. We will not suit."

"My dear girl," drawled her uncle, the slight tic at the side of his mouth betraying his anger, "have I never taught you that actions speak louder than words? After that outrageous display, you are most definitely affianced. And I now think that perhaps Sir Frederick spoke the truth. In any event, your choices were narrowed. Rothsea or Sir Frederick. You have chosen the only acceptable option."

Benedict stilled and she understood his discomposure. It was no great matter to be compared to Sir Frederick. His voice was cool when he spoke. "Eloise and I shall stay here for the remainder of the house party. Given the potential for Sir Frederick to cause trouble, I suggest we then journey to Town to commence the wedding preparations. I also have some business to attend to. In addition to my family, perhaps Lady Bentley will accompany us as chaperone?"

Before Aunt Harriet could say a word, her uncle answered. "Lady Bentley will be delighted to accompany you, as shall I. I refuse to let the two of you out of my sight until the wedding has been held! Now I need to deal with poor Sarah. I have heard from Dr Weston, and we are to meet in the woods. Benedict, you will come with me. You could probably do with the fresh air."

Benedict's voice was grim as he agreed, but Eloise had no words as the rest of her life was decided upon by Benedict and her uncle.

She fled to her room, brushing aside her aunt's offer to

accompany her. She gently touched her lips and ran her finger across their swollen plumpness. Her mouth still tingled from his touch, and as she closed her eyes, she relived those moments before they had been disturbed. Truth told, she found it hard to concentrate when Benedict was near. What did that mean for the future?

CHAPTER FOURTEEN

The Huntley woods were a jungled mass of soaring ancient trees and dense undergrowth blanketed by wildflowers. Some said the woods were haunted, others that strange noises could be heard. Few ventured there unless they had good reason, and those reasons were usually of an illicit nature.

Benedict stood beside Westbury and Strathleven as they looked upon Sarah's body, which lay in a crumpled heap at the base of a large oak.

Strathleven said, "I covered the girl with my coat but did not disturb the area. This is how she was found."

Westbury removed the coat and visibly flinched. She lay as before, dress open to the waist, her breasts almost exposed and her skirts hitched around her thighs.

Doctor Weston came up behind him and knelt as he carefully examined the body, paying particular attention to the head. With a groan, he placed his hand on the ground and pushed to his feet. Benedict heard the creak of aged bones as the doctor straightened. He crossed to his horse and returned with a rolled-up blanket that he shook out and draped over the body, leaving the head uncovered. "The girl should be afforded some dignity at least."

They all nodded, but it was Westbury who responded. "Well thought of. What is your professional opinion?"

"Look, here on the side of the head. She suffered a massive blow that would have killed her almost instantly. And here, see the blood on the tree trunk. It looks like she fell against it."

Benedict glanced at the body. "It could have been an accident, but her clothes are in considerable disarray. More than one would expect from a fall."

The doctor's eyes flicked towards him. "To sustain a wound like this, and for death to result, the girl would need to have hit the tree with a high degree of force, and a simple fall would not necessarily have resulted in death."

Westbury's face was grim. "Very well, we'll keep it quiet for the moment as I don't want to frighten my guests unnecessarily. I'll get some men looking into the situation."

The doctor stood up, brushing leaves and earth from his trousers. "If this was caused by human hands, they will probably be long gone. The Gypsies are always travelling through these woods. It's not uncommon for a local lass to be seduced by them."

"I know, Doctor, I know. However, if this is a deliberate act, I'll do all I can to bring the perpetrator to justice if they are still in the vicinity. Now I need to return home and await the magistrate."

"Ah, there is a problem. The magistrate is Sir Jonathan Carmichael and his sister passed away last week. He and his family went north. They will not return for several weeks."

Westbury frowned and shook his head. "Well, I am sorry for the circumstances, but this is inconvenient. Whoever is deputising will not have the experience to deal with what is obviously not an accident. Sarah worked for me; her family have lived and worked at Huntley for generations. I owe it to her to make sure the circumstances of her death are brought to light. I have a suggestion."

He turned to Benedict, who had an inkling what he was going to be asked. "You took over from your father and have acted as a senior magistrate for several years. Can I count on you to assist?"

Benedict heard the question and knew it was not a request but a demand. From the glint in his eyes, so did Westbury. He executed a brief bow. "Of course. I will help in any way I can, although I do not have vast experience in investigating such a serious matter as death."

"I recall that you have had more exposure than I, so I will lean on your knowledge. I will ride over to see Sarah's parents. They deserve to hear this tragic news directly from me. I leave the investigation to you. Go where you want and speak to whomsoever you see fit."

"Thank you. I'll join you in speaking to the parents. Let us see what they can tell us about Sarah."

The weight of responsibility pressed upon him. A girl was dead. He hadn't known her well in life, but in death she was now his to champion as he sought to determine the truth of her last moments.

* * *

Isaac Carpenter held on to his wife as she sobbed in his arms, shaking as tears racked her plump body. Benedict had stayed in the background of the cramped kitchen as Westbury solemnly told the Carpenters that their only daughter was dead. He moved forward at Westbury's signal.

"This is the Earl of Rothsea. He will help find out what happened to Sarah."

Benedict addressed the stricken couple. "I am sorry for your bereavement. If you do not mind, I have a few questions to ask."

Carpenter's face was blank, and it took him a moment to respond. "Of course, m'lord."

"When did you last see your daughter?"

The man looked at his wife, and it was she who answered. "Sarah had a half-day last month. She came to see us for the afternoon." Her voice cracked.

"Did she seem concerned about anything?"

"No, she was just herself. Laughing and joking. Same as always." She briefly closed her eyes and shook her head.

"Did Sarah have any close friends or a young man?"

Her father shook his head. "She had no time for friends except the other maids at Huntley. She didn't have a young man either. My Sarah was a good girl."

Benedict sighed. A good girl she may have been, but someone had reason to kill her. "Thank you. Do you have any ideas about anyone who would want to do Sarah harm?"

Carpenter shook his head, "No, not at all. Who could have wanted to harm her? Who?"

Now it was the father's turn to express despair as his shoulders shook and his body trembled with unshed tears. His wife was now the one to give comfort as she held him close against her chest. "Hush there, hush." Her voice was weary. "You always did only see the good in Sarah."

She looked at Benedict, and her shoulders slumped. "I loved my daughter, m'lord, but I knew her for what she was. Sarah wasn't one to mind her station or be happy with her lot. She had all sorts of funny ideas. Said she was meant for better. For a girl who looked like Sarah that meant only one thing."

Carpenter pulled back from his wife. "What's this nonsense, Mary? Don't be daft, talking about our Sarah that way."

She turned to him with what looked like pity in her eyes. "Isaac, Sarah was not a good girl, not these past years at least. She went . . ." She paused and a sob escaped. "Sarah went with men. They gave her money. She thought I didn't know, but, well, wait here."

She walked the few paces to where two threadbare and mismatched armchairs were the only comfortable seating. Between them, against the small window, was a low bench. She knelt, puffing as she did so, and pushed the bench to the side. Her hand pressed on one end of a wooden floor plank, and the other end popped up. Her arm disappeared into the exposed hole and pulled out a small drawstring bag.

Carpenter had been watching, and his mouth dropped open. "What you got there?"

She laughed, but it was a broken, mirthless sound. "This is what Sarah was worth to those who used her."

She upended the bag, and the contents clattered onto the floor. Coins. The floor was covered in them. There was more money there than Sarah could have dreamed of earning the entire time she had been working. Benedict was at a loss for words.

Carpenter bent and picked up a handful of coins that he let trickle through his fingers. They clinked on the wooden floor and the sound reverberated in the small room. He looked at his wife. "Where on earth would Sarah have got this from?"

"Don't be a fool. Sarah was selling herself for coin." Her voice was a hiss. She looked at Westbury. "I'm sorry to speak of my daughter's shame, but a girl that looked like her was only going to get money one way."

"No! Don't speak such filth of our girl." Carpenter's voice was a roar and his face was purple, his mouth mottled with spittle.

His wife shook her head, and her sadness filled the room. "I loved Sarah, but I won't run from what she was or what she did." She looked at Benedict. "Might this be something to do with what happened to her?"

"I don't know, but any information is helpful. Please, I know this must be distressing, but did Sarah mention anyone to you? Was she seeing someone in particular?"

"Sarah never said a word to me, but I saw her mooning all over the place whenever she came home. She wasn't a bad girl. She just wanted a better life."

And yet all she got was a violent death.

* * *

At the doctor's request, Sarah's body had been transported to the Rise, where a more detailed examination would be carried out. Benedict parted from Westbury in the main hall. He needed to find out if anyone knew what may have happened to Sarah. To that end, his first port of call was the servants' area.

The houseguests were in the lazy afternoon lull between tea and dinner. The men would be lounging in the library or playing billiards, the ladies resting in their rooms or gossiping in the parlour. The perfect time to gather the servants together.

Benedict addressed the crowded servants' hall, where kitchen staff sat next to stable grooms, groundsmen, footmen and ladies' maids. For once, all hierarchy was forgotten as Benedict spoke. "Thank you for gathering so quickly. You will all be aware of the tragedy that has befallen this house. Sarah Carpenter has been found dead, and we suspect it may not have been an accident. His Grace has asked that I assist him in finding whoever was involved. We need to determine who was the last to see Sarah. She served drinks in the drawing room before dinner. Who saw her after that?"

There was a heavy silence. He sensed it was a natural reluctance to make themselves visible; to be the one who speaks out.

"Please, all I want is to determine when and where Sarah was last seen."

There was a general shuffling of feet, and then a young maid spoke, her face scarlet and her voice a whisper. "I know when I didn't see Sarah, if that would help, m'lord? I share a room with her, and Sarah wasn't there at bedtime."

"Thank you, that is helpful."

A woman dressed entirely in black with chatelaine's keys hanging from a chain around her neck spoke up. "I am Mrs Havers, the housekeeper, m'lord. I set Sarah to dusting the lower parlours. She started the task not long after supper. I would have expected her to finish the job and head to bed."

"Thank you. Did anyone else see Sarah after you had all eaten?"

There were general mumbles and shaking of heads. The servants would eat after the household and their guests, and by his reckoning that meant that no one had seen Sarah after around eight o'clock. Apart from her killer, of course.

* * *

The servants went back to their own places and chores. Work continued no matter what had happened to a foolish girl. John Coachman waited until Hannah walked passed him. The cook had her own rooms off the kitchen, and he motioned with a nod of his head and a flick of an eye for her to meet him there. Her voice rang out as she ordered the kitchen staff. "I've something to do, so get on with your jobs and no slacking. I'll know."

A chorus of "Yes, Mrs Oaks" followed her as she left the kitchen. He waited a respectable moment before slipping past the bustling servants, each intent on their own tasks. The narrow corridor led to the tradesmen's entrance and the cook's small bedroom and sitting room. He entered without knocking. Hannah was waiting for him, and he settled into the chair opposite her.

Her smile lit her plump face, and he thanked his lucky stars that she had taken him on. Things were looking up all round.

"What you want, John? I can't be gone too long. Not long enough for what you likes best." Her saucy words were accompanied by a broad wink.

"Now's not the time for any of that. I saw Sarah by the woods last night. And I followed her."

Hannah gasped, and her hand flew to her mouth. "You haven't done anything stupid, have you?"

He brushed away her words with a dismissive flick of his hand. "Don't be daft. I hid in the bushes and saw who she waited for. Then I left, quiet as I could."

"You didn't see them harm her, did you?"

"That doesn't matter. I saw who they were, and I saw them with Sarah months and months ago. There'll be money in this, I reckon."

She leant forward, her tongue flicking out and wetting her lips as her eyes sparkled with the avarice he knew would be mirrored in his own. "Tell me, who did you see?"

"Never you mind. I'll deal with this, but it's our ticket out of here. Just you wait and see."

CHAPTER FIFTEEN

The evening saw the houseguests being joined by the estate's nearest neighbours. And Eloise knew this night would irrevocably seal her fate.

The air still held considerable warmth, and everyone assembled for drinks on the lower terrace that ran towards the gardens.

Eloise surreptitiously kept an eye on the doors leading from the house, her heart pounding faster with each long moment that passed. Then stilled as Benedict approached the group with whom she conversed; Bellingham and Gooding were among them, as was Sir Frederick. The latter had stood inappropriately close to her on occasion and had even attempted to answer remarks addressed to her in a proprietary manner. She had rebuffed him as best she could but longed for him to desist. The engagement announcement would cure his pretensions.

Eloise tensed as Benedict approached and drew her aside. What did you say to a man you barely knew who would soon be your husband? "Good evening. I trust your afternoon was well spent? Is there news of what happened to Sarah?"

Benedict shook his head. "No, we have nothing as of yet, I am afraid. I spent this afternoon discussing the marriage settlements with Westbury."

Ah, the real cut and thrust of the matter. No one of their status would think of marrying without ensuring that the financial arrangements were in order and enshrined in legal documents. She knew her uncle would look after her as much as possible, but the fact was that her fortune would automatically be Benedict's property once they were wed.

Benedict looked away as he replied. "There are a couple of matters we need to resolve, but I am sure Westbury will see my point."

"I am confident my uncle will do what is correct. He always does." Eloise heard the coolness in her voice, but she did not know how to act. Her stomach churned and her heartbeat quickened as her uncle looked her way and, inclining his head, indicated that they should join him.

* * *

Benedict knew his path was irrevocably set as Westbury took position on the top steps that led out from the wide glass doors, giving all the guests a perfect view of the proceedings. "Friends, I must thank you for joining us. Although tonight was intended merely as a way of bringing together our houseguests and neighbours, it now has a great deal more meaning for my family."

Benedict caught a glimpse of Sir Frederick out of the corner of his eye. The fool was preening and looking around as if he expected Westbury to call him forward.

With a raised hand, Westbury beckoned for Eloise and Benedict to come closer. Soft whispers and murmurs spread through the assembled group. Sir Frederick's face was a study of confusion.

Westbury gave them a long look before saying, "I am delighted to announce the forthcoming marriage of my niece, Miss Eloise Camarthon, to the Earl of Rothsea. I am sure you will all join me in extending your congratulations."

The gathering's gasps of surprise were quickly covered and words of well wishes and congratulations rang out as Eloise and Benedict were surrounded by the guests. Not all faces looked pleased at the announcement. Eloise's suitors, most significantly Gooding and Bellingham, looked taken aback, as if they couldn't believe that their hopes were dashed so quickly. However, it was Sir Frederick who was most affected. His look of puzzlement turned to one of anger as he saw his hopes disperse like mist. His threats held no water now; surely, even he was smart enough to see that.

Eloise was by Benedict's side. His chest tightened, and his heartbeat quickened. It felt right.

* * *

As they entered the dining room to join the other guests, they were waylaid by a stone-faced Sir Frederick Richards. With a bow to Eloise and a nod to Benedict, he said,

"Congratulations are in order. I must say it is a—surprise—but, well, I must congratulate you on your forthcoming marriage."

Benedict simply inclined his head briefly as Eloise dropped a light curtsy. Inside, she seethed. This fool was the reason their lives had been turned upside-down.

"Thank you, my lord. Do you stay with us long?"

"Unfortunately, the wheelwright says it may take a few days to fix the problem of my carriage, so I shall not be leaving for the moment. If I may render you any service, you only have to say. I believe you will be aware that I hoped for a closer association with you."

She wasn't sure if she was imagining it, but there seemed to be a smirk in his voice, a taunt.

Eloise's hand rested on Benedict's arm and his tension was unmistakeable. She spoke quickly to ease the situation. "Why, thank you, Sir Frederick, but I am sure Lord Benedict will be most happy to provide anything I require."

With a brief bow, he left them alone.

Benedict's growl matched his frowning face. "How Westbury can stand having him here, I do not know. The rancid little toad sought to blackmail your uncle into giving you to him. I would never have stood by and let that happen, never!"

* * *

Dinner was bearable, but Eloise was tiring of the speculative glances and questioning smiles. Uncensored looks came from those men she may have been inclined to consider as a husband courtesy of her uncle's machinations. Looks of disappointment and regret and, from some, unconcealed anger that the prize had been plucked from beneath their noses. Eloise knew she wasn't the reward sought—that honour was reserved for her fortune, the very fortune that had held her hostage and resulted in her having to marry this summer at her uncle's bidding.

She shivered as Benedict whispered in her ear, hot breath feathering across her skin. "I would like you to smile prettily at me, as if what I am saying is most pleasing to you. Let us give the impression that we are overjoyed at the circumstances we find ourselves in."

She did as he commanded and, turning, whispered back, "Like this?"

Her smile was wide, and she caught his gaze in her own. One moment stretched into another and then another, increasing the intimacy between them. He looked away first, coughing as he did so. His smile was broad. "Perhaps you are already too good at this. You are a quick learner, and I will need to watch my step."

Eloise beamed back, and not all of it was play-acting. Perhaps this marriage wouldn't be so bad after all.

* * *

Westbury was amongst the last to exit the dining room. Someone was waiting for him in the hallway. Sir Frederick.

"Ah, Richards. To what do I owe this pleasure?"

"I want to know what you play at, my lord. Eloise was to be mine!"

He held himself at ease and resisted the rage that threatened to erupt at the whelp's disrespect. "Come in here where we can be private." Westbury opened the door to a small sitting room and let loose as he closed it behind them. "You bloody fool. What are you going to say? That Rothsea was alone with my niece? That he compromised her? They'll be married within weeks. Can't you get it into your thick head? You have no power—nothing at all."

His mouth flapped opened and closed like a floundering trout. "But there will be scandal that Rothsea is being forced to marry your niece. None of you will want that."

"And again you do not see what is in front of your eyes. Rothsea has done a good job of making it look like a love match. Your game is over."

Sir Frederick deflated before his eyes, and Westbury experienced a modicum of pity. "Stop gambling; repair to the country for a bit and let your finances recover. Take the time to help your father with the estate. I hear it is ailing, but you can improve matters. You can't blackmail your way out of this."

There was a desperate look in Sir Frederick's eyes. "If I could stay here until my carriage is fixed?"

"Very well, but keep out of my way and no more of your tricks."

"No, my lord, no tricks."

* * *

The evening was almost over. The local neighbours took their leave, mindful of the distance their carriages would have to travel in the dark. Shortly after, tired but happy houseguests retired to their chambers, where biscuits and fortifying decanters of brandy and wine awaited them.

Benedict didn't have another chance to speak privately to Eloise, to probe and prod and try and understand her thoughts about their changed circumstances, and for him to test further this overwhelming pull that drew him towards her. He briefly raised her hand to his lips as he bade her good night under the watchful eyes of Westbury.

Refusing a last glass of brandy in the smoking room, he left the other men and climbed to his room. He had told Groves not to wait up for him. He slipped off his jacket and laid it over one of the chairs, moved towards the bed, and reached to undo his cravat. As he sat, he heard a rustling noise and, looking down, saw that he had crumpled a piece of paper, rolled and tied with a ribbon.

B, I must speak with you. Meet me by the side entrance to the stables at midnight. Please don't let me down. E

Benedict stared at the note and frowned. She must have slipped away during the evening and left this note for him. Would she have been so outrageous as to enter his room? Or send her maid? Either was fraught with the danger of discovery.

Benedict checked the ornate clock on the mantel. He had half an hour, plenty of time if he left right away.

The moon was obscured by heavy clouds threatening rain. As Benedict carefully made his way across the lawns to the stables, he hoped that Eloise had the foresight to wear a cloak. The second this thought entered his mind, the first droplet of rain hit his head. Pulling his jacket collar up, he picked up speed and swiftly made his way to the yard.

The side entrance of the long, low stable building opened directly onto the tack room, a large wooden-panelled equestrian treasure trove filled from floor to ceiling with hooks and shelves to hold the many bridles, stirrups and saddles required by the master of a fine country estate. Wooden benches ranged around the outside walls, but there was nowhere to sit, covered as they were with baskets of horse blankets and currying tools.

Benedict looked around with a rueful sigh—not exactly the most romantic place to schedule an encounter, but then he didn't know what Eloise had in mind. He certainly knew what he intended the outcome of their meeting to be. He wanted her in his arms again, to explore what he hoped was a growing mutual attraction. He didn't want to frighten her off, so he would take it slowly. Very slowly.

Benedict stood with his back to the door and, hearing a noise, turned with a lazy smile to greet Eloise. The smile froze as he took in the tall, cloaked and hooded figure coming towards him, barely discernible in the dark of the night. The figure raised one arm high, a long club in the outstretched hand and before Benedict could defend himself, his assailant brought the weapon crashing down upon his skull with a loud crack. Benedict crumpled to the ground, senseless, as the fleeing figure silently melted into the night.

* * *

Eloise had lain awake for what seemed like hours. The window drapes were drawn tight, and only a sliver of light crept across the room. Her mind was a jumbled mess. She would consider her own predicament and a melancholy would cloud her thoughts, and then the realisation that Sarah was dead would dislodge any concern for herself. What had happened to her? She couldn't erase the image of Sarah as she had last seen her. Not the vivacious and saucy maid, but the husk, the shell of what had once been a vibrant living being. She knew she should believe that Sarah was in a better place now but she was gone so young. What had she endured before her death?

She was roused from her musings by the wild clang of the stable bell. What on earth was wrong? She jumped out of bed and opened her armoire, grabbing a heavy chenille dressing robe. She pulled it over her nightdress, wrapping it around her body and tightly tying the matching belt. She would look respectable enough in what was no doubt an emergency. Slipping her feet into light slippers, she ran into the corridor and hurried to catch up with a harassed-looking Aunt Harriet, who was scurrying along the corridor ahead of her. From their vantage point at the top of the stairs, they looked upon a scene of unmitigated chaos. Most of the houseguests and a number of the staff were milling around in the main hall, the double-fronted doors wide-open to the night. The noise was deafening as puzzled questions were addressed to all and sundry as they tried to find out what was going on.

Her uncle strode in to the melee from outside and stopped short at the sight of his nightwear-attired guests and staff, holding candles aloft as they surged towards him.

With a shake of his head, he raised his voice to be heard. "Enough! The Earl of Rothsea has befallen a slight mishap. May I ask please that you all return to your rooms? Higgins, please have hot brandies and fortifying wines delivered to our guests to aid them on their way to sleep." With that, the efficient butler started to herd the guests into the appropriate wings as maids and footmen flew to dress appropriately before providing refreshments.

Eloise's gasp caught in her throat, and her legs threatened to give way beneath her. Aunt Harriet clutched at her throat in horror as she placed her other arm around Eloise's shoulders. "Come, my dear. You must be brave. Your uncle said a slight mishap, so that is what we must believe until, and by that I mean if, we know otherwise."

The hall was almost empty as Benedict was carried in on a long wooden board serving as a makeshift stretcher by two burly stable hands. Strathleven was beside him.

Eloise followed her aunt down the staircase, caring little for the informality of her dress. The men halted as she approached them. Her aunt giving directions for them to deliver Benedict to what she deemed a more comfortable room. He was pale, lying still. His fair hair matted with sticky blood, and rivulets streamed across one side of his face. Apart from the vivid slashes of blood, he was colourless, and Eloise suppressed a shudder. He looked as if the very life had escaped him.

CHAPTER SIXTEEN

Doctor Weston had attended that evening's dinner, and a groom had been dispatched to try and catch the doctor along the road home. Benedict lay pale and still in the middle of the four-poster bed. His hands rested atop the counterpane, and Eloise's fingers itched to touch him. But she didn't.

Doctor Weston bustled into the room, flustered, although it was unclear whether his high colour was the result of his unexpected dash back to Huntley or the wine he had consumed during the evening. He looked at the ladies, but before he could speak, Aunt Harriet advised, "We're not going anywhere, so get on with it."

Weston was well-known for his strong belief that ladies were too weak and tender-hearted to be faced with any unpleasantness, but he capitulated under her aunt's stern gaze. He quietly and methodically probed and prodded at Benedict, carefully feeling his way, testing bones and taking his time over the wound on Benedict's head. Eloise was maddened as he "humphed" and "aha-ed" his way through the examination without saying anything that would let them know how Benedict actually was.

With an "mmm," the doctor finished lightly tying a bandage around Benedict's head, carefully washed his hands in the bowl brought in for that purpose, re-donned his evening jacket and, with barely a nod in the ladies' direction, turned to leave the room. "I must speak to Westbury. I suggest you both get some sleep."

He had barely exited when Eloise jumped to her feet. "I must know what he says." She turned to Benedict's man, Groves, and said, "Please stay with the earl and call for assistance if aught is amiss."

"Of course, miss. I will not leave him."

Her aunt urged her on. "Hurry up and hear what he says. I will wait here."

Eloise moved quickly and, upon reaching her uncle's study, simply opened the door and walked in. Her uncle was speaking.

"Doctor, how is the earl?" Before the physician could respond, her uncle saw her and his brow lowered. "What on earth are you doing here? I did not invite you to this conversation."

"No, but you should have done. I am betrothed to Benedict and naturally anxious to know what has happened." She crossed her arms against her chest and stared at her uncle. After what seemed like an eternity, but could only have been mere moments, he shrugged and indicated the sofa. "Sit, and let the doctor begin."

The doctor looked from one to the other and sighed. "Well, he's taken a good whack. Mind you, it could have been worse. Either the assailant missed his aim, or Rothsea moved at the last minute, for the blow glanced across the side of his head, above his left ear, and across his shoulder. Yes, he was knocked out; however, as far as I can see, no real damage has been done. Though he'll need to rest for a day or so and take it easy when I do say he can get up."

"Assailant?" The word escaped before Eloise could stop it. Her hand flew to her throat.

Her uncle said, "There is no way it could have been an accident? Perhaps Rothsea went for a walk to get some air and may have stumbled. We had our fair share of wine this evening, and the ground was wet from the rain."

Weston shook his head. "I am afraid, Your Grace, that a blunt object was used by the looks of the wound, shallow though it is. This was not an accident." He rubbed at his eyes. "It grows late, or should that be early? I have left something for the pain, but it should be used sparingly, otherwise it'll finish the boy off. I'll be back in the morning to see how he fares."

As the two men rose, the elder steadying himself on the arms of the chair, Westbury pulled the bell cord, and in moments Higgins appeared at the door to escort the doctor out.

Weston stopped at the study door and said, "By the way, who found the earl? I have to say it was incredibly handy that someone got to him in time."

Her uncle stared, his face unreadable. "Strathleven. It was the Earl of Strathleven who found him."

* * *

Eloise awoke after a restless night and bathed and dressed in record time.

Benedict's new quarters were at the far end of the corridor from Eloise's own suite. Her brief smile was weak as she considered that even in the midst of last night's event's her aunt had retained sufficient sense of the proprieties to have Benedict directed to a room as far from Eloise's as possible.

The door to his suite was ajar. Eloise entered and, passing through the small sitting room, paused before the closed bedroom door. She knocked lightly. "May I enter?"

It was Groves who replied in the positive. He was sitting on a chair by the side of the bed, and Eloise could see from his reddened eyes and drooping countenance that the manservant must have been there all night. He jumped from the chair and bowed his head.

"Miss Camarthon, my master briefly woke up, just a flutter of the eyes and a smile, and then he fell asleep again." His voice was joyful, and Eloise was taken aback to note that there seemed to be real affection here. You could tell a great deal about someone by how their servants thought of them.

An iron weight was lifted from her heart. "Groves, I beg of you, find some rest. Please ask my maid, Anna, to come and join me in sitting with the earl. It will all be quite proper." No one was more of a stickler for the proprieties than a servant. Groves wavered for a moment, and Eloise's voice was gentle. "I shall tell your master that you were most diligent."

"Thank you, miss." He left the bedroom door and the sitting room door open.

It would take some minutes for Groves to find Anna, and Eloise was not going to waste the opportunity. She sat in one of the chairs by the side of the bed and took her fill of Benedict. He seemed younger as he lay sleeping; a wash of light colour dusted his cheeks, for the room was indeed warm, and there was a day's growth of fine hairs along his jawline. What would those whiskers feel like against her skin?

Before she could think better of it, Eloise tenderly stroked the back of her hand along the side of his cheek, relishing in the soft abrasion of his beard. Her eyes were drawn to his mouth, sensuously full, and she drew the pad of one finger gently across his lips, relishing in the freedom of touching him as she wished.

A gasp of breath escaped his mouth, whispering across her hand, and she looked up in surprise to see Benedict's blue eyes staring back at her. "Hello," he managed, his voice raspy. "Am I in heaven, or has the world tilted on its axis, for I do believe I am in bed and you are fondling me, madam?"

Eloise blushed and swiftly removed her hands, setting both primly on her lap. "Well, I am glad to see that you are undoubtedly feeling better, my lord."

Benedict made to sit but fell back onto the pillows, clutching the side of his head. "Ow. That hurts like the devil. What the hell happened?"

She ignored his language. "You were found by the stables. It is believed that you were attacked."

Benedict paled even further, a feat she would have thought impossible. His hand shot out and grasped her wrist in a surprisingly strong lock. "Did you see anyone by the stables? You are unhurt?"

Eloise was puzzled. Had his mind been affected? "Of course I am well. It is you who has had the accident. I was not by the stables and was in my room, abed, when the alarm was raised. The more pertinent question would be, sir, what you were doing lurking in the stables after the ball?"

Now that Benedict was patently on the mend, Eloise could let her mind move to other topics, such as what he had been doing in the deserted stables in the first place. Had he arranged an assignation with another lady? It was possible. She knew little of him, and he was only marrying her to satisfy his honour. The idea of him making advances to another, touching them in the way he had touched her, caused a leaden weight to settle in her stomach.

"Eloise," Benedict said impatiently, "this is no time for coyness. I was in the stables at your invitation."

Her eyebrows lifted in surprise. "My lord, I cannot imagine what I said to you that could have been construed as a desire to meet you in the stables, in the dark, and, let us not forget, in the rain and also unchaperoned."

Benedict sighed, his frustration evident. "Your note, Eloise. Your damned note asked me to meet you at the stables."

Pieces of the puzzle clicked into place. "I did not send you a note. So who did? What did it say?"

At that moment, Anna walked into the room, carrying a basket of mending, and dropped a blushing, bobbed curtsey.

"Girl—what is your name?"

The blush deepened. "Anna, my lord."

"Well, Anna, I have a commission for you to undertake. You must go to the bedroom I was previously staying in and bring the note that I placed on the bedside table. Please hurry." Anna turned in a flurry of petticoats, bobbing as she left the room.

So much for protecting my virtue, thought Eloise as Benedict sat up fully in the bed, the open neck of his nightshirt gaping wide to reveal a smooth chest covered in the finest of blond hairs. Benedict looked down at the ruffled-front nightshirt in apparent disgust. "What am I doing wearing this monstrosity?" He picked at the front of it with a thumb and forefinger as if he could barely stomach touching it.

Eloise blushed. "I assume, sir, that your man saw fit to dress you appropriately for the company of ladies."

"Yes, well. He keeps packing the damned things, and I never wear them. He must be delighted at having got his way."

The bedroom door banged against the wall, and a deep voice growled, "If you were not already injured, I would knock you out myself. How many times will you compromise my niece before you are legally wed?"

Her uncle entered, closely followed by an out-of-breath Anna, who presented a folded-up note to Benedict before bobbing and exiting. Benedict handed the note to Westbury, who quickly unfolded it. "This note awaited me when I retired last night."

Her uncle scanned the page and, thrusting the note

towards her, said, "What is this?"

"I have no idea. I certainly did not pen this. Why on earth would I? Surely, anything I had to say to Benedict could wait until the morning."

He glared at her familiar address. "Yes, it is certainly hoped that would be the case." He glared at Benedict. "Yet, my friend, I understand that you believed it was from Eloise and went haring off to the stables. For a midnight meeting. Unchaperoned."

"The note was in my room when I retired. I had already dismissed Groves and was readying for bed when I found the missive. On reading it, I didn't know what to think, but I assumed, obviously incorrectly, that Eloise wished to speak to me in private."

Her uncle's face was a study in simmering rage as his expression darkened. Benedict spoke firmly, "Eloise and I are engaged to be married, so whilst not of the first order, a brief, private meeting is not completely frowned upon, I believe? In any event, how could I have taken the chance that Eloise was wandering the grounds at night, waiting for me to join her? Dark, deserted stables are no place for a lady."

Her uncle stiffly inclined his head in reluctant agreement and turned to Eloise. "My dear, as you did not send the note, I believe you may now leave us to discuss the matter."

Eloise, used to her uncle's dominating and dictatorial nature, rose to leave the room, and then, looking at Benedict's amused smile, promptly sat down again. "No."

"What do you mean no? Do as I say, Eloise. That is final."

Eloise smiled and stiffened her resolve. "I think not. I am to marry Lord Rothsea. You have been firm on that point, therefore anything that impacts on his well-being concerns me, for I assume that the very existence of a note purporting to be from me is suspicious in the extreme."

She looked to Benedict for support and her stomach somersaulted. Was she wrong about his nature? Had she overstepped the boundaries?

"Eloise is a grown woman and soon to be my wife. I would like her to have knowledge of the circumstances."

"You're a fool, man! She'll tie you in knots if you aren't careful." With a resigned shake of his head, her uncle strode to the bottom of the bed and perched on the mattress. "Carry on."

"Having received the note, I went to the stables, to the side entrance as directed, and entered the tack room." Benedict took a sip of water from the glass by his bedside and continued.

"I was thinking . . ." He paused. "Anyway, I was slightly distracted and heard footsteps behind me. I turned to greet Eloise, but instead I saw a cloaked and hooded figure, and that was the last I recall."

Her uncle's voice was solemn. "That's twice in a week you could have died. The shooting and then this. I am sorry, but we have to consider that these are related incidents and face some harsh facts."

"Which are?" queried Eloise.

Her uncle glanced at her and hesitated.

Benedict smiled. "I am going to have a very unconventional marriage. I find that I have no objection to discussing any matters whatsoever with my future wife, and therefore let us speak plainly. That is what you wish, is it not, Eloise? I will leave to your judgment as to what you wish to be involved in and what you wish to leave to me."

Another chink in her armour was vanquished at Benedict's words. "Yes, my lord. I wish to know all."

Her eyes caught Benedict's, and they stared at each other for a long moment, a dawning realisation that perhaps, just perhaps, they could work this out and have a marriage that was more than an arrangement, much more than convenience.

Her uncle coughed. "Very well. I must speak of my concerns. Rothsea, you were found by Strathleven. It was he who raised the alarm."

Benedict smiled. "I have to thank my distant cousin, for without him I may not be here."

Her uncle did not smile back.

"What is it?"

"I had the area searched. The rain washed away any tracks. There was therefore no sign of anyone approaching the stables. We have no idea where your assailant went to or where he came from."

Benedict stilled. "What are you saying?" He sounded slightly belligerent.

Her uncle raised his arms in supplication. "We need to speak to Strathleven."

"Very well. If you will both excuse me and send Groves in, I shall get dressed."

Eloise interjected, "My lord, that is not acceptable. Doctor Weston will be coming to see you this morning, and I insist that you do not move from this bed until he does."

"Eloise, I am getting out of this bed. If you do not leave the room immediately, I cannot vouch for what you will see."

Benedict looked expectantly at her, and she assumed he waited for her to make her gentle excuses.

"I will leave the room, yes, but I shall not leave this matter alone. I find that I am not interested in being a wife who is only seen and is neither heard nor given the courtesy of being listened to. I shall therefore speak to you later, my lord."

CHAPTER SEVENTEEN

Several hours, and one relatively heated argument later, Benedict had persuaded Doctor Weston to release him from his sickbed, on the condition that he was to sit and rest, perhaps read something soothing, in the library or the duke's study, where he would be uninterrupted by the other houseguests.

"It was a tap on the head. I am absolutely fine," Benedict grumbled his protestations as he brushed aside the doctor's best attempts to persuade his patient to at least let himself be assisted in descending the staircase that led from his rooms. "I can manage one flight of stairs without your hanging on my arm." Benedict could not help glancing at the aging doctor, whose slight frame suggested that he might buckle under Benedict's weight were his kindly, though insufficient, offer of assistance to be accepted.

Dressed in buff breeches and a dark indoor jacket over a pristine shirt, Benedict's cravat was more simply tied than usual, betraying the fact that even Groves' implacable manner had been shaken by his master's mishap, and he had not the heart to truss Benedict up in one of the latest, more modish styles of neck attire.

With one hand firmly placed on the banister, he slowly but easily made his way to the ground floor and the duke's study. The location suited Benedict's plans for the morning, but he had no intention of resting. Westbury met him at the study door as if he had been waiting for him, which his words confirmed.

"Glad you were able to make it. Shall we get on?"

At Benedict's nod of acquiescence, the two men entered the study and made themselves comfortable. Westbury tugged the velvet bell-pull and a footman silently appeared as if conjured.

"James, kindly inform the Earl of Strathleven that we are now ready for him and should be pleased if he would be good enough to join us—immediately, please."

At Benedict's raised eyebrow, Westbury smiled and explained. "I sent Strathleven a note advising that we would wish to speak to him once you had risen and asked that he keep himself available to meet us at short notice. I didn't want him hieing off on the gentlemen's morning riding party until we have heard what he has to say."

Benedict nodded. "I am in total agreement. Any light Strathleven is able to shed on the events of last night will be welcome indeed."

Before they could discourse further, there was a brisk knock on the study door, and a solemn-faced Strathleven entered at Westbury's bidding. Strathleven closed the door behind him as his grave eyes sought out Benedict. Long-limbed and broad-shouldered, the younger man was a fine specimen of manhood to look at, but as to his deeper nature, Benedict had no clue as to whether he could be trusted or not. He was Rothsea's heir, and his turning up unexpectedly at the same time as these accidents started to occur was too much of a coincidence.

Strathleven moved toward him. "Cousin—let me address you thus, for surely that is what we are—how are you? I cannot tell you how glad I am to see you up and about. I trust there are no lasting effects?"

"None at all. I am a very lucky man."

At this, Westbury interrupted, "Thank you for your time, Strathleven. Please be seated." His accompanying wave indicated the matching partner to the armchair in which Rothsea sat. Strathleven crossed the room and settled his length onto the padded, high-backed chair. Westbury himself perched on the edge of his desk, his long legs stretched in front of him and crossed at the ankles, mirroring the arms folded across his chest.

"It is that very luck that we wish to discuss, Strathleven. We are attempting to piece together the events of last night. How did you come to be out by the stables and in the fortuitous position to come to Rothsea's aid?"

"I was having a nightcap in the smoking room. The room was a little hazy from the cigar smoke and I fancied some air. I walked to the open terrace doors and stepped outside for a moment. It was raining, and I noticed a figure moving towards the stables, obviously someone from the house. I thought nothing of this until a hooded figure came around the side of the house and made their way after the first figure. They looked furtive, and so I decided to follow the two. It did not look like a lovers' tryst, nor did it have the hallmark of a conventional meeting."

Benedict leaned forward. "Would you recognise the hooded figure?"

Strathleven shook his head. "I am afraid not. I did not even realise the first figure was you until I came upon you on the ground."

"Carry on."

"I followed a little behind the second figure, for I did not wish to be seen. As I passed through the yew walk that conceals the entrance to the stable yard, I saw the cloaked figure enter the stable. Then I heard a sound—a dull thud—which I now assume was you falling to the ground. As I ran towards the stable door, the cloaked figure came running out and barrelled past me. I went inside and saw you lying there and immediately raised the alarm."

"I am indeed grateful. Thank you."

Strathleven asked, "Could this be connected to what happened to the girl?"

Benedict shrugged. "I cannot think how, but too many incidents are happening for them to be unconnected."

"If that is all, I shall leave you to your rest, but I am at your disposal."

Westbury rose. "We now have a clearer picture of what happened, thank you."

There was a momentary pause whilst Strathleven exited the room and closed the door behind him.

Westbury turned to Benedict, his gaze searching. "Well, what are your thoughts?"

"I don't know. Strathleven seems too direct to go about this in a hidden way, to conceal features. Then again, he would certainly gain from my death. I would imagine he'd be capable of anything if he put his mind to it, and it is damned strange that he turned up like this. He must be after something. I don't really know him at all, so who am I to guess his motives and capabilities?"

"He bears watching. We cannot escape from the facts. Attempts would appear to have been made on your life twice, and all within a short while of your heir being informed of his good fortune. Perhaps I am too suspicious, my friend, but someone wants you dead, and with two attempts behind them, we can only hope we discover who they are before the next one."

Benedict looked up. "Well, I didn't fare too well in getting my hands on them last night," he said drily.

"No, but you were lucky. There is too much death surrounding us. First Bartholomew and then poor Sarah. Have you news?"

"No. Sarah knew Bartholomew, and they had contact within the last months, but there is nothing to connect their deaths."

"Should there be? Is it not far-fetched to consider the deaths to be linked?"

Benedict ran a hand through his hair. "Perhaps, but it doesn't sit right. They were childhood friends, and now both are dead in suspicious circumstances. Also, why the attacks on me? Is it because I am investigating Bartholomew's death?"

He moved and winced as a sharp pain shot across his temple. "Ouch. I can't believe I was so distracted that I didn't see who came upon me last night."

"Yes," Westbury said suspiciously. "You mentioned

that your thoughts were far away . . ."

He tailed off as Benedict tried, unsuccessfully, to stifle the guilty expression that he was sure had flitted across his face.

"Never mind, I imagine I don't want to hear what was occupying your mind. Do you wish to stay in here this afternoon or join the others in the gardens?"

"The blow wasn't so bad, you know. I may take it easy though. Has Gareth Jones returned yet? You said you expected him today."

"Yes. He arrived earlier. I requested that he rest and refresh himself, and join us here. I have some matters to attend to, but I shall return with Gareth. Shall I arrange for luncheon to be served to you in here?"

"Thank you—wait. It is probably best if I update Eloise about our conversation with Strathleven. Perhaps you could mention to her where I will be?"

Westbury smiled briefly. "Of course. Should I speak to Eloise, I shall let her know you are asking for her."

* * *

An early luncheon was served on the terrace, to allow the ladies time to rest before their preparations for that evening's ball. As Eloise approached the buffet table, Lord Gooding moved in front of her, blocking her progress. He gave an extravagant bow and indicated the empty plate in his hand. "Please, may I serve you?"

This was the last thing Eloise needed as she wasn't in the mood for small talk, but she smiled in acceptance. "Of course, thank you."

Her plate was soon groaning with tempting treats and delicacies, but she feared she'd not eat a bite. Gooding pulled out two chairs at the long table, and she sat next to him. She glanced around at the other guests. The atmosphere was subdued. Although no formal announcement had been made, the news of Sarah's death would have flown on the wind. The Huntley staff would have discussed it with the visiting maids, valets and grooms, and they, in turn, would have passed all the gory details, factual or not, on to their masters and mistresses. As for Benedict, they had simply said he had slipped in the muddy yard, but it would still be another incident for the guests to gossip over.

Gooding's voice broke across her musings, "I must confess I was surprised to hear of your sudden engagement to Rothsea."

Eloise resisted the temptation to say she had experienced the same emotion. She simply smiled and dipped her head. This was not a conversation she wished to partake of.

"My lord, I believe you know this area well."

She relaxed as he accepted the change in subject without a quibble. "Yes, indeed I do. A dear maiden aunt resides nearby, and I spent many a summer month with her as a young boy."

"Were there other children around to keep you company?"

"No, my aunt lived alone, but I made friends with local children and ran through the woods with them. I am afraid we were a little wild."

This intrigued her. Her own childhood had been

sheltered to say the least. "Did you stay friends as you grew?"

"No, our lives took very different paths, as is the order of such things."

Gooding's shoulders were tight and the muscles in his neck bunched. He opened his mouth to speak, then closed it and looked away. Then appeared to steel himself. "I must confess that I had certain expectations for my stay at Huntley that have been dashed. I had hoped to get to know you better." He stopped, and the silence lengthened. "And suddenly you are betrothed to Rothsea."

The bitterness of his words lingered in the air and Eloise made to rise. "If you will please excuse me, I must speak with my aunt."

His hand shot out and grabbed her wrist and she sank into her chair to avoid a scene. She could handle this.

"Of course, I should not be surprised that Rothsea moved so quickly, given his circumstances."

She tensed. "To what do you allude?"

He leaned in and whispered, "It is not widely known, but there are rumours of Rothsea debts. I would urge you to consider if you know the man to whom you are promising your life."

She kept her smile even and her features neutral. "Thank you, my lord. I know all I need to of the Earl of Rothsea. Good day."

She moved with carefully controlled steps to hide the fact that she was shaking. Was it true? Had Rothsea seen her as a way to settle his debts? Yet again she was hostage to her fortune.

* * *

Gareth Jones was a tall, thin Welshman whose black hair was speckled with grey. His eyes were sunken and shadowed with the grief that was etched in the craggy lines of his face. He sat opposite Benedict, shoulders slumped, and carefully sipped at a brandy Westbury had pressed upon him. He coughed and answered Benedict's question. "I don't know of anyone who would have wanted to harm Bartholomew." He briefly looked at the floor, and when his gaze met Benedict's, there was resignation in his eyes. "But that doesn't mean very much. I rarely saw my son, and he was not a reliable correspondent. He had taken over his father-in-law's moneylending business, so who knows what kind of people he was dealing with."

"You had little knowledge of his business dealings?"

"I had none. My son was the beneficiary of a good education and had all the attributes to be a fine private secretary. He left here to take up an excellent position but resigned barely a year later to work alongside his new wife's father."

There was an undercurrent rippling through the words. "You did not approve?"

Gareth sighed. "I did not approve of the wife, the father-in-law or his business, but who am I to be listened to? Bartholomew made his own bed."

Westbury asked, "Who did Bartholomew work for in London?"

Gareth answered, brows drawn together, "Apologies. I thought I had told you. He was private secretary to Lord Everton."

Benedict sat up straight, and the claret in his glass sloshed and spilled over onto his hand, which he hastily wiped. "Lord Everton is one of the guests here. I did not know he had a connection with your son. How did they meet? Did they stay in touch?"

"I do not know if contact was maintained, but I would doubt it. As regards how they met, you should speak to Lord Gooding. It was he who introduced Bartholomew to Lord Everton in the first place."

* * *

Eloise found her aunt in her elegant private parlour. She was lying on the sofa with a muslin cloth covering her eyes. Eloise backed towards the door. She would give her aunt some peace.

"Eloise, come in, please."

Her aunt swung her slipper-clad feet to the floor and sat up, the eye mask discarded. She patted the sofa. "Come sit next to me. I was grabbing forty winks before checking all is in order for this evening."

"Thank you. I won't keep you but a moment. Have you seen Rothsea? He was not at luncheon, and his rooms were empty when I passed by a moment ago."

Her aunt raised her brows. "For someone who was bemoaning a forced engagement, you seem excessively interested in Rothsea's whereabouts."

Eloise cursed the heat that flamed her cheeks. "I am mindful of the position I am placed in and seek only to make the best of it. It is simply that the earl has been injured, and I was curious as to how he was, in a charitable way." Her words sounded lacklustre, even to her own ears.

Her aunt's "humph" and rolled eyes made her regret broaching the topic. "I should go now and let you rest."

A gentle hand on her arm prevented her from rising. "Be careful you don't push Rothsea away. I know the circumstances are not ideal, and I do not agree with how Westbury has gone about managing your future, but neither you nor Rothsea are without fault. He is a good man, and I think you could be happy. Do not look for problems where there are none."

"I can hardly find a problem with Rothsea when I haven't spoken to him since this morning. There is surely a great deal to consider and discuss, yet he does not seem eager to seek me out."

"Do not act the shrew, I beg of you. Are you sure you do not simply miss Rothsea and desire his company?"

"Of course not. I hardly know the man and have not had the opportunity to form any strong opinion of him." The lie coated her tongue.

"Perhaps you should have considered that before you ended up in his arms."

The dry tone dripped with sarcasm, and Eloise figured she wasn't going to get any sympathy here.

She shifted, ready to rise, when her aunt's words stopped her.

"Wait. We must speak, I cannot hold my tongue."

She shivered as a cold dread iced her blood. If her aunt's thoughts were heading to past times she had no desire to discuss them.

Gentle hands held her own. "Your parents had an unusual connection. No, don't turn away from me!" The sharp reprimand gave her pause.

Her aunt continued, "We should have spoken much earlier. Your mother's death has undoubtedly impacted upon you. I have eyes and some knowledge of matters between a husband and wife, albeit I've been a widow these long years."

Eloise wanted to clasp her hands against her ears to block out what was coming next. "Aunt, please. There is no need to open old wounds."

"Rather air them than let them fester. The Earl of Rothsea is a man you could build a fine life with. From the circumstances that led to your betrothal there is undoubtedly passion between you."

Eloise burned with embarrassment. "Aunt, matters were not quite what they seemed."

"No false protestations, you know what I mean. All I want to say is don't run from this man, do not push him away. Give whatever is between you a chance to grow. Your mother followed her own path; you don't have to copy her."

"But…"

"No, let us be frank. Your mother taking her own life was, in my opinion, an act of betrayal. She left two children orphaned because she couldn't bear to live without her husband. I cannot forgive her that act."

Eloise beseeched, "Uncle Richard said we must never speak of this."

"And I agreed. It had to be kept quiet but not to the extent that you ruin your chance to have a good future. It is alright to care for someone, to love them. Please, mind how you act."

She left with a heavy heart. She had come here thinking that if Rothsea had no interest in being in her company, then did it mean that yet again it was her fortune that was the lure? Now she must reflect on why she should care. Of course she wanted her husband to be fond of her but not in a way that made them think only of each other. Certainly not the way her parent's had loved, that had been too much and too powerful. From the hollowness in her stomach and the confusion in her head she must surmise that she no longer knew what she wanted.

* * *

Benedict was exhausted and his head ached, but he was fired with anticipation as he stared at the two men in front of him. Gooding had adopted a seemingly relaxed, louche pose, yet his fingers drummed on the wooden armrest of his chair. Everton looked from Westbury to Benedict as his brows drew together in a dark look. "What is this about?"

Benedict stood and faced them. "Bartholomew Jones was introduced to you by Gooding, and I believe he was taken into your household as your private secretary."

"Yes, that is correct, but what does that signify?"

"That you both knew a man who was recently murdered. Why did he leave your employ?"

Everton flicked what was presumably an imaginary piece of lint from his pristine breeches. "He went to work with his future father-in-law. He'd barely been with me a year. It was incredibly inconvenient."

"When did you last see him?"

"On the day he handed in his notice. I told him I had no more need of him and he could leave immediately."

"So you haven't seen him since?"

"That is what I said."

Benedict looked at Gooding, who was listening to the conversation with a bored look on his face. "You claimed mere acquaintance with Bartholomew and that you hadn't seen him in years. Yet you apparently got him a job with Everton?"

"That was years ago, and I haven't seen him since. The last I saw him he said he was moving to London and seeking a position. I promised to send letters of introduction to a few people I knew who may have use of him for an administrative role. Everton was one of them. I had no further contact with him, although I did hear he was married."

Everton stood. "I am late for a game of croquet. I assume you are done with us?"

"For the moment."

They left, and he stared out the window, arms rigid by his side and fists curled tight. Either of them could have bankrolled Bartholomew Jones. But could they also be capable of murder?

CHAPTER EIGHTEEN

Eloise walked into the drawing room, a serene smile on her face and a temper bubbling away inside. She had gone in search of Benedict earlier, but he wasn't in his rooms, he had not attended luncheon and none of the other guests had seen him. Her uncle had not been visible either; perhaps they had been together?

It was certainly not that she had any particular urge to see him. Not at all. But surely they should keep up their agreed pretence of a happy couple? She had to concede that the discussion with her aunt had shaken her, and opened up emotions she did not wish to consider. She was not her mother and never would be. Caring too much was not an option.

Benedict was now standing in a group with Bellingham and Strathleven.

"My lords, I am sorry to interrupt, but may I drag my fiancé from your side? There are some matters I must discuss with him. About the wedding, you know."

Her smile was wide, but she avoided eye contact in case any latent rage simmered in her gaze. Strathleven was all accommodation; Bellingham's face was stern and unyielding.

Benedict took hold of Eloise's arm and, turning her, said, "Shall we stroll amongst the roses? It is a fine evening."

She nodded her acceptance, her jaw aching from keeping a smile on her face and her temper in check. She didn't dare say anything in case she betrayed herself whilst the guests on the terrace were still in full hearing of them.

Her body responded to his proximity, to the strength of his arm beneath hers. The smooth material of his evening jacket was sensuous beneath her fingertips, causing her to wonder what his bare skin felt like. Would the hairs on his arms be fine, like hers, or coarse, like the shirtless farmers who toiled in the summer heat? Were his muscles finely hewn like the smooth, elegant marble statues of David or taut and well-developed, and savage, like the painting of the near-naked Spartans that could be found at the British Museum?

Dear heavens, she was hot. Eloise swept the back of her hand across her brow as she tamped down these traitorous thoughts and unwanted desires. It meant nothing, nothing at all, that he provoked such a strong reaction in her. All she had to do was focus. Concentrate on why he wanted her, and it had nothing to do with honour or even desire, and everything to do with cold, hard cash and the valuable dirt of the land.

A few short steps from the terrace, they entered the

rose walk. A mass of heavily scented blooms were trained over wicker archways to create a colourful and fragrant passage. The arches were spaced slightly apart, which meant that a strolling couple could still be seen and yet enjoy some semblance of privacy. The heady scent assailed Eloise as they walked along the flagstone pathway under the floral arbours but she was in no mood to appreciate the normally intoxicating fragrance. Taking a deep breath, she began, "I wish us to be perfectly frank with each other. I would ask that there be honesty between us."

His smile was wide. "I am all for that. I cannot see how a marriage can truly survive without the principal parties speaking their minds, at least with each other."

She took another deep breath. "I know of your financial position and can see that my fortune is a great inducement to you. I have to say that I am angered that you sought my hand by trickery, by placing me in the very same sort of compromising situation that you had previously warned me of. No doubt you found me an easy mark, my lord?" Eloise could not help the bitterness, and disappointment, that crept into her voice. "It must have been a great relief to you that Sir Frederick arrived here and told my uncle that we were together on the balcony. Dear Lord, are you in cahoots with him?" Her mind was whirring.

Benedict's face betrayed no emotion. "What on earth are you talking about?"

"I must confess that I overheard you speaking to my uncle on the day you arrived; you said you could not afford for your sister to make her come-out and spoke of finding a rich wife. I believed you may have been making a joke."

The last was said with bitterness and a hint of futility for her situation. "I have also recently heard that there are rumours of Rothsea debts."

He was completely still, and the tendons in his neck were taut. A pulse throbbed at the side of his mouth. "I see. So you believe I deliberately compromised you?"

Eloise laughed, although it was devoid of mirth. "I am not a fool, sir. You have no doubt avoided many a matrimonial trap in your time, and yet you expect me to believe that you were unaware of the position your attentions would put us in?"

Benedict's face was impassive, his voice brusque as he spoke. "Your mind is obviously made up, then, as to my designs. You are a silly eavesdropping little fool. At least have the goodness to tell me who believes they have knowledge of my private financial position."

"It matters not, but it was Lord Gooding."

"Ah, wise words from a man who is dependent upon his father for every penny he spends and who himself has designs on either you or your fortune." He placed his hand on her arm and turned her around to go back to the house. "There are several things you should know, although you deserve to be left in the dark with your suspicions." His next words were bitten out, and she could not miss the controlled anger. "My wealth is greater than yours. We were temporarily constrained after my father died, but I worked tirelessly to reverse our fortunes, which has been successful." He paused. "My family circumstances were not publicly known, no matter what Gooding insinuates. I indeed cannot afford to debut my sister this year, but only because she is a hoyden and would have no chance of snagging a husband and would no doubt ruin her chances of ever hoping to get married once it was put about that she is a tomboyish terror. So I have decided to wait at least a year before her presentation." He stopped and held her firmly by the upper arms as he gazed into her face. "And finally, I wish it were different, but I find I am drawn to you. I cannot seem to help myself where you are concerned."

He drew back and dropped his hands from her as if scalded. "However, you have obviously made your mind up that I am a scoundrel, so a fine start to married life we shall have."

They had recommenced walking and, all too soon, Benedict swiftly escorted her back onto the terrace, where he bowed and, speaking louder so he could be overheard, said, "Please forgive me, my dear, I promised Strathleven I would tell him some of the family history." And with that he was gone, leaving a stunned and startled Eloise looking after him in confusion.

If Benedict didn't need her money, why on earth did he want to marry her? For honour alone? And why did he look so hurt, as if she had let him down?

* * *

Benedict was near to death with boredom.

He was no prude but, good God, he could almost see his dinner guest's nipples every time she bent forward. He was fairly sure the young Countess of Harewood was aware of this, as she did seem to bend forward more than was warranted. He kept his eyes firmly on her face, or rather on the large ornate mirror on the wall behind her. The huge gilt-edged mirror reflected the lights of the candelabra, the wall sconces and, pleasingly, the entire far end of the dining table. Benedict had played at attentiveness to his dinner partner while his eyes strayed time and time again to the mirror, reflecting Eloise and her constant glances towards him. She clearly wasn't as indifferent as she made out.

Benedict had been shocked and confused by how Eloise's words had affected him. He wanted a companionable marriage with real affection. But how could this be if his intended thought him a penniless fortune hunter without honour?

He cast another glance at the mirror. Eloise looked anxious, and he could see she was growing increasingly perturbed by the countess and her extravagant behaviour. Good! She had hurt him with her accusations, and even though he knew it was petty, he wanted her to suffer as well.

* * *

Eloise was seated by Bellingham, who, after dispensing with generalities and pleasantries, broached a much more personal subject. "Miss Camarthon, I have earlier proffered my felicitations for your recent engagement, but there is something weighing heavily upon which I must speak."

Eloise hid her surprise at this turn of conversation and reluctantly withdrew her gaze from the goings-on at the other end of the table. "Pray, sir, to what do you refer?"

He moved closer and kept his voice low. "My dear, I hold you in especially high regard and had hoped that we could perhaps reach a more permanent understanding during my visit. Alas for me, Rothsea stole a march, and you are farther from me than ever before. However, I do want you to know that should matters not progress as intended, I would wish to request the duke's permission to make my addresses to you."

Eloise schooled her features so as to not betray any emotion, which wasn't easy. However, as she made to speak, hoping to change the subject, Bellingham continued, "I have considered much of what you said regarding the role of a politician's wife, and I would be happy to accept whatever support a wife may have to offer."

"I am flattered. However, I am engaged to marry the Earl of Rothsea."

"I am happy to wait and see the outcome. For my hopes will not be dashed until you are actually wed."

Eloise was at a loss for words. As providence would have it, their plates were removed and the next course served, allowing her to turn to Colonel Eastleigh, who was the dinner partner on her other side. As Eloise listened to the elderly colonel's monologue on his prize roses, she couldn't help but let her mind flit back to the odd conversation with Bellingham.

Bellingham was more the sort of husband she had imagined. But it was already too late. Even without considering the scandal of a broken engagement, Eloise knew her emotions were already too deeply involved to countenance any other husband than the one she was engaged to have. She had fallen too far to save herself.

Benedict sat next to the Countess of Harewood, who, in Eloise's opinion, was no better than she should be. The young wife of a septuagenarian earl, the countess was red-headed, buxom and known to be shamelessly flirtatious. Eloise hadn't given the young matron's antics a second thought before this evening. Now she tried to stop looking but found she couldn't. Her gaze was drawn time and time again to where Benedict sat, being fawned over by the voluptuous siren. Not once did he look at Eloise.

The time at the table was interminable. Listening to her dinner partners with half an ear, her eyes strayed far too frequently to the far side of the room, her thoughts returning to their conversation of earlier. Benedict said he was wealthy and, if she was honest, there was nothing to have led her to believe otherwise. Even she could see that Gooding had an ulterior motive in trying to discredit the man she was to marry. After all, he had come to this house party with the expectation that he was in the running for her hand. For Benedict's manner, his bearing, his clothing all suggested that he was exactly what he appeared to be—an aristocratic landowner, a successful man with a large fortune. His horseflesh was incomparable, his carriages of the first order.

She hated being wrong, but it seemed that's exactly what she was. She would have to apologise to Benedict, and the sooner the better.

At her aunt's signal, the ladies rose and retired to the drawing room. Eloise was careful to catch Benedict's eye and dipped her head in acknowledgement. The gaze he returned was cool, his shuttered eyes betraying nothing.

Eloise was disappointed that his usual easy smile wasn't available to her.

The wide terrace windows were flung open, letting in the night breeze, which gently set the long gauze curtains dancing to and fro. The laden tea trolley was ready and waiting, and the ladies were helped to refreshments by her aunt and waiting footmen who dispensed delicate cups and saucers.

She couldn't settle and restlessly flitted from one group to the next, joining a conversation here, making a passing comment there, before moving on. She surely appeared the consummate hostess-in-waiting, helping her aunt and practising for running her own establishments. Yet she was moving and acting automatically. The serene social smile hid the tumultuous storm inside her. What if Benedict was very angry with her? Surely not, it had all been a mistake. But she had to acknowledge that she had insulted his honour, had insinuated that he was no better than a fortune hunter who had schemed to marry her for her fortune. Her damned fortune again held her trapped in its coils, never allowing her the privilege of knowing if she was liked or wanted for herself or her monetary value.

Her patience was rewarded moments later as the gentlemen joined them. Strathleven came in first, in what appeared to be an animated conversation with Gooding about the legendary London-to-Glasgow horse race. No one appeared to know anyone who had actually taken part in the notorious race. The rest of the gentleman followed them, quite a few congregating round the two to add in their knowledge of the phantom-like proceedings.

In a group of several others, Benedict entered the

room, caught Eloise's eye, dipped his head in acknowledgement and went to join the Strathleven group. If Eloise hadn't been so well-brought up, her mouth would have fallen open in astonishment. The dratted man materialised uninvited whenever she didn't want him near her. Yet now she did, he was happily playing the bachelor.

She stood, excused herself to the ladies whose circle she had joined, drew her shoulders back and slowly walked towards her betrothed. Head held high and a charming smile on her face, Eloise valiantly hid the storm of fierce emotions raging inside her.

As she neared Benedict, she noticed that others had joined the group, and to her horror, the young countess had insinuated herself into the space next to Benedict. She stood far too close to him, resting a small hand on his arm, gazing into his eyes in blatant invitation.

In the years to come, Eloise, ever cool, calm and unflustered, would undoubtedly remember this as the day the red mist descended on her. There was a thunderous roaring in her brain, like a dark, northern sea crashing and battering against the rocks, and, for just a moment, her eyes were clouded and it was as if she could not see. The roaring in her ears quietened; her eyes cleared as a white hot fury engulfed her. How dare she? She approached her erstwhile fiancé and the simpering lady hanging on his every word. "Ah, there you are Rothsea. I am sorry I could not join you earlier; I was detained."

The young countess unwisely chose that moment to speak. "Lord Rothsea and I have been keeping each other most entertained. Have we not?" She finished with a coquettish upwards glance at Benedict.

“I must thank you for your kindness. However, now that I am here, I fear I have to beg my fiancé’s indulgence and steal him away to speak for a few moments.”

“Of course, my dear. Lord Rothsea, I am sure Miss Camarthon has much to do in assisting Lady Bentley, but never fear, I shall be happy to do my part and share in keeping you company and your spirits up.”

Eloise smiled widely, although her eyes were cold. She carefully moved in between the countess and Benedict, trapping his arm with hers and saying, “Why, that is most kind of you, but you know something?” Eloise bent closer and whispered in the countess's ear. “I fear I am most diligent and never shirk my duties, especially the most pleasurable ones, so your . . .” Eloise paused for effect and cast a sideways glance at her sparring partner, “services . . . shall not be required.”

The countess flushed dark red at the insult and was stuck for words as Eloise pressed against Benedict, and with bobs and bows the two made their way onto the terrace.

* * *

Benedict's ire of earlier that day had already started to subside during dinner. Eloise's furtive glances his way, her acknowledgement of him as the ladies withdrew and her seeking him out unbidden was most gratifying. Surely, she must care for him a little and not only as someone for whom she felt a newly fledged desire. Her treatment of the countess gave away the truth of her emotions. Whether Eloise knew it or not, her words had been driven by a jealous tongue. She had firmly, albeit barely within the bounds of politeness, put the countess in her place; her actions indicating to anyone who overheard that this was more than an arranged marriage.

They strolled out the terrace doors proffering greetings here and there, although neither stopped to indulge anyone who wished to speak to the newly affianced couple. Eloise's arm lay across his sleeve, his other hand placed on top of hers as if seeking to anchor her to him. He could feel the tautness with which she held herself.

Instead of strolling on the terrace, for he feared what temper she would unleash, Benedict suggested they stroll across the lawns towards the raised flower beds filled with life-sized statuary. The guests often ambled in this direction, so no one would consider anything amiss in their doing so. In any event, they would still be in full view, and their way was lit by a series of outdoor lanterns scattered around for exactly that purpose. The air had turned cooler as the heat of the sun left the day, and Benedict noted with satisfaction that they were the only ones brave enough to venture into the gardens.

Once they had cleared the grounds closest to the house, Benedict spoke. "You wished to speak with me?"

His face was half caught in the shadows, which made it easy for him to conceal the grin that threatened to break out all over his face. She was no doubt about to start spitting fire. He had kept the countess at bay, had not encouraged that lady—if one could use that term for her—one whit. However, Eloise was only interested in what she thought she had seen. For, after all, she didn't really know him. Didn't yet appreciate or understand where his moral code lay.

He turned so that their upper halves were concealed by the shadows. To anyone watching, it would seem like they remained in proper view. He raised his hand and gently stroked Eloise's face, running one finger from brow to chin. The air had stilled, seemed to cover them, envelop them in a world, a place, a time of their own.

He leant forward and whispered, "I have not encouraged anyone's attentions. In truth, I found the countess obvious and overblown. Even if we were not promised to each other, I would not have dallied with her. I would not want to touch her, hold her." His hand trailed downwards as he lightly caressed her breast with the back of his hand. Back and forth, he traced a lazy pattern, his knuckles brushing over her nipple in a sweeping motion. He felt the bud tighten. His voice was husky. "I would not wish her come alive at my touch."

He turned his hand and, deliberately not breaking eye contact with her, cupped her breast. The fullness settled into his hand, and he momentarily closed his eyes. Eloise's shocked gasp recalled him to his senses.

He needed control here. "We should perhaps be more circumspect and finish our discussion nearer the house."

Eloise simply nodded, her gaze straight ahead as they retraced their steps.

Benedict's face was impassive, betraying nothing of the turbulent emotions coursing through him. He had aimed to cast a spell of seduction, to enflame Eloise's desires, to draw her closer to him—but before he had even begun, he had also caught himself in the snare he sought to set. Never had he been so unsure, so less in control, struggling against his desire to have her as his—and only his—forever. It was a sobering thought that it was not merely physical possession he desired.

He knew Eloise was attracted to him, that during their married life he could call on his undoubted skills as a lover to make her forget all but lying in his arms. But that was not everything he sought to achieve. He wanted Eloise to want him, not just on a physical level but on every other level as well. He wanted her to respect him, to like him, to show real affection for him. His previous idea of what constituted a good marriage now seemed tame and unsatisfying, as if he would be selling himself short by settling for such an arrangement. Good God, the realisation forcibly struck him as though he had been doused with ice cold water, he wanted her to love him.

Benedict schooled his face. He was being a fanciful fool. Love had no place in a marriage amongst their kind. Their marriage would be based on honour and underpinned with lineage, wealth and the responsibility it brought. Eloise would make an excellent countess and would grace his table, and he had to admit it would be no hardship fathering his heir. She would be horrified to find how his mind was heading. Eloise was a properly brought-up lady, and he should simply be grateful that she seemed to find him attractive and, hopefully, would not have a disgust of the marriage bed. Who was he to wish for anything more?

* * *

Eloise's gait was slow. She had been shocked to her core

when Benedict had openly caressed her, even though she knew they were screened by the lengthening shadows. His touch had been fleeting, and she was now bereft—as if something had ended before it had even begun. Her nerves quivered with the tension that swirled in the air around them; the light silk of her dress rasped like the heaviest of rough homespun as it brushed against her highly sensitised skin.

As her tumultuous emotions calmed, she recalled what she had intended to say to him before the predatory countess had riled her temper. Before Benedict's touch had made her forget even her anger. She stopped and turned to him. "My lord, I owe you an apology from earlier today. It was wrong of me to jump to conclusions and to castigate you without allowing you an opportunity to explain matters. I realise that you are not interested in me for my fortune."

She waited for him to say what he was interested in. Why her?

Benedict looked calmly into her face, lifted her hand and bestowed a soft kiss on the back of it. "Thank you for your apology. All is forgiven and forgotten. Now come, let us join the others. The evening will draw to a close soon, and we do not wish our absence to be remarked on."

Eloise had no choice but to blindly follow him to the house. She was no closer to understanding what he wanted of her, why he specifically wanted her. For that was certainly how it seemed. Gentlemen of his ilk did not dally with well-bred young ladies, for they knew the consequences all too well. Yet they had ended up in a compromising situation, and, apparently, Benedict was showing some fondness for her. Her mind was whirring with questions, as her body ached for answers of its own. What more could he, would he, do to her?

These tumultuous emotions were so far from the sort she had imagined would be present in her marriage, and she didn't know whether to be glad—or terrified.

As they climbed the stairs to the terrace, she gently touched his arm. "What have you learned this day? Did you speak to Gareth Jones?"

"Yes, and it was most illuminating. Bartholomew Jones was once employed by our very own Everton, and Gooding and the late Mr Jones were more than mere acquaintances. They were childhood friends, and he introduced Bartholomew to Everton."

She stopped. "That seems odd. Could either of them have something to do with his death? What reason could be had for such an act?"

"Bartholomew wasn't solely a simple moneylender. He loaned money to my cousin's husband to cover some gambling debts."

He paused, as if unsure whether to proceed, and she gently squeezed his hand, immediately drawing away as a bolt of longing surged through her.

He cleared his throat and carried on. "He took his own life and left a note indicating he was being blackmailed. If he didn't hand over some of my cousin's jewels, it would become public knowledge that he was unable to settle his debts and was having dealings with a moneylender. You appreciate how that would have been enough to taint his name."

Her blood chilled. This tragic event was too close to

home. She pushed back at the bile in her throat. She had to stay calm. "I am so sorry. Thank you for your confidence. This conversation is, of course, between us. I assure you I will not speak of this with anyone else. But what could this possibly have to do with Everton or Gooding?"

"Someone had to be financing Bartholomew. He didn't have enough cash to do this on his own."

"And Sarah? Does she fit into any of this?"

"Sarah knew Bartholomew from childhood and she certainly had contact with him in the months before he was killed, but her death could be an unconnected tragedy. These are mere threads, but if we pull hard enough, they will surely unravel."

CHAPTER NINETEEN

Friends and close acquaintances from neighbouring properties joined the houseguests in the ballroom. The room shone with the flickering glow from dozens of chandeliers and wall candelabra; the dancing flames cast a magical sheen over the gleaming silver wall sconces, and the polished parquet floor. Delicate, gilt-edged high-backed chairs were set around the edges of the room in small groupings, the golden gleam of their spindled legs even brighter in the blaze of candlelight.

The musicians sat on a raised dais at one end of the room, readying their instruments to keep everyone dancing until late. Liveried and bewigged waiters proffered trays of champagne, ratafia and amber-coloured wines. A gentlemen's smoking room had been set aside in an antechamber with long glass doors that opened onto the terrace, mirroring those which led from the ballroom itself. This room would gain in popularity as the evening progressed, a welcome respite from the ladies, the dancing and the heat from the mass of bodies in the ballroom.

News of Eloise's engagement had flown fast. Mrs Pettifer, the wife of a neighbouring squire, had a hard gleam in her avaricious eyes as she took in Benedict's fine figure. "Why, Miss Camarthon, I hear congratulations are in order." Her eyes flickered to the side, and she openly admired the groom-to-be. Eloise gritted her teeth. She'd just have to get used to this.

"My lord, this is Mrs Pettifer, a near neighbour, and this is the Earl of Rothsea, my betrothed." Eloise had the uncomfortable notion that she had betrayed a previously unbeknown possessiveness in her tone. A quick glance at Benedict confirmed that he had picked this up, and a smirk hovered at the corner of his mouth.

A spiteful look came into Mrs Pettifer's eyes. Her two meek daughters trailed behind her, and jealousy laced her words. "My dear, well, all I can say is well done. Of course, one such as you was always going to marry quickly and well. I mean, your father was a very, very clever man, and his legacy has stood you in good stead."

Eloise tensed. She hadn't fully appreciated how many people knew of her father's whim. His will had obviously been registered, and all it took was a little gossip here and there for the information to out. Under cover of praising the late Viscount Barchester, Mrs Pettifer had neatly insulted Eloise, whose stomach lurched as she sought to recover her wits. She had no need.

Benedict's voice was loud enough to be heard by the surrounding groups. "Why, thank you for your kind words of congratulations, madam. However, I believe you meant to say that the legacy from Viscountess Barchester has led us to this happy state. And indeed you would be correct, for the lady was renowned for her beauty, her intelligence and her kind heart. All of which have been passed on to her daughter."

Benedict took Eloise's gloved hand and, bringing it to his lips, bestowed a gentle kiss. "Which I noticed the second I met Eloise. What a surprise it was to later learn she was my good friend's niece, for I had spent a week haunting the ton for another glimpse of my lady. As soon as I found her again, I knew we were meant to be together."

Mrs Pettifer, and the ladies surrounding them, gasped. Eloise could almost hear their thoughts. It was indeed a love match. Didn't Eloise Camarthon have enough already? Now she had to have true love as well!

Eloise flashed a grateful look at Benedict. What a load of nonsense he spouted, and a pity it wasn't true!

* * *

A whirling mass of couples executed the intricate steps and dips of a quadrille. Eloise had been whisked away by the first of many dance partners, and Benedict hadn't been able to get near her. He caught snatched images of her as she was swept from one end of the ballroom to the next, either in a sedate set piece or a boisterous country reel. She seemed to have danced with half the men here already. She was certainly fulfilling her duty as the host's niece.

At that, the musicians struck up a waltz, which although becoming commonplace and acceptable in Town was still seen as a tiny bit scandalous in the shires. Benedict pushed himself off the wall he'd been lounging against and, catching sight of Eloise's tawny curls, made a beeline towards her, confident that she would have saved the waltzes for her fiancé. He hadn't actually asked her to do so, but it was obviously something she would do instinctively. This would give them a chance to be close, the very idea of which had him hurrying towards his affianced—who, to his utter shock, was smiling at Lord Bellingham as he led her onto the dance floor and assumed the correct waltz position. With his brows drawn, a black, thunderous cloud settled itself on Benedict's face as he positioned himself near the edge of the dance floor and stared at the offenders as the music rose and they moved past in a twirling waltz.

* * *

Eloise had been unable to refuse Bellingham. It would have been unconscionably rude to do so. She would have to make the best of it and keep the conversation on appropriate subjects, although his previous comments could not be forgotten. "So, my lord, how fares your family? They are from Cambridgeshire, I believe."

"Yes, I have an estate there. A fair size, but it has to be, for the life of a politician is one of great expense."

They fell into silence as they danced.

"Miss Camarthon, if I may, I would like to make some reassurances to you regarding our last conversation. The subject is rather indelicate, but I do wish you to be aware of my true feelings."

Eloise kept a smile on her face and discomfort hidden

as Bellingham continued. "Should matters of a personal nature have progressed between Rothsea and yourself, I would be willing to overlook any indiscretion on your part."

Pardon! Surely he did not mean what she thought?

"And should there be any unavoidable repercussions, well, I can assure you that I am not above bringing up a cuckoo in the nest. So, my dear, I have made myself clear, and you can consider my offer?"

Eloise had gone cold and almost stumbled as they turned around the room. If she could believe her ears, this "gentleman"—and she really used the term in its loosest form—had boldly said that he would not mind in the slightest if she came to their marriage bed unchaste, having anticipated her vows with Rothsea, nor would he be concerned if she bore Rothsea's child in wedlock with Bellingham. She wished she had the courage to slap him and cause a scene but that would never do.

"My lord, I thank you for your consideration." At Bellingham's beaming smile, she continued, "However, I am to marry the Earl of Rothsea, and that is exactly what will happen. I must ask you never to speak to me in such a way again, and in return, I shall do you the courtesy of forgetting your insulting comments to me."

He stiffened. "I apologise for offending you. However, my offer remains on the table. Who knows, you may have need to take me up on it one day."

His words had an undertone of threat, and Eloise longed to be rid of him. At this closing remark, the music stopped and Eloise allowed Bellingham to properly escort her from the floor. A large hand appeared in front of them, neatly removing Eloise's gloved fingertips from Bellingham's arm and placing them on his own.

"Ah, thank you for returning my fiancé to me. My dear, there is someone I want you to meet. Please excuse us, Bellingham."

Eloise mentally sagged with relief.

With an incline of his head, Bellingham acquiesced to Benedict's stronger claim and, bowing over Eloise's hand with a mumbled, "Until later," and with that he left them to it.

She could not imagine who on earth Benedict would want her to meet, for surely she knew the majority of the guests far better than he?

At her enquiry, Benedict responded matter-of-factly. "I am afraid that was a falsehood. I wanted to get you away from Bellingham. I surmise he is disappointed that I am to be your groom and not him."

"I have to agree. I would prefer not to be in his company again."

She would keep her counsel. There was no need to enflame Benedict, for she was sure he would be enraged at Bellingham's comments.

* * *

The musicians took up a new tune, and it was with a possessive, predatory grasp that Benedict led her to join the other dancers. One hand settled lightly against her waist, as he placed the other in hers and they began to waltz as the music started to rise. He pulled Eloise closer until his thigh rode against hers and the tips of her silk-clad breasts were grazed by his jacket. Eloise tried to move away to create more distance between them but was prevented by his large hand moving into the small of her back, where he laid his palm flat and, with gentle pressure, pulled her closer towards him.

They settled into the rhythm and glided around the room; their swaying bodies touched time and time again. Eloise was hot and flustered and, for the first time ever, understood why there was a very, very good reason that young ladies should not waltz until permission was granted by the patronesses of Almacks. And even then the girls were expected to keep a respectable distance between themselves and their partners. For a completely green and impressionable girl to undergo the same experience that Eloise was currently facing would be almost unbearable. She was near to fainting herself. No wonder so many fell prey to charming rakes. Her senses were on fire, heightened by the silence between them.

Benedict had not yet spoken, and the lack of words cast an intimate spell. She was forced to concentrate on their movements, their bodies touching, the sensations coursing through her. They were, it seemed, alone in their own world as they swept across the dance floor. Benedict slightly bent his head and focussed his gaze on her, a gentle smile lifting the corners of his mouth as he gazed into her eyes. There was a connection between them, so palpable she could almost touch it.

As the strains of the waltz faded, they stood still for a moment, just a fraction longer than propriety accepted. With a sigh of what sounded like regret, Benedict broke their gaze and gently released her, keeping one hand locked in his, which he placed on his arm as he escorted her around the room. This had been the final dance of the evening.

Her uncle entered the room and, with a slightly raised voice, called for silence.

"Friends, I have been persuaded that we need a little more excitement and fresh air, so I have agreed to a horse race tomorrow morning." Over the excited oohs and ahhs, he continued, "Any gentleman may enter."

Eloise stilled. Her uncle had locked eyes with Benedict as he made his announcement. What were they up to?

She turned to Benedict. "I trust you do not take part in this race; the gentlemen all seem excited."

"There is nothing like a hard ride to banish the cobwebs."

"You must jest, my lord; after last evening you would exert yourself in such a manner?"

"My dear, I am flattered that you show such consideration for me, but your fears are unfounded. I have a hard enough head and have sustained a knock or two before."

Was there no end to this man's stubbornness? "I'm not an idiot. It is best you understand that before the wedding."

He raised a brow. "I am afraid I do not follow you."

"You and my uncle are planning something. What is the meaning behind this horse race?"

He opened his mouth to speak, but before he could do so, she jabbed a finger into his side as she propelled him into a corner by the musician's stand where no one could overhear them. "Please carry on, and mind you tell me the truth."

She wanted to laugh when he spluttered out an aggrieved sound, but didn't.

"Very well." His voice was low. "There have been two attempts made on my life, and we must expect there will be a third. Westbury and I have therefore decided to put an opportunity in place that my attacker would be unable to ignore."

A sharp, jagged pain stabbed at her heart. "The race?"

"Yes, Westbury will have men hidden along the course so that the riders will always be in sight of someone. If anyone attempts to attack me, they will be seen."

She simply stared. "And what if they shoot at you?"

"We'll be riding fast. Someone would have to be an exceptional shot to fatally wound me."

She could not believe she was hearing this. "What if they are?"

He shrugged; an insouciant lift of shoulders accompanied his careless words. "Well, they only winged me last time."

She shook her head. How could he be so cavalier? His hand lightly caressed her arm, and she almost jumped. "Hush, don't worry. I will take care. I promise you it will be fine. There is something else—the house party breaks up the day after tomorrow. I would like it to be known that we are heading to London. We do have a wedding to plan."

Now that they were discussing the formalities, it all seemed far too real. Before long, she would be this man's wife and under his complete control and authority. The thought was sobering, but not unpleasant—in fact, it was quite the reverse.

Eloise's voice remained calm and even as she replied, "Yes, I have no objections."

He bobbed his head, made as if to speak and then sharply closed his mouth. After a brief pause, he obviously thought better of his hesitation and spoke. "We need to make plans, decide on where and when we will be married."

"Oh yes, of course."

"Would a week be long enough?"

"A week! Seven days?"

"Yes, is that too long? We can make it sooner if you like. I can easily obtain a special licence from my godfather. Who'd have thought having connections to a bishop would come in handy?"

"No, no! A week is scant enough time as is. Should we not wait a little longer? What is the rush?"

He simply looked at her, really looked at her. It was as if all the layers of society and behaviour were peeled away, layer by layer, to reveal the truth between them, to lay bare the shimmering connection that had lured and bound them over the past days. Eloise felt as if there were no one in the room but the two of them and raw, naked emotion.

"I don't want to wait." He supplied in an even, honest tone. "And I don't think you do either."

Eloise held his gaze for several heartbeats before looking away. "Yes. Well. I am sure your family and my aunt will have an absolute fit. That is no time whatsoever."

He took her hand in his and gently stroked his thumb across her palm. Heat blazed through the satin material of her glove. "Eloise. It is plenty of time. I shall easily obtain the appropriate licence. The modistes would resort to fisticuffs to obtain the honour of making your wedding gown and work all hours to do so. Everyone is in Town anyway, so there will be no problem with the guest list and Westbury's staff is more than capable of supplying a wedding breakfast at a day's notice, far less a whole week."

"You've spoken to my uncle already, haven't you?" She knew when she was vanquished.

He had the grace to look abashed. "Ah, yes I have. I also need to be in London to further investigate Bartholomew's death. We do have another motive in mind. If my attacker is indeed a member of the house party, they will realise they are running out of time. London is a more claustrophobic existence and not as free as the country. If they wish to see me gone, then they must act soon, and that leads us back to the race."

CHAPTER TWENTY

The sun had not long risen, its amber glow glinting off the dew-laden grass, and yet most of the houseguests were milling around the courtyard.

Seven men had put their name down for the race, Benedict, Sir Frederick Richards, Strathleven, Bellingham, Gooding, Everton and Lord Stanhope. Benedict trotted his horse towards the start line and couldn't help but question if one of the men beside him wanted him dead. Or did that person lurk along the course?

Westbury's voice boomed out, "Steady, gentlemen. One, Two, Three." On the three, the riders surged forward. Half-risen out of their saddles, bent low across their horses' backs, the riders raced towards the woods. Benedict was elated as he raced along, feeling the harnessed power of the animal beneath him. Crisp, fresh air caressed his skin as he bent over his stallion's back and urged the magnificent beast on, faster and faster.

He was ahead, the others somewhat behind. The

blurred countryside flashed past in a medley of muted greens and subdued browns; his whole being focussed on the path ahead and the thundering hooves to his rear, drawing closer. Benedict loved the challenge, pitting Gilgamesh against these other fine beasts and allowing his steed to draw on all its magnificence and master the road in front of them.

They were out of the first part of the woods now and would have to pass through narrow hedgerow-edged lanes until they made their way into the bluebell carpeted woods, farther along the course.

As Benedict rounded a corner, he saw that the road ahead was blocked by a large mound of debris; the bank must have been loosened by the recent rains. Westbury's men had checked the course at first light so the collapse must have been within the last hour. He cursed their bad luck.

Not wanting to risk any damage to the stallion's legs in riding through the stone-laden mound, Benedict gripped tight to his reins, lifted his seat fully out of the saddle and, pulling back, man and beast soared into the air and easily cleared the obstruction.

As Gilgamesh's back hooves followed the front in finding solid ground, Benedict sat heavily in the saddle. As his full weight settled on the horse's back, Gilgamesh let out a high-pitched neigh, laced with distress, and bucked frantically.

Benedict flew through the air and landed, thankfully, on the soft rain-soaked soil of the opposite bank. He laid spread-eagled for a moment, his breath caught in his lungs. As he expelled air, he instinctively flexed his fingers and toes. No damage there, although he ached like he had gone a round in the boxing ring. He raised himself on his elbows and considered what had happened. What *could* have happened if he had landed on the hard ground or fallen awkwardly? However, he was fine, so no need for undue concern. Here he was expecting an attack, and yet he'd still managed to unseat himself like an untrained youth.

Moments later, the sound of thundering hooves drawing nearer announced the imminent arrival of the rest of the field.

"To the devil, Rothsea, you're an accident-prone one!" Stanhope's jesting words inadequately concealed the concern in his voice.

Benedict could only smile. He was certainly looking a bit of a clod. Any other day, he would have laughed at his clumsiness. Dismounting, Stanhope quickly moved to Benedict and offered his arm, which Benedict grabbed and allowed his friend to haul him to his feet.

"How are you?" Stanhope's tone was grave.

Benedict smiled as he dusted himself down. "All that is hurt is my pride."

Before any more could be said, the others came barrelling up, Strathleven in the lead. He swung his leg over and dismounted before the animal had fully stopped. Striding forward, he demanded, "Good God, Rothsea, what has occurred? How fare you?"

"I fell off my horse. I came down too hard on his back after I jumped over that." He waved dismissively at the offending mound in front of them.

By now, the other riders had dismounted and swarmed

around him. Having confirmed his well-being to all concerned, Benedict, not a little sheepishly, said, "Afraid I've mucked up the race. Stanhope, I was unseated, and if you had carried on instead of coming to my aid, you'd have won."

"There is no issue, Rothsea. It is all harmless fun. It is not as if any wagers are attached."

"Indeed," inserted Sir Frederick, "let us name Stanhope the winner."

Benedict slowly approached Gil and stroked a careful hand gently over his nose and ruffled his ears. With the softest of touches, he gently ran his hands over and under the very edges of the saddle. Gil bucked and reared, and Benedict held tight to the reins.

"Something's wrong with him. Can someone hold him whilst I get the saddle off?"

Strathleven took over the reins, and Benedict unlashed the smooth leather straps, freeing the saddle sufficiently to lift it clear off the horse's back.

He gasped and made soft shushing noises to soothe his horse. "Gentlemen, here is the problem." He pointed to several twigs, which had pierced Gil's flesh, small rivulets of blood surrounding each intruding object. He carefully eased out the twigs one by one. The stallion shifted a little but seemed too relieved to cause much of a fuss.

He held out his palm to show the others the offending items. "What bad luck is this? An accident like this happens once in a lifetime." Benedict spoke the words in a careless tone. He didn't believe in coincidences, and there had been far too many "accidents" recently.

Stanhope bent forward and picked one twig up,

carefully holding it between his forefinger and thumb, and pointed out, "Look here, this was no accident—the ends have been whittled into points as sharp as a razor."

Benedict carefully ran the pad of his thumb over one of the doctored spikes. "I am sure it is all harmless. Come on, you go on ahead and let everyone know what has happened. I shall walk Gil back as I don't want to put too much pressure on his back until he's been looked at. If you would send a groom with an extra horse, I'll meet him on the path."

The group agreed and mounted their horses. As they galloped off, Benedict noticed that Strathleven still stood by him, and he lifted one eyebrow in sardonic enquiry at the younger man. Strathleven quirked the corners of his mouth in a smile, but it did not reach his eyes, which remained sombre. "I will keep you company whilst you walk, Cousin."

"If you wish, although I would not mind if you had ridden off. It is a long walk." They turned to follow the trail of dust left in the wake of the other riders. For a moment, silence reigned until Strathleven let out a long, low sigh. Benedict glanced at the younger man. "You have something you wish to say?"

"Yes, yes, I do." Meeting Benedict's eyes, he simply said, "I do not like coincidences, and nor, I think, do you."

This so perfectly mirrored Benedict's thoughts of moments earlier that he threw his cousin a startled look as he questioned whether the Scot had some form of second sight, or, more logically, perhaps blood really was thicker than water. He took in the dark looks of his relation, those black eyes inscrutable, giving nothing away. Truly, was this man friend or foe? Benedict decided to go with his gut instinct and walk the direct road.

"Why did you come here? What caused you to seek me out?"

"Sisters." The word shot out of Strathleven's mouth with a sneer. "I am plagued by sisters. I imagine you know what that is like?"

"Yes, but what does that have to do with you coming to see me, to establish the connection I asked for, as my heir, but you did not wish to give?"

Strathleven sighed. "I have three sisters. Three! The unholy trinity are much younger than I am. Annabelle is sixteen, Catriona fourteen and the baby, Heather, is twelve. They have, well, I suppose you would say they are each one ambitious in regard to their futures."

At Benedict's puzzled glance, Strathleven continued, "Anyway at the moment it is Annabelle's ambitions I am forced to deal with. She is hell bent on leaving Scotland and sees herself as a fine English lady, and I do mean lady with a capital L. Although in Annabelle's world, being a lady is the consolation prize, for she'd rather be a duchess or a marchioness." Strathleven paused to consider what he'd said and conceded. "At a push, she'd probably find being a countess acceptable, so let us thank the Lord she hasn't laid eyes on you, for she'd have tied you up well and proper before Miss Camarthon had even had the passing notion that perhaps she liked your smile."

Benedict was suddenly troubled by whether Eloise had even noticed his smile, far less admired it. In fact, now he considered it, he had no idea what she truly thought of him. The concern that it may not actually be as much as he hoped had his stomach lurching uncomfortably. He was drawn from his reverie by Strathleven as he continued with his tale of woe.

"Fact is, I have no desire to be an English lord. I am a man who takes his responsibilities seriously, but my heart aches at having to be part of your formal society. I am a Scot through and through, though half the blood running through my veins is English. I have oft paid for that in my homeland, being seen as an English half-blood, and I have striven to make my mother's people respect me. I would ruin that were I to take on the responsibilities of an English earldom, taking me away from those who owe loyalty to Strathleven. I have titles, land and riches enough. I neither need, nor desire, any more." His words were simple but heartfelt, and Benedict truly believed this man would not willingly wish to harm him.

"It sounds like you have every reason to stay away from me and mine. So I must ask again, why are you here, Strathleven?"

"Debuts. I am here for debuts, Rothsea, for balls and fripperies and a turn around the park. I am here for marriage. I am sent to court the patronage of my English relations to beg their indulgence in sponsoring my lovely sisters at the English court and in that most English of events, the Season. Annabelle wants an English husband, and I am here to further the acquaintance of our branch of the family with yours to gain an entrée into the highest levels of society for her. I have aunts who have married well, very well, into the aristocracy, but they were Scots-born, and sometimes that can count against someone. Your mother comes from a fine lineage and is well-connected to all the major hostesses, even though I understand she has been in seclusion this past while. I am hoping that may change."

All was silent. All that could be heard were the sounds of heavy male boots crushing against the ground, the horses' hooves following in their wake. "So, if I get this right, you have travelled almost the length of the kingdom to arrange for my mother—and I, where required—to debut your sisters in a manner fitting those doubly related to earls?"

"Yes" was the terse, short response.

"So having decided you wanted nothing to do with us—what is it the Scots call us—yes, so wanting nothing to do with us mere Sassenachs, your sixteen-year-old sister routed you—a what, twenty-seven-year-old earl, the head of the family—and demanded you get on your horse, travel to England and open relations with our branch of the family to further her matrimonial ambitions?"

"That is what I said." Benedict could almost hear his companion's teeth grit as he spat out the confirmation of his mission.

Mirth erupted. Benedict was bent over, holding his sides, desperately trying to ease the aches as waves of unabashed laughter lapped through him, again and again.

A severely affronted Strathleven rounded on Benedict in outrage. "Now look here. I only did what any man would do—the harpies would not give up! It was all about how all I had to do was this tiny little thing, didn't I love them? Was I deliberately ruining Annabelle's chances of happiness and then, well, then she started crying, as did Catriona, and Heather howled that I was a big bully, and she started crying as well, and they just would not stop." The final words were ground out.

Benedict laughed all the harder, tears streaming down his face.

"Oh stop. Please, I beg you—stop! I can't take any more. The big brave Highlander, brought to book by three wee lassies, as you'd say," Benedict howled.

A look as black as thunder ran across Strathlevens's face as he scowled at his laughing companion, and then his lips twitched, his eyes closed and his broad chest heaved. The two men, strangers these long years but cousins now, held on to each other and laughed until the tears ran down their faces. For Benedict, the tension of the last few life-changing days was released, uncertainty ebbing from him. At least he knew he could trust Strathleven.

* * *

Eloise waited, surrounded by the guests, on the back terrace that overlooked the pathway leading to the stables, her palm lifted to shield her eyes as she stared straight ahead, scanning the horizon for a familiar figure on horseback. The others had returned with news of the mishap. A groom had immediately been dispatched with a spare horse, and she watched for Benedict's return. Was it truly an accident, or had yet another attempt been made on his life?

She squinted, trying to make out the moving shadows. It was him. Benedict rode a borrowed grey horse and led his own by its reins. He was accompanied by Strathleven.

Picking up her skirts, she pushed past those closest to

her and ran down the steps and across the lawns towards the stables. She did not care for impropriety. She wanted to see Benedict, and her heart told her she needed to see him, to know all was well. She looked behind and saw the others followed her. She turned into the stables and ran straight into a broad chest, comforting arms reaching out to steady her. His voice was a soothing balm. "Whoa, slow down. All is well."

She searched Benedict's face for sign of injury or pain. None of which were apparent. "Are you all right? What happened?"

"I am fine. A burr was lodged under Gil's saddle."

"Rothsea! What the devil happened?"

Benedict moved away from her and turned to Colonel Eastleigh. "I am well, sir, simply a tumble from my horse."

"My word, you are prone to accidents are you not?"

Bellingham spoke next, "And you had the misfortune to buy a horse that habitually unseats you."

Eloise stayed silent as the gathered guests smiled and laughed at the apparently clumsy earl.

Her uncle joined the group. "My friend, come and join me for a brandy. I do believe you have need of it." He turned to Eloise. "After all this excitement, perhaps we should bring lunch forward. Would you kindly lead our guests in?"

Eloise smiled and said, "Of course," but inside her a tight knot of dread burrowed deeper.

CHAPTER TWENTY-ONE

Benedict nursed his glass of brandy as he lounged in one of the well-used, comfortably padded wingchairs in Westbury's private study. The owner of said room paced up and down in front of Benedict as he finished spilling out his tale of the morning's events.

"Let's get this clear. You saddled the horse yourself. One of my grooms walked it around the yard as a warm-up, and everyone agrees that apart from the stable hands the only people near the horses were the race participants?"

"That is correct."

"So," came Westbury's measured response, "you have yet another 'accident', Strathleven is present—again—and yet you don't believe he has anything to do with it, even though he has the most to gain from your untimely demise? An interesting deduction. May I enquire how you arrived at your conclusion of his innocence?" Sarcasm laced his words.

Benedict smiled. He supposed it did seem odd when put that way, so he answered as best, and as honestly, as he could. "Gut feeling, nothing more or less. Although the facts do support my instincts. He comes across as a steady man, enmeshed in his Scottish heritage, albeit his father was an Englishman. The carnage of the defeat in 1745 isn't that far in the past, and I hear the Scots have long memories. To us, 'tis simply history, a turn on the path towards the Union that is Scotland and England today. To the Scots, almost to a man, the bitterness of defeat runs deep, and they have no liking for the English, whom they believe 'stole' their country. So yes, I can understand Strathleven not wanting to take up the mantle of an English title, to keep his own people from knowing that he is heir to one of the hated English lords."

The duke paused in his criss-crossing of the room and looked reflective. "You're entirely correct. Strathleven's initial rejection of your hand of friendship seems logical under the circumstances. Can you truly believe that he hied halfway down the country to satisfy his sister's desire for an English husband? Especially if, as you say, he hates the English with a passion."

"He doesn't. Hate us, that is. I do, however, think he is a careful man, and he can see how his own people might react. I would imagine there are long-memoried people who comment that he, himself, is not pure-bred Scots and that the blood of the English aristocracy runs through his veins. As for the sister part, well, I can tell you that when Beth and Maddie start up, I'd as soon give them whatever they ask for than listen to them berate me for days on end.

The complaining and whining I could stand, but the tears, ugh, that finishes me off." Benedict downed the remains of his brandy in one gulp, the better to assert his manhood.

"So he doesn't like the English all that much, or his people don't, and he is generous to his sisters. I don't suppose he kicks small animals either. Oh well, he must be innocent." Westbury smiled with a sardonic glance.

"Look, I know it doesn't sound that rational, but this man could be a good friend, certainly not an enemy."

"You trust too easy, Ben," the friendly address took any sting from the words, "and I hope to God you are right. But this doesn't detract from the fact that you have had several attempts on your life recently. So if not Strathleven—and I tell you I am still keeping an eye on him—then who? Who does you harm?"

"It is too much of a coincidence that these attacks follow on from my investigation into Bartholomew's death. One of the men present today is, I believe, at least connected to what happened to Bartholomew and could even be the banker behind his business—and perhaps his killer. Let us not forget Sarah. She fits into this somehow, but I cannot see in which way."

"My concern is that Eloise may get caught in their machinations, either deliberately or simply by virtue of being in your company. I therefore suggest that we postpone any wedding plans and, in fact," Westbury paused and looked Benedict full in the eye, his expression unreadable, "perhaps we should reconsider the whole matter?"

"What do you mean by *reconsider*?"

"Perhaps I may have been too hasty. I should have dealt with Sir Frederick in a more direct manner, even paid off his debts. What I mean to say is that I don't believe the two of you will suit. A broken engagement is not unheard of. Let us say you will allow Eloise to cry off, and I can get her married to someone more suitable by summer's end."

His stomach somersaulted as dread rose. The denial tumbled forth in an explosion. "NO!" Benedict rose to his feet, tension writ across his face and rigid frame. "No, I am afraid that will not do. I have offered my hand, and your niece has accepted it. In my mind, that is an end to the matter. And there will be no future husband apart from me!"

"I do not want Eloise in danger. What do you mean to do about that? She is under twenty-one. I can refuse to give my permission and marry her off to someone else before she comes of age." The late afternoon sunlight filtered into the room through the half-closed wooden window slats, casting shadows over Westbury's face, obscuring and distorting his expressions.

"Let us ask her if she wants to go ahead with our marriage. It should be Eloise's choice."

"Yet this engagement was not of her choosing. I have forced her hand too much in this. Really, if I think about it, the decision was made for you both—and by me."

"It would be far worse for Eloise to be thought a flirt who pulls out of an engagement after a few days!"

"Nonsense. She's one of the richest girls in England. If she can't be capricious, then who can? Anyway, let us be honest on that score. Eloise could be the hoyden and flirt of the year and still there would be a queue of suitors all the way to Land's End willing to marry her."

As Benedict went to speak, Westbury raised his hand and motioned him to silence.

"I must confess that I have, on occasion, let fear of scandal and a rigid adherence to the proprieties influence my decisions. And that must have happened in this situation, for the lord knows I do not see that you and Eloise could ever suit. She can be headstrong and wilful, and you, as you have rightly stated, want a pleasant woman as your wife who'll look after your name, your houses and your children. Surely, that is what every man wants. Pleasures can be found elsewhere. Well, I can—and I shall—remedy that." He tugged the tapestry bell pull to summon Higgins, who was sent to find Eloise and have her attend them post-haste.

As they waited for Eloise to arrive, Benedict found that he could not speak, did not have the ability to form the right words, not without erupting in rage at Westbury's meddling. He simply stood, hands behind his rigid back, legs planted wide, as he looked out through the slatted shutters to the gardens beyond. The idea of losing Eloise as his wife made bile rise in his throat. The decision was made, his path was set, and he would not move from it. Now he only had to hope that Eloise would take the same stance.

A soft knock on the study door alerted them to Eloise's arrival.

Eloise's gaze was direct and steady as she looked into Benedict's face. "About time too. I have been near driven to distraction waiting to speak with you in private. How dare he? How does this villain have the audacity to attack you on Westbury's estate?"

Westbury immediately rose and, placing his arms around Eloise's shoulders, led her towards a chair, into which he gently pushed her. She looked up into her uncle's face. Her question of moments before being asked again in her anxious gaze.

"The only thing we can be sure about is that we don't actually know anything—except that someone apparently means Rothsea harm. And it is that very matter I wish to speak to you about."

Her head slightly bent to one side, Eloise waited for her uncle to speak. She shifted her eyes by a hair's breadth towards Benedict, but he stood straight, keeping his face immobile, giving nothing away.

"I am concerned that your present involvement with Rothsea may bring you harm. You could be injured were there another attempt on his life or even targeted yourself. I have also been reconsidering my position."

"Your position on what?" Eloise asked, her voice wary.

"I may have been slightly short-sighted in forcing you to become betrothed to Rothsea. From the distance of a few days, I can see that the . . . well . . . the situation may not have been as bad as it seemed at the time. I should have taken time to consider how to deal with Sir Frederick's threats and not simply jumped upon a betrothal between you and Rothsea as the easy way out. There is no real damage done, and obviously it is best that you distance yourself from the danger surrounding Rothsea at the moment. You can be forgiven one broken engagement," Westbury smiled as he warmed to his theme, "especially as we'll make the next one a nice short betrothal. By the time you're married, this broken engagement to Rothsea will be yesterday's news."

* * *

Eloise simply stared at her uncle. *What!* Where had all of this come from? She looked at Benedict. So he would renege on his offer. What price honour now?

Eloise's eyes linked with Benedict's as, unblinking, she stared at him, her own face betraying none of the chaotic emotions that were coursing through her. "My lord? What think you of this pronouncement?"

Benedict's voice was even, but his eyes burned with determination. "I have to tell you that I am not in accord with Westbury. No irrefutable damage may have been caused, but I find I cannot agree that our betrothal was not the necessary step to take."

He moved until only a foot separated them. "I believe you know my position?"

Yes, she thought. *I do now. You apparently do want to marry me.* What she couldn't figure out was why, especially when he had a golden opportunity to simply walk away. She knew with blinding clarity that this was the last thing she wanted. "Yes, my lord, I understand your position. I really do. And that, Uncle, is what I shall shortly be saying as I become the Countess of Rothsea. I do."

"Eloise . . ."

She raised a hand to ward off her uncle's words. "My mind is made up. Since we have finished our discussion, I shall leave you as I have a great deal to organise before we leave for Town in the morning." Her voice was cool, her diction clipped as she rose and dropped a brief curtsey.

CHAPTER TWENTY-TWO

Dinner was a quiet affair as the guests discussed their travel plans for the next day. Eloise would have liked to say that the spectre of Sarah's death hovered over those assembled, but she knew that most of the guests would not give a second thought to the passing of a servant girl. The Huntley household mourned Sarah, and Benedict had investigated as much as he could. Would they ever find out the events that had led to Sarah being killed?

"Miss Camarthon?"

Lord Everton addressed Eloise from across the table. "I hear you are for London?"

So the word had spread. Would it have reached the ears of Benedict's attacker? "That is correct. We travel there tomorrow."

"And, if I may be so bold, would the plan be to organise your wedding at that time, or do you wait?"

Benedict was seated next to Eloise at dinner, and even

though there was a respectable distance between them, she sensed him tensing before he answered in her stead. "Yes, indeed. We will finalise our wedding plans in London and would expect a swift marriage. I have no desire for a long engagement."

Benedict's voice had carried along the table, and Eloise decided they could all make of that what they wanted.

Everton dabbed at the corner of his mouth with his napkin. "I am sure it will be an outstanding day."

Her uncle's voice cut across all conversation as he rose to his feet, glass in hand. "My dear friends, if I may, I would like to take the opportunity to thank you for your company these past days. I appreciate that many of you will be making an early start in the morning, so I have arranged for drinks and tea to be laid out in the drawing room, but please retire when you see fit."

Benedict rose and pulled out Eloise's chair, offering her his arm as she rose. There had been no opportunity to speak in private after their discussion in Westbury's study. As they left the room, he bent his head and quickly whispered, "Shall we take a turn on the terrace? I would like to speak to you without interruption."

Her smile was soft and accompanied by a light in her eyes that made clear her desire to be alone with him.

"Ahem," Aunt Harriet interjected. "We have a lot to organise tomorrow before our journey. Perhaps you should call it a night, Eloise? I will be up shortly myself once I have seen to our guests."

"Of course. We shall have to be early risers." Eloise left him with a whispered good night and a regretful look as she headed towards the stairs and the family's private wing.

* * *

Eloise lay awake, her restless eyes tracking the moonbeams that cascaded through the mullioned windows and illuminated her bedspread in a shifting pattern. She had opened the curtains earlier and forgotten to draw them tight. She was far too cosy to get up and block the light. She'd simply duck beneath the covers.

Her eyes drifted closed as she allowed tiredness to overcome her. Almost asleep, a now-familiar face crowded her mind. Benedict. She relived their encounters so far, the ones where he touched her, caressed her and made her feel more alive than in any of her previous twenty years.

A hot blush infused her body as she remembered the liberties he had taken, what he had done. The kisses were shocking enough, the way his tongue had tangled with hers, how he had invaded her with his seeking mouth, but the touch of his large hand on her breasts had undone her. She tried to push the image away but the memory of his capable hands stroking her breasts, cupping their fullness, caused her heartbeat to quicken, and an almost unbearable ache was rising. She had a yearning, but she knew not what for.

She thought of nothing but him. His teasing caresses had aroused her passions and played with her emotions. She knew she was in too deep and there was no way back.

A gentle sigh escaped her lips as she imagined Benedict touching her. A blush burned her flesh as she conjured memories of scandalous touches. Touches she knew she would welcome again. She was going to seek her fill of the pleasures he rained on her. Where was he right now and what was he doing? Did he think of her?

The sound of a shifting floorboard broke into the silence. Someone was outside her door. A creak of wood accompanied the opening of the bedroom door, followed by its closure as a gentle click signified the lock being engaged. Her heart thundered, and her skin chilled. She lay still and silent, too frightened to move.

"Eloise, are you awake?" The soft whisper and familiar voice had her throw back the covers and sit up.

She kept her voice low. "What are you doing here? Is something wrong?"

Benedict crossed the room and loomed over the bed. "No. All is well. It is simply that I had hoped to speak to you this evening, but your aunt thwarted my plans. When we are in Town, we will not have as much freedom as is afforded here. There are eyes everywhere."

She knew this to be true. Their lives were always played out in front of the servants, but in the claustrophobic society of London, little was overlooked.

He glanced at the bottom of the bed. "May I?"

"Oh yes, of course, please do sit."

She wanted to slap herself. Had she just invited him to sit on her bed as if they were in a formal drawing room? She was chilled and looked down. The covers had fallen to her waist and exposed her fine lawn nightgown. She instinctively crossed her arms, covering her breasts. The air grew heavy, pressing in on her as it trapped her in place. She spoke, surprised that she managed to maintain a calm tone. "What did you wish to speak about?"

He didn't say anything for a moment and seemed, in

fact, to be at a loss for words. He cleared his throat, and his gaze was direct, trapping her eyes with his own. "You had an opportunity to escape our engagement earlier today. Why didn't you?"

Eloise sucked in a breath at his directness. Could she open herself to him completely? Tell him of her deepest emotions and desires? She braced herself and took the leap. "Despite the circumstances, I find that I do want to marry you. We suit well."

"Yes, I agree." He looked away, and his gaze rested on his hand, which absently played with the corded tassels of her bedcover. When he looked up, there was a depth of desire in his eyes that almost scared her. "We do suit, and in many ways. I desire you very much, I think about you almost constantly and I would like to hope that you feel the same. Do you?"

The silence pressed upon her. His words, and their present circumstances, stripped away any social barriers. The darkness, alleviated only by moonbeams, emboldened her, gave her courage and bravado to speak freely. "Yes, I must confess that I am drawn to you. This was not something I expected in marriage, but I am happy to have it."

Never breaking eye contact, he shrugged his jacket from his shoulders, discarding it on the side of bed, and then proceeded to undo his perfectly tied cravat.

"What are you doing?" Eloise squeaked.

"I am making myself a little more comfortable. We will be married in a week or so, but for most of that time we will be separated either physically or by society's rules. I would like a small memory to keep me warm."

He moved towards her, eyes shuttered, like a sleek predator approaching his prey. He sat beside her, and the traitorous mattress sank beneath his weight and propelled her towards him. He gently pulled her into his arms and swiftly bent his lips to hers. Eloise gasped as he covered her mouth, delicately brushing his lips against hers. His hands were around her waist, and he tightened his grasp as he pulled her flush against his chest, deepening the kiss and stealing the very breath from her. Waves of sensation lapped over and swept through her.

As her mind clouded and clarity fled, her passions rose, and a tension overtook her. She was a novice in these matters and did not know where they were going. Oh, she had an idea of what the end outcome would be. But of how they would travel there, she had not a clue. She struggled to maintain a semblance of control as his lips pressed firmly against hers, and his tongue insinuated itself between her lips, easing her mouth open, giving him greater access to lick and tease as he willed. For it was indeed as he willed. Eloise had no strength, no desire and, shockingly, to her distant sane mind, no intention of stopping him. She longed to know what happened next, needed to assuage the burning desire that had arisen and would not abate. Not easily. This was not an unpleasant feeling, but strange, unknown.

Sweeping his hands upwards from her waist, Benedict possessively caressed her breasts, cupping them in his hands. He drew back slightly, brushing his fingers against the buttons that fastened the front of her nightgown. His eyes trapped hers, and she easily recognised the question in them as he silently asked her approval. She was in no mood to deny him anything this night. Her answer was a whispered "yes". His hands travelled lower, loosening each button until her bodice gaped and drooped open, exposing the tops of her breasts. Her window was slightly open and a cooling breeze filled the room. She should be cold, but wasn't.

Breaking the kiss, Benedict moved back and whispered, "I need to look at you. Please?" His voice hitched on the entreaty, betraying vulnerability. He waited for her answer, his eyes never leaving hers.

Drawn by his broken tone, Eloise instinctively arched her back, causing her nightgown to slip lower still, barely covering her breasts, the rasping of the material against her tender flesh increasing her rising excitement. Her whispered "yes" floated on the still air.

With one swift movement, Benedict spread the cloth apart and exposed her breasts to his gaze. Appreciation shone from his passion-filled eyes as he bent his head and gently feathered kisses across her chest. Her senses were already maddened by his touch and heightened by his seduction. Eloise arched, her hands clasping his head and urging him nearer, pulling him closer still.

He pulled back slightly, and Eloise was filled with an aching loss as her hands fell to his shoulders. The feelings he aroused in her, the desires he set coursing through her, were unknown territory. Yet she was neither afraid nor apprehensive, she was . . . well, she was curious, intrigued, willing to be taught and to learn.

He caught her gaze, a passionate haze cloaking his eyes. "Tell me you want this?" His voice was hoarse. "Give me your permission to carry on." The last was more a command than a request, but Eloise didn't care. Wild horses could not have dragged her away from this moment, from this man. She nodded her head and willingly stepped into the abyss.

Sensation layered upon sensation, as burning desire swept through her. Her mind a haze, there was no yesterday, nor tomorrow. Time was suspended as her entire being was focussed, centred on this one moment—the here and now. No thought of anything other than exquisite sensory pleasure. He could make her ache with a gentle sweep of his hand across her waist or a butterfly kiss to her forehead. What he was now doing to her, with his hands, mouth and tongue, was indescribable.

* * *

Her skin was as soft as the finest silk, her creamy flesh highlighted by the rosy flush of rising passion. His tongue tenderly grazed the tight bud of her nipple. He was in no rush, they had a lifetime to enjoy each other, to explore. He knew this was why he had sought her out. Yes, he had wanted to clearly understand why they had chosen to go forward with their marriage, but in his heart he knew that was only an excuse to be with her, to infiltrate her private rooms, to further explore what was growing between them.

Raising his head, he saw the same desire shining from her eyes, the same need to touch, to explore, to adventure together. Benedict drew back the covers and moved closer. He wanted no barrier between them. He let one hand slide downwards, skimming over her hip and thigh until it caught the hem of her dress. Plunging beneath it, his fingers weaved up and over her long, slender legs.

He leaned forward and kissed her full on the mouth as he caught her by the waist and tumbled her backward, so she was lying full length on the bed. Toeing off his boots, he settled beside her. She lay flat on her back, staring at him with wide eyes, seemingly oblivious that her bodice lay open to the waist, exposing her to the air and to his eyes. Her nightdress was ruched around her thighs, revealing her long, slender silken legs.

Benedict revelled in the sight that only his eyes had seen and only he would ever see. Ever. The word imprinted itself on his brain, seared itself into his subconscious. A surge of masculine possessiveness coursed through him. She was his. Forever. Perhaps not today in the physical sense, for he knew he should go slow to catch her, enslave her, but the fact was inescapable that he was binding Eloise to him with the invisible cords of passion, desire and need.

Leaning over, he once again captured her mouth. The kiss possessive and claiming, hard and demanding, betraying a need he had not meant to declare to her. Not yet, if indeed ever.

* * *

Eloise marvelled that his desire for her was so evident. She saw it in his trembling hand, in his darkened eyes, in his uneasy breathing. This was not a man in full control of his senses, nor of himself.

She shivered at the soft, silken glance of his fingertips

over her bared thigh. Back and forth he stroked as the kiss deepened, his tongue probed, caught and feasted daringly with hers in a dance of seduction. His large body covered hers and pinned her in place. One muscular thigh inserted itself between her legs, gently pushing, intruding and opening her thighs to allow him to press closer, deeper.

His hand continued to caress and cajole, stroking, teasing, enticing her flesh to new experiences, to a heightened level of awareness. She was aflame with desire and burned with a radiating heat.

He slipped his hand between her thighs with gentle, circling, teasing strokes. As his hand continued towards the apex of her thighs, Eloise gasped. His fingers gently fondled the softness between her legs. "Benedict!" His name flew from her lips in shocked surprise, even as she thrilled to his touch as he showed her how little she knew, how much there was to learn, to enjoy, to embrace. Firm but gentle strokes teased her aching flesh. Sensations swept through her from the rhythmic motion and gentle pressure of his clever fingers.

* * *

To his great surprise, Benedict was shaky, unsure of himself and teetering on the verge of losing what little of his control remained. How different from his usual liaisons with past mistresses, experienced widows who knew what they were getting into, who may have expected more but knew they would never receive it, who knew the rules of the game. For him, it had been an arrangement necessary for mechanical release and involved his emotions to a level of fondness—certainly in no way affected him or unmanned him, as his intimacy with Eloise threatened to do.

He tried to marshal his defences. This was far enough for today. Enough to have her aching, demanding more. He went to move from her, but, fast as a whip, her hand shot out and anchored his hand against the soft underside of her breast. His startled eyes leapt to her face. Through desire-laden eyes, she communicated her needs and then reinforced them with her words. "Please, Benedict, touch me. Keep touching me." As she pressed his hand closer, her head fell back, and a moan escaped her lips.

His control snapped. Desire flooded him, carried him away and he reacted only as he could.

* * *

Eloise was engulfed by a rising tide of tension; she was searching out for something but didn't know what it was or how to get it. Her body bucked against Benedict's hand as he cupped her more firmly, creating pressure that instead of providing relief simply increased the unbearable ache of tension.

She beseeched, "Please, Benedict—please." She didn't know what she was asking for. But Benedict obviously did, and her begging made him throw caution and restraint to the wind as he gently and carefully brought her the satisfaction she craved. Her emotions were in chaos; her sense fled along with her willpower. She couldn't stop this, didn't know how, and if she were truly honest with herself, she didn't want him to stop.

As Eloise moaned in pleasure, Benedict whispered, "Come on, darling, let go; that's my girl. Come on. Let fly." Eloise didn't understand the words, but her body was acting on intuition, obeying an instinct as old as time itself. There was a rising tension, an aching need deep inside that pulsated and throbbed. Panic rose and her heart thundered. "I can't bear this. Stop."

His hand stilled and he laid his forehead against hers. His warm breath whispered against her skin. "Hush, don't worry. Let me hold you. I won't do anything else."

The loss was overwhelming and she pulled him closer. "No, don't stop!"

He did as he was told and her mind went blank as sensation after sensation lifted her higher. He captured her mouth in time to muffle her scream of pleasure as she came apart in his arms.

Benedict held her close. She was floating, drifting on a wave of pleasure. She turned to him, her eyes already fluttering closed as sleep started to claim her. Her words burst forth before she could stop them. "This is what I was trying to avoid. I want a comfortable marriage. The way you make me feel is too . . . well, too much."

* * *

Benedict's initial reaction was to laugh. He hadn't been looking for this depth of connection but he found he was pleased to have it. Then he saw the sadness in her eyes. "What is wrong? Have I upset you?"

She sighed, as a broken breath escaped. "No, it is nothing."

"I don't believe you. We are to be married. What did you want to avoid?"

She sat up, leaned back against the headboard and covered herself with the eiderdown, clutching it tight to her chest. She seemed withdrawn and their closeness of mere moments ago had disappeared. She was cloaked in tension.

He shook his head, unsure of what had happened to spoil the mood. "Please, just tell me?"

She bit her lip and briefly closed her eyes. When she opened them her gaze was blank; when she spoke her voice was monotone. "You are correct, but when you hear what I must say you will understand why no-one, especially my uncle, must know of what I tell you."

He nodded. "Of course."

Her eyes locked onto his. "My parents didn't die together in an accident. My father's carriage overturned in a storm. He was so close to home; he was on the estate and the house was in sight. He died immediately. My mother was distraught. She adored my father and couldn't live without him."

He tensed, and reached out and gently stroked her hand. "Go on."

She spoke on a monotone. "She fled to her room. I found her there hours later. She was dead, the blood pooling from her wrists.

He pulled her into his arms and held her tight as she sobbed. He said nothing, just made comforting sounds as she let herself go.

Eventually she quietened, her breath short and jagged. "My uncle arrived shortly afterward. He took care of everything and soon the news spread that both my parents had perished in the accident. I have barely spoken of it since."

The agony in her eyes was a bolt to his heart. She was in pain yet there was little he could do, except try and reassure her. "I am so sorry for what you have gone through and I appreciate your frankness. No-one will know we have spoken of this tragedy." He paused, "You are not your mother."

"I know, but I don't want that passion. I don't want to care about someone above all else. I just don't."

She sounded as if she was trying to convince herself.

Benedict kissed her soundly and, laying her farther into the pillows, covered her with the blankets and kissed her gently on her head with a whispered, "Rest well. I will see you in the morning. All will be well. I promise you."

CHAPTER TWENTY-THREE

John Coachman bided his time, waiting for the right moment, the exact circumstances that would further his plan and net him the most gain. He had almost approached him earlier. A group of men had left the terrace to stroll the gardens, the smouldering tips of their cigars marking their way. John had followed them, but the group stayed together. He had no way of making contact. A guest of His Grace rarely crossed paths with a lowly coachman. He hadn't thought this through properly. Tomorrow all the house-party would depart, and his chance would be gone. He downed the dregs of ale and dropped the tankard onto the table. He'd joined Hannah in her rooms for some supper, but she'd been called away to see the housekeeper.

"John, you'll never guess what," she said when she came back. "Higgins will be looking for you."

"What's he want? I haven't done anything."

Her eyes sparkled with a tease. "That'll make a change."

Hannah smiled and drew a finger down his cheek. "Don't worry. Seems that Miss Eloise is to be married sharpish-like, and it's all hands on deck. I've to go to London in the morning and take my pick of helpers with me. I'm to bake the wedding cake. I'm ever so excited. I hope I don't mess it up."

"You won't do that, girl. Your sponges float, they're so light. But what's Higgins want with me?"

"Ah, that's the best part. You've to drive us there in one of the coaches. How exciting is that?"

She would mean them being together. But he was thinking of something else entirely. He knew where to find him in London. No one would miss him for an hour here and there. He needed to have a word with him about Sarah, then he and Hannah would get what they deserved. There'd be no stopping them. Their lives were about to change for the better.

* * *

They arrived at Westbury's townhouse mid-afternoon. The traffic got worse the closer they got to London, and they'd been stuck behind an overturned cart for the better part of half an hour. Benedict dismounted and helped first Lady Bentley and then Eloise from the carriage. She placed her hand in his and flashed him a quick look that spoke volumes—a look he hoped signalled she was thinking of the previous night. Not just the passion, but their new-found closeness from the confidences she had shared. He longed for everyone else to disappear and for them to be alone again. The damned wedding couldn't come soon enough.

The front door swung open, and Higgins appeared in the doorway. He must have left Huntley in the middle of the night to get here before them.

Eloise climbed the front steps behind her aunt and paused to look back at him. "I shall see you this evening at Lady Featherington's ball?"

"Indeed, I have arranged with Westbury that we all travel together and will meet you here beforehand."

"Excellent. And now? What are your plans?"

"I must visit Whitehall and determine what, if anything, they have discovered." He bowed over her hand. "Until later." They lingered for a moment, and a wave of prescience swept through him at the years, days and nights that they would spend together. He smiled and headed to his destination.

He decided against hailing a hackney or going on horseback. He'd walk. Sauntering through the streets of Mayfair, Benedict drew in the sights, smells and sounds of London, the capital of their, and perhaps the entire, world. Porticoed white stone mansions rose several storeys high; hidden behind their painted front doors and brass knockers were spacious, elegant rooms, and the terraces behind led to long manicured gardens. The streets were quiet, with only hurrying servants returning from errands, the occasional rumble of carriages or a cantering horse breaking the silence. Yet if one were to take a wrong turning, walk along a narrow lane and exit into an unknown area, the sophisticated and refined veneer fell away, peeled back like the curtains of a theatre stage to reveal the real foundations of London beneath the patina of the ton.

The city may be mainly populated by honest, decent people, but they lived cheek by jowl alongside thieves, con men, tricksters and those who travelled the hell route of kidnap, rape and murder. The lanes and alleyways were shadowed, even at the height of day, and occasionally their darkness spilled onto the well-swept paving stones of Mayfair.

The shadows were lengthening as the sun started its late afternoon descent. This was the perfect location for someone to attack Benedict. Anyone could have been watching their arrival, seen him leave, alone and on foot, and stealthily followed. Long, narrow alleys ran between the tall, stately town houses, dark passages leading to tradesmen's entrances and walled gardens. These were perfect places for mischief and murder; it taking but an instant to draw an unsuspecting victim into the gloom of the underworld. A swift slash of a blade, the dull thud of a club and the light of life could be extinguished in moments.

However, reflected Benedict as he turned from the street to climb the wide, steep steps leading to the discreet ministerial office, that hadn't happened today. This in a way was disappointing as it meant the two men following him, supplied by Westbury, had wasted their time. His would-be attacker hadn't shown up, even though his stroll through Town had presented the perfect opportunity. Or if they had, they lurked in the shadows and thought better of it. Perhaps they had recognised his protective tail?

The two men who now dogged his steps were from Huntley's stables and had discreetly accompanied them to

Town. These young men would, as directed, wait and follow him home again, but he feared there would be no action seen on the journey. He wanted this madman stopped, and stopped right now, without the cloud of attack hanging over his head as he and Eloise started married life.

Benedict did not like the inexplicable. In his mind, "unexpected" events were considered all too reasonable and expected with hindsight when all the facts were known.

So the very fact that his would-be assailant had not ventured forth in the last twenty-four hours told Benedict that something had changed, but was it only that they had left Huntley, or was it something else entirely?

* * *

The minister looked up, his face alight with anticipation as he rose to greet Benedict. "I'm glad to see you. I hope you have some news, for we are getting nowhere. We have pored through Jones' records, but the client names are disguised. There are tally records of what has been loaned to whom and details of repayments. There are also notes of where extras have been paid."

"More blackmail?"

"That's the assumption we have made. Someone had to have been providing the money for the ever-increasing size of the loans. Jones simply did not have these sums available. In the days of his wife's father, they lent money to merchants and tradesmen secured on the next shipment or month's trade. Bartholomew Jones inherits the business, and suddenly he is dealing with the aristocracy and lending them multiples of what he previously had available. Where did he get the introductions and the money? That person could very well be the killer as well."

"And are you any closer to identifying that individual?"

A mouth that was a sharp tight line was the initial reaction to his question. With a sigh, the minister responded, "Not at the moment. We have exhausted all avenues. The wife says she had nothing to do with the business and was not at all forthcoming."

"Did you visit her yourself?"

The minister sniffed. "Of course not. I've attached two runners to this investigation, and they met with Mrs Jones. She ended up calling in a neighbour's husband and refusing to speak."

No doubt the rough investigators-for-hire had tried to intimidate the woman with bluster and bullying. "Do you have any objection to my speaking with her?"

"I cannot see what you will achieve, but I have no objection. Now what do you have to report?"

"Jones spent the latter part of his childhood at Huntley. He became friendly with Lord Gooding, who often visited relatives at a nearby family estate. Interestingly, Gooding was a guest of Westbury's house party. He claims they outgrew their boyish friendship and had not seen each other in some time."

"We will have a closer look at him. His family has no lack of money, so I cannot see him as Jones' backer. He certainly didn't need the money from the blackmail."

"There is someone else you need to look at. Jones' father said that his son worked as a private secretary when he first arrived in London. He joined the household of Lord Everton."

"We should speak to him."

"I already have. He was at the house party as well. Everton says Bartholomew stayed with him for under a year before leaving to get married and join his father-in-law's business."

"Fine. Do let me know if you find out anything else."

The tone of dismissal was plain, but Benedict hadn't finished yet.

"Jones had another childhood friend. She became a maid at Huntley and was found dead a few days ago."

The minister stared at him, boredom in his arrogant gaze. "And how does this concern me?"

He tamped down his anger. "Apart from the fact that a healthy young woman is found dead in the woods, it does seem a coincidence that both Bartholomew and his childhood friend are murdered within a week of each other." He paused for a moment. "We also have to consider the attempts on my life."

"What do you mean? What has happened?"

"There have been three incidents, two of which could only have been carried out by someone staying at or connected to Huntley. However, the first exercises my mind. If not for the other attacks, I would have deemed it being in the wrong place at the very wrong time. I was shot at as I journeyed to Huntley. No one could have known at that point that I was interested in the death of Bartholomew Jones."

The minister glanced away and shuffled in his seat. His cheeks were stained with twin patches of red. "I had people to update. They had to know what was going on."

He took a moment to understand this. "So you are saying that various people knew I was involved, and any of them could have spoken out of turn and leaked this information to interested ears?"

The minister had the grace to look away. "I am afraid so."

"I started out wanting to know who had been financing Jones and was therefore culpable in my relative's death, but now I have other compelling reasons to bring this person to justice. Someone tried to kill me and succeeded in ending a young girl's life. I will discover who is responsible. This is personal."

* * *

Eloise had been prodded, pinned and draped in silk by Madam Veronique as she and her aunt discussed her wedding dress. The jubilant dressmaker left promises in her wake that the dress would be ready to fit in two days. No doubt her uncle would pay a hearty premium for such service.

A brief knock on the door preceded Higgins. "Miss Eloise, the Earl of Rothsea is here to see you. Shall I show him in?"

She jumped up. "Yes, please do."

Benedict must have been sure of his welcome, for he entered the room before she had a chance to consider why he would be here.

Higgins bowed and exited the room, leaving the door slightly ajar to maintain respectability. Eloise's heart beat a little faster. "This is a surprise. Is something amiss?"

His face was serious. "No, but I have need of your assistance. I must speak with the widow of Bartholomew Jones, and I believe she may be more forthcoming if I am accompanied by a lady."

"Of course. I shall meet you in the hall. It will only take a moment to ready myself." She marvelled at the calmness of her voice as her heart fluttered and flipped in amazement at how a person whom she had known for barely a week could affect her so badly. But enough of that—Benedict needed her help.

* * *

The late Bartholomew Jones had lived in a promising area rife with merchants and those whose industrious nature and brains kept commerce flowing. The terraced house was double-fronted, and a young maid had shown them into a pretty parlour. They were soon joined by a birdlike woman dressed in black who compulsively rubbed her hands together as if to combat nervousness.

She cleared her throat. "I am Abigail Jones. How may I help you?"

Eloise knew Bartholomew Jones had been twenty-five, yet his widow had to be a decade older. "Thank you for your time. I am Miss Camarthon and," she waved a hand in Benedict's direction, "this is the Earl of Rothsea."

Mrs Jones bobbed and curtseyed and, from the quick light that brightened her eyes, Eloise thought that, grieving though she was, the widow was in awe that an earl was in her parlour.

Her thin hands fluttered towards two armchairs. "Please, please be seated."

Eloise seated herself and took the lead. "Please accept my condolences for your loss. I believe my uncle, the Duke of Westbury, sent you a note on behalf of the family."

"Yes, he did." Her eyes flicked nervously between them in rapid succession, and her tongue darted out to moisten dry lips. Her face was shuttered and closed. Eloise understood only too well why Benedict had requested her assistance.

Benedict spoke, "If you do not mind, we have a few questions about your late husband's business."

She avoided their eyes and stared at the rug. "My husband never spoke of such matters with me."

Eloise moved closer to her. "This must be such a dreadful time for you. Often we do not know what tiny snippet of information may be of value or of interest to the matter in question. Who was your husband's business associate?" Perhaps a direct question would solicit more of a response.

She kept her eyes on Eloise. It was as if Benedict did not exist. "My husband did not have a partner. He worked alone. My father always said a man should keep his own counsel in business."

"Did your husband have any close associates? Anyone who may have been involved in the business? Someone with access to money?"

She shook her head and wrung her hands, the knuckles white. "Please, I don't know anything."

They'd get no more out of her today. Eloise removed

her calling card from her reticule and pressed it into Mrs Jones' hand. "If you recall anything that may help us, please let me know." She moved towards the door, Benedict in her wake, then stopped and turned. "A young woman has been killed at Huntley, and there have been attacks on the earl's life. It may be the same person who killed your husband, so if you recall anything, anything at all, no matter how insignificant, I urge you to let us know."

CHAPTER TWENTY-FOUR

Benedict turned as a whisper of satin and tulle, accompanied by the intoxicating scent of rose water and violets, drew his eyes to the sweeping staircase. Lady Bentley descended first. She wore a midnight-blue wide-skirted gown, draped across the shoulders to form a wide neckline, the front of which was trimmed in delicate lace dyed to match the colour of her gown.

Westbury smiled, genuine affection and warmth in his voice. "Aunt, you look lovely."

Lady Bentley blushed a little.

"Why, thank you." She smiled a little self-consciously as she moved to smooth the folds of her gown. "I ordered this gown some while back, although at the time I had no event in mind. However, it seemed perfect for tonight."

Benedict swept a long, low bow and gently placed a courtly kiss on her gloved hand. "My lady, you do indeed look lovely. Westbury and I are honoured in escorting you this evening."

Lady Bentley lightly swatted Benedict with her fan. "You are an outrageous boy." But her smile betrayed her pleasure at the compliment.

As Benedict straightened, he turned towards the stairs to greet Eloise—and froze. He was rendered immobile at the sight that greeted him. Blood fled his brain and rested where it would, but he had enough sanity left to know he was done for.

Eloise's gentle curves were draped in ice-blue satin, gathered over one shoulder, leaving the other daringly, shockingly bare. The dress fitted lightly to her waist and flared to the floor, longer in the back to create a small train. Her only adornment was a superb diamond brooch in the shape of a full-blown rose, blue-tinged diamonds clustered together to create the petals with dew-effect droplets of white diamonds. Her hair was swept upwards at the sides, the curls tamed and caught into a low, tight chignon that nestled in the delicately curved nape of her neck.

Her gaze was steady and straight as she descended the staircase, one hand holding her train slightly aloft to the side, the other trailing along the highly polished mahogany banister. His eyes were caught in her gaze as if an invisible thread connected them, and he couldn't pull away, couldn't escape the taut bands that connected them.

She looked alluring and sensual—and far too damned transparent. He smiled; Eloise clearly carried her heart in her eyes. And her heart was saying that she was connected to the man in her sight. In the same way that her innocence had shone through, now her irrevocable attachment to Benedict was plain for all to see. Well, Benedict hoped not all, as he glanced at Westbury, who, luckily, was laughing with his aunt and had turned to escort her to the front entrance and the waiting carriage.

Benedict quickly covered the ground to the bottom of the stairs and, bowing low, placed his lips in a gentle caress on Eloise's gloved hand and whispered, "You look beautiful, but be careful, love, your thoughts shine out of your eyes."

* * *

His voice was a husk of a whisper, and she shivered, but not from the cold. She had drunk in the very sight of him until her head was spinning, and she held on tight to the banister lest she fall. She descended the last step, her hand still held in his, and considered his words.

They stood alone as the others exited the front door. "I suggest you look in your own eyes, my lord, and consider the truth that is also in them."

He looked startled for a moment and then laughed, placed her hand on his arm and steered her towards the door and the waiting carriage. "We will suit very well indeed."

* * *

They had danced and conversed and been the recipients of felicitations and well wishes. Eloise smiled and thanked and was gliding on a wave of heightened emotions when a voice caused her to steel herself.

"May I have the honour of this dance?"

She was not already engaged for the quadrille, and, under society's gaze, she could not think of a way to politely refuse Bellingham. Even with his previous apology, his coarse proposal—if that is what one could call it—still rang in her ears, and she had to garner all her social strength to smile brightly and follow the flow of the music. There was silence between them as they mastered the intricate dance steps. As they settled into the routine, Bellingham's voice broke into her thoughts.

"Being engaged obviously suits you." His eyes admired her, yet there was a bitter underlay to his tone.

"I am content with my circumstances, my lord. I trust that one day you too shall know such joy in your choice of a marriage partner."

Bellingham gave a rare grin, which softened the severity of his features. "I don't know about joy, but yes, I am sure I shall be content."

As the dance finished and the requisite curtsey and bow were exchanged, Eloise knew she would never be comfortable in this man's company.

* * *

Benedict sipped at his wine as Eloise left Bellingham and joined a group of ladies conversing with her aunt. Knowing where she was, having her in his sight, gave him a sense of peace that he hadn't known he was missing. He smiled at his foolishness and idly gazed around the room—and froze.

He knew Bellingham was here, but this was the first he

had seen of Everton. He was talking to a younger, wilder crowd, and in their midst was Gooding. This meant that three of the men from the house party were here. He better be on his guard.

* * *

The evening was growing hotter, cheeks becoming pink and eyes glittering with the effects of alcohol. The windowed doors were open to the gardens, and the revelries had spilled onto the wide lawns, the secluded rose arbours and tree-lined walks ringing with laughter and merriment.

Eloise and Benedict had ventured outside with Lady Bentley, and the ladies were sitting by a tinkling fountain as they took advantage of the welcoming coolness of the night breeze.

Lady Bentley tuned to Benedict, wisps of hair being blown hither and thither as she rapidly waved her fan in front of her face.

"I don't know about you two, but I've had enough. Rothsea, be a dear, won't you, and go and find Westbury and ask him to have the carriage brought round. I imagine he won't complain." Eloise didn't even try to conceal her laughter. Her uncle would have been ready to leave shortly after he arrived and would jump to do his aunt's bidding if it meant he could get home to the peace of his study.

Eloise watched Benedict as his long limbs quickly covered the ground to the house. Her heart quickened a little, and she smiled. She would soon be this man's wife.

Her aunt's gentle exclamation interrupted her musing.

"Oh look. There is Lady Somerset. I want a quick word with her. The flowers for her daughter's wedding last year were spectacular, and I would like to ask if she'll let us borrow whoever organised them. I believe it was her housekeeper." Lady Bentley turned her gaze to Eloise. "Darling, sit here for one second. I shall be back shortly."

As her aunt's figure receded into the gloom of the evening, becoming a little indistinct and hazy, Eloise was pulled to her feet with a sharp, hard tug, and before she could even collect her thoughts, she was pushed behind a box-cut hedge that bordered one long side of the gardens.

She was backed up against the close-clipped foliage before her vision cleared and she could see who stood in front of her. Sir Frederick Richards!

Outraged, and more than a little nervous, Eloise demanded, "What are you doing?" She struggled to loosen the hard grip on each wrist that held her immobile.

Sir Frederick smiled. "I know that you are being forced into marrying Rothsea. Yet it was meant to be me. I have come to rescue you."

She simply stared. Was he mad? She looked out the corner of her eye but couldn't see into the gardens beyond, which probably meant that no one could see her. Sir Frederick lunged towards her and pressed wet lips against hers, all the while whispering, "Oh, Eloise. We were meant to be together."

To the devil with scandal. She had to do something about this. Eloise drew back and, tilting her face to the sky, opened her mouth to scream when Sir Frederick was brusquely pulled from her and flung backward, squealing in outrage as he fell in an ungainly heap at the feet of the figure, taut with rage, which now loomed over him.

Benedict's voice was low and tightly controlled as he spat out his words. "You bloody fool, Richards. I've had just about enough of you. She does not love you, you imbecile."

Sir Frederick looked at her. "You don't?"

Eloise gave a most unladylike snort. "I do not care for you, sir, nor shall I ever have any feelings for you apart from mild revulsion. You, sir, are a blackmailer and a rogue." The ice dripped from her voice, and Sir Frederick's colour rose.

"But I love you—you danced with me, smiled at me. We spoke about my horses, for heaven's sake."

"I was being polite and treated you no differently than any other. Do not give me any nonsense either. I know for a fact you offered for me before you had even seen me." This last was hissed.

If it was possible, Sir Frederick's skin took on an even rosier hue at being so thoroughly caught out. He slowly pushed himself up on his elbows and into a sitting position. Looking nervously at the silent, watchful Benedict, he tugged at his cravat as if he sought to loosen it from choking him.

"Ah yes, well. Never quite have enough funds, you see. I'm the youngest son and that means you got to marry a rich wife. So yes, I did offer for you. But I still would have done the same once I'd seen you, especially once I'd really looked at you."

There was a slightly lecherous look in his eye, which was swiftly extinguished as Benedict stepped towards him, fists curled at his sides. Sir Frederick spoke in a rush, his words tumbling over each other in his haste.

"I'm sorry. Really, I am. I need your money, and I assumed there was a little something between us. Who can blame me for trying?" He looked up at Eloise, eyes like a contrite puppy. Her look was dismissive. "I was wrong. Obviously very, very wrong. So please," here he glanced at Benedict, "let me go, and I'll keep my distance."

Benedict bent, grabbing the front of Sir Frederick's shirt and roughly hauling him to his feet. The younger man rocked back on his heels as he was set down, but Benedict pulled him forward until their eyes were bare inches apart.

"Do you hear what she said? Did you actually listen?"

Eloise could feel the suppressed violence shimmer in the air as Benedict held on to his control, barely held it in check, shaking Sir Frederick until his teeth rattled.

"Please . . . yes . . . I heard and . . . and I understand. Please let me go, and I promise I will never bother you again." The words were directed towards Eloise, but the plea for leniency was meant for Benedict.

With a muffled curse, Benedict threw Sir Frederick from him, disgust etched in the stark lines of his handsome face.

"Go, but mark my words. If you ever try to harm me or mine, or if I gain proof that you have tried to do me harm, I shall come after you—personally and with the most fatal of intent."

The foolish young man ran across the now-empty gardens, stumbling and falling as he tried to put as much distance between himself and Rothsea as he possibly could.

* * *

Benedict stared after him until his slight figure disappeared into the night. A weary sound behind him made him recall who else was there and what she had been through.

"Eloise, come here." Benedict pulled her close and rested his chin on the top of her head. His own heart was beating a wild tattoo, from the remnants of the rage that had flowed through him like poison when he had seen Eloise being manhandled.

"Benedict, how could he be so deluded as to think I had strong regard for him? Remember the night we met? It was obvious I wanted nothing to do with him and his machinations."

"I believe Sir Frederick was trying to justify his advances. He wanted your money, badly, and perhaps he sought to assuage what conscience he has by imagining you in love with him, that you actually wanted to marry him."

"Do you think he was the one trying to harm you?"

"I don't know. The first incident was on my way to Huntley, and there was no known connection between us at that point. No, I cannot see how that fits, but I shall investigate it. Come on, before we're missed."

At that, her aunt popped her head around the hedging. "Good heavens, there you are. Out, out now, before someone realises you are missing. And Rothsea . . ." The name and tone were informal, but the glint in her eye was anything but. "Do be a dear and get your hands off my niece. You aren't married yet!"

Eloise took her aunt's arm, and the pair sauntered out

of the bushes as if they had been walking quietly through the gardens, their handsome escort following meekly behind.

* * *

It had taken but a moment's work for John Coachman to visit the stables used by a certain town house. He'd slipped away in the afternoon lull, armed with a flask of brandy filched from His Grace's own stock. He'd singled out the man he needed and shared a tot or two with this fellow coachman and discovered his master was to attend the same ball as the Westbury party. His new friend boasted that his work was done until later as he had readied the coach that morning. A few more brandy slugs and his drinking partner lumbered off to piss behind the stables. John quietly hopped into the coach and left a note on the velvet-covered seat.

Now he waited in the cooling night air, his jacket collar turned up against the chill. He'd chosen this spot as it was a mere five-minute walk from the mansion where the ball was in full throw. He'd easily slid through the shadows of the gardens that surrounded the house. He'd dodged through the lanes around Shepherds Market, each step taking him farther from the privileged realm of his masters as he entered a world where the air was perfumed by jellied eels and sewage, and the sounds of base nature carried on the air as streetwalkers serviced their customers in shadowed corners. The hawkers and flower-sellers had packed away for the day, and there was little footfall. This wasn't the place to be when the dark came, but he'd been born near here. He'd joined the previous duke's household when he was a lad, but his family had stayed in the area and were well-known. No one would touch him here. These streets had eyes and ears, but they'd glance away when they recognised him as one of their own.

Echoing footsteps disrupted the silence, and he quickly turned.

The man's eyes were chips of ice, his face expressionless, his voice cold and autocratic. "What is the meaning of this? How dare you summon me?"

John quickly shook off the chill that ran through him. This man may be far above him in society, but he held the winning hand.

"I saw you. You were in the woods with Sarah Carpenter the night she was murdered. I reckon there are a few that would want to know if it was you who killed her. Not that I'm saying you did, but you being with her in the woods and then she's dead, well, might look strange, eh?"

"Are you attempting to blackmail me?" The voice was more pleasant, the tone calm. This was going much better than he had expected.

"I'm only asking for a little something to help me keep my mouth shut. Did you bring me anything?"

"Yes, I did."

"Good. We can talk proper numbers later on, but give me what you've got right now."

"With pleasure."

John tingled with anticipation as the man pulled aside his elegant evening coat and reached into an inside pocket. The whisper of steel being unsheathed and a glint of moonlight on a flat blade confused him.

"No need for any of that. Give me what I'm due, and we'll say no more about it."

The smile was feral. "Very well. Take your due. It is what you deserve."

The stiletto blade flashed, and John instinctively took a step back, landing against the wall. His attacker grabbed him by the neck, fingers pressing tight against his windpipe. His throat burned, and his eyes watered. He was a weakling compared to this man, but he had to fight back. It was his only option.

He twisted to the side as his assailant pushed against him, pinning him to the wall. The knife pierced his flesh and pressed in deep, and the sharp, blinding pain was overwhelming. The blade twisted, and he opened his mouth to scream, to shout for help, but all that came out was a choked wheeze as strong fingers cut off his breath. The pain consumed him, devoured him as his eyesight cleared momentarily and he gazed at the grim face contorted with rage. It was the last he saw.

CHAPTER TWENTY-FIVE

Benedict sipped at his brandy as Westbury raged.

"It is unconscionable that John abandoned his duties and left our carriage waiting in line. I am indebted to our hosts for offering one of their men to ferry us home."

Benedict was regretting his acceptance of the nightcap, no matter how fine the brandy was.

Lady Bentley's voice was edged with weariness as she moved towards the drawing room door. "I find I am consumed by fatigue. I am for my bed. Good night."

She looked at Eloise, who was settled in one of the comfortable brocade armchairs.

Eloise's reply was quick. "I am not yet tired."

Westbury simply raised a brow and poured her a small glass of claret.

Lady Bentley was almost at the door as Higgins came rushing into the room. "Your Grace, please forgive me, but there is something you must hear." At that, he pushed a red-eyed woman into the room. Benedict recognised her from speaking to the Huntley staff; it was the cook. She had obviously been crying.

Westbury's voice was gentle. "What do you have to say, Mrs Oaks?"

"Begging your pardon, but it's about John—John Coachman." Her voice broke, and she stifled a sob. "He's a good man, and he was trying to better himself." A dark red stain mottled her cheeks. "He was trying to provide for our future, that's all. He saw who was with young Sarah the night she was killed."

That got Benedict's full attention. "Who was it?"

She slowly shook her head. "I just know that he was a proper gent. John was going to get money for us. I wrote a note." She looked at the floor, and her words were mumbled. "I am sorry. I know it was wrong." She raised her eyes and beseeched. "But where is John? What has happened to him?"

"What did the note say?"

"That the gent was to meet John at Shepherds Market. He was to bring money."

"You have no clue as to who this man was?"

"No, but it was someone as was going to be at the fancy party you went to this night."

Benedict turned to Westbury. "May I beg assistance from some of your footmen? I will call upon the Bow Street Runners as well, but we need to have Shepherds Market searched as a priority."

As Eloise and her aunt led the sobbing woman from the room, Benedict feared the worst.

* * *

After a long night Benedict gratefully sipped at the cup of coffee pressed into his hand by Lady Bentley. He had returned to his home before dawn and risen mere hours later, quickly changing and arriving at the Westbury household as breakfast was being served.

He knew directness was the only option. "I am afraid that we discovered John's body in Shepherds Market. There is no doubt. He was murdered."

Westbury sucked in a breath of air, and the noise reverberated in the still room. "This is madness. A man killed because he opened his mouth to the wrong person."

Lady Bentley pressed a trembling hand to her breast. "Poor John. Mrs Oaks will be distraught. I must tell her in person. Excuse me."

Eloise sat across from him, her face pale. "How does this connect? From Bartholomew to Sarah and then John?"

"I don't know, but it has to be tied to Bartholomew Jones' business and the financial backer."

The door swung open, and Higgins entered followed by an ashen-faced Mrs Jones.

"Miss Camarthon, I believe this is the lady you advised may visit you."

"Thank you. Mrs Jones, please come in and take a seat."

Abigail Jones held herself straight, tension writ in every taut movement. "I shall stand, thank you. I won't be long, but I did think of something. You asked if my husband was being financed by someone. Well, I still don't believe anything like that was happening, but I suddenly realised who may know."

Benedict questioned if the woman really did have something to tell them or if she wanted to maintain a connection with the Westbury household. "And that would be?"

"Lord Gooding. My husband's best friend."

He sat up straight. "They were in contact? I understood your husband had not seen Lord Gooding for some time."

The woman smiled and puffed with pride. "Barely a week went past that Lord Gooding did not meet with my husband. Their boyhood friendship has remained true all these years."

Benedict tensed. "Thank you. You have been most helpful."

* * *

Gooding's father owned a large mansion that occupied a massive corner plot near the Thames. The house was set back from the busy road and surrounded by manicured gardens that stretched to the river itself. Benedict concealed himself across the street under the canopy of a towering oak that spread its shadow towards Gooding's gates. He'd called at the house earlier, but an imperious butler had declared his master not at home. Benedict knew that could mean that Gooding wasn't receiving or perhaps was about to leave for one of the clubs. If it was the latter, he'd be waiting for him.

Carriages and loaded carts rumbled past in a steady stream, and merchants, goodwives and urchins crowded the pavements and spilled onto the road as the dirty, chaotic city went about its business.

Benedict questioned his reasoning. What would cause Gooding to kill his partner? He had no doubt that Gooding was the backer. It all fell too neatly into place. Yes, Gooding had a wealthy father and would have access to a generous allowance, but the rumour was his father held the purse strings—and held them tight. Was the moneylending business and subsequent blackmail an attempt to fill his own coffers without going cap in hand to his father?

A movement at the mansion drew his attention. The front door had opened, and two liveried footmen raced to open the tall gates. They were followed by an elegantly dressed man. Gooding. Benedict moved out of the dappled shade and, dodging the oncoming carriages, ran across the road and called out, "Gooding. Wait."

He was greeted with an affable smile as Gooding turned. "Rothsea, this is a surprise. What brings you this way?"

"I wanted a word with you. May we talk inside?" He gestured to the house.

"I am afraid I am on my way to an appointment. Can this wait?"

"No, I need to speak to you now. It is about your relationship with Bartholomew Jones."

Only the slightest slippage of Gooding's smile betrayed his surprise. "Very well, but I must hurry. I am due to picnic at Vauxhall Gardens, and a boat awaits me."

Gooding venturing to the scandalous gardens told him more about the kind of man he was. Vauxhall was a licentious place where the classes could freely mix and morals were relaxed. "I will walk with you. I believe you knew Jones more than you previously indicated. I hear you met him frequently, at least once a week. Yet that is not what you told me."

His smile was easy. "Well, I have to say, and I am not proud of this, but I was a little ashamed of my old friend. He was not from our class, and moneylending has a taint of the streets. It was not a connection I wanted to overly publicise."

"You stayed in touch over the years and were good friends, I assume, given the frequency of your contact."

"That is correct. I would ask you to keep this information to yourself. There is no need for this connection to become wider knowledge."

They were nearing the Thames boarding jetty, where a cluster of small boats waited to ferry their passengers across the dark, putrid Thames—London's lifeblood. Gooding pointed along the river path to a luxurious vessel floating in splendid isolation. "I have engaged the services of one of the Vauxhall barges."

Another indication that Gooding preferred more exotic pursuits. The Vauxhall amenities were only available to their most frequent—and high-spending—customers.

As Gooding stepped aboard, Benedict took his chance. "And were you also Bartholomew's backer? Did you supply the funds to tie up your victims in debt, before blackmailing them to steal from their families and estates?"

Gooding faltered and stumbled, throwing a hand out to hold on to the railing that ran along the perimeter of the boat. When he straightened, his face was blank—

undoubtedly on purpose. "What nonsense. I have no idea what you're talking about. You have gone mad." He looked to the bargeman. "Let's go. Now!"

The man jumped to attention and, snapping his fingers, indicated for the oarsmen to take position as he wielded a long pole to push away from the riverbank. Benedict saw opportunity slipping away with the tide and leapt across the widening gap, landing on the deck.

Gooding turned, his nose tilted and a haughty expression on his face. "Leave me alone. My dealings with Jones are my business."

"Your so-called dealings with Jones led to the death of someone I cared about. I want justice."

"Justice?" His lips curled in a sneer. "Yes, I funded the lending. I took Jones' father-in-law's business to another level, and we were making good money. If you are implying that someone took their life because they couldn't pay their debts, that is not my concern, nor is it a crime that you can lay at my door."

"Perhaps not, but blackmail is a crime, and one I believe you colluded in with Jones."

Gooding smirked. "And how could you even begin to prove that? Jones is dead, and I doubt anyone being blackmailed would come forward to tell tales on us. They were stupid enough to get in over their heads, and all we were doing was asking for a little more interest to be paid. No, I don't think you'll get anywhere with that."

"What about multiple murders?"

Gooding spun round and drew his lips back in a sneer. "You are scraping the barrel now, and you have even less chance of trying to tie me to the murder of a moneylender, a little slut and an old coachman."

Benedict stilled. "How did you know about John?"

Gooding laughed, a harsh sound that lifted above the tide as it slapped against the narrow hull of the boat. "Don't be naive. A little coin spread here and there results in anything worth knowing coming out. The majority of London knew the mighty Duke of Westbury was left standing on the steps without his carriage. It added to the tale when news of the coachman's death came by first light."

Benedict cursed the busybodies and gossipmongers. "Perhaps I don't need proof. We both know that it will be enough for you to be rumoured to be involved in blackmail for society invitations to start dropping off and you receiving the cut direct."

Gooding's neck corded and his flesh mottled with an unsightly flush. When he spoke his voice was tight and the words bitten out. "I demand your silence. You will say nothing."

Now it was Benedict's turn to laugh at foolish words. "Or what? I hear your father is sparing with his fortune, and he is a moral man. He may even decide to cut you off, especially if the rumours also name you a murderer."

Benedict knew he was taunting, but he wanted a reaction. "You were at the house party. You knew Bartholomew Jones and Sarah Carpenter, and it is said that John Coachman spied on Sarah and saw her with a man the night she was murdered. Was that man you? Did you murder John Coachman to keep him quiet? Were the attacks on me to prevent me investigating Jones' death?"

Gooding's eyes darted around as if seeking an escape,

but the boat was in the midst of the river, at its deepest part. His shoulders slumped, and his gaze locked onto Benedict's. "You think you know everything, but Lord Bellingham and Sir Frederick Richards were also at Huntley."

Benedict took a moment for the words to sink in before he shook his head. "What does that signify?"

"They both knew Bartholomew Jones and were his clients. There are a lot more people in need of funds than you could imagine."

Hearing of Sir Frederick did not surprise him, but Bellingham did. "I am sure you have a long list of clients. Let us not forget that you funded Jones."

"Yes, I did. So what? I will not have my life ruined because of you." His face reddened, and spittle dripped from the side of his mouth as he spat out the words. With quicker movements than Benedict thought him capable of, Gooding launched an attack and landed a strong jab to Benedict's stomach. He doubled over, but as he crumpled, he grabbed Gooding's calf and pulled, causing him to lose his feet, and they both tumbled to the floor.

Benedict loomed over Gooding and pinned him to the deck, forcing his weight onto his opponent's shoulders. "Don't be so stupid. This won't change anything."

Gooding bucked and kicked as he struggled to free himself. He swivelled his head and clamped his teeth around Benedict's wrist. The pain was intense, and he let go in shock. Gooding pushed himself up and turned the tables. He sat astride Benedict's chest and used a forearm to press against his throat and keep him trapped. Benedict gagged as he struggled to take a breath, then stilled as he saw the flash of light on a rapier-sharp blade. "You bloody fool. This is going too far."

A sly smile was the only response before Gooding called over his shoulder to the oarsmen. "There will be hefty coin for your silence today. This is none of your business."

The men turned away. Gooding raised his arm high and stabbed the vicious blade towards Benedict's chest. Benedict bucked with all the strength he had, dislodging Gooding, who fell to the side. The knife dropped to the ground and skittered across the deck towards the prow.

Benedict was first to gain his wits and jumped to his feet, pulling on Gooding's jacket to bring him with him. He smashed his fist into Gooding's face, drew back and landed a sharp uppercut to the jaw. Gooding crashed to the deck, and Benedict bent over to catch his breath. A scrambling noise alerted him that Gooding was on the move. He was crawling to the prow, and the discarded knife was back in his hand. He held the blade aloft as he swayed from foot to foot, a vicious, dark look in his eyes. "Only one of us will be walking off this boat, and it isn't going to be you."

He ran towards Benedict, who quickly glanced around for something to use as a weapon. He caught the gaze of the ancient bargeman, who, to his surprise, repeatedly flicked his eyes to Benedict's feet. He looked down and saw a spare oar tucked against the side of the boat. He grabbed it with both hands and held it horizontal in front of his chest. It was more for defence, but it would do. Gooding rushed forward, and Benedict met him head on, brandishing the oar to deflect the knife. Gooding was stabbing the weapon in a frenzy, here and there, left and right, but Benedict blocked his attack each time. Gooding moved backward, inching along the flat stern of the barge, swaying as he jabbed the knife into the air, warding off Benedict. One false move and the fool would be overboard. Benedict called out, "Watch your feet."

A mocking laugh greeted him. "You don't get me that easy. I'm keeping my eyes on you."

A large cargo boat sailed past, too far away to see what was happening but close enough for its wake to surge their way. The barge tilted. Gooding wobbled and lost his feet. Benedict tried to grab him, but Gooding swatted his hand away, still brandishing the knife. The movement was too much, and he fell head-first into the river. After a moment, his head reappeared, but in a blink he went under again before reappearing moments later. He was thrashing and screaming. Realisation slammed into Benedict. Gooding couldn't swim.

He dived into the putrid, foul-smelling Thames, but he was too late. Gooding didn't surface again.

CHAPTER TWENTY-SIX

Eloise clutched at her chest as she listened to Benedict's description of his day.

". . . and so I called in the runners and the minister. He has organised for men to drag the Thames, but it flows fast, and the body may never be recovered."

Eloise shook her head. "Gooding—of all people. He certainly gave off quite a different impression. I assume he was dallying with Sarah, and John was blackmailing him, but what reason did he have to kill Bartholomew Jones?"

"We may never know. I am sure the minister will have questions, but I have achieved what I set out to do."

"What about Bellingham and Sir Frederick?"

"I should imagine they will be delighted that they don't have to pay back their debt. There were no proper business records kept."

"I am not at all surprised about Sir Frederick, but I am taken aback that Bellingham would be reduced to borrowing funds."

Benedict shrugged. "I hear it is expensive to be a politician. But enough of them; I have something else occupying my mind."

His eyes were burning, trapping her gaze, and he had moved closer to stand a hair's breadth from her. He reached out and, taking her hand in his, gently rubbed his thumb across her palm. "We will be married soon, and I find I cannot wait. I want you as my wife and in my bed. I want you near me during the day and even closer at night. I ache for you." He paused and cleared his throat. "I love you."

He stopped, as if surprised that he had spoken aloud. The words lifted into the air and took her breath. Her heart leapt, and warm joy spread through every part of her. He stood still, suddenly looking boyish and unsure.

She closed the small gap between them and boldly placed her arms around his neck, pulling his head towards her, and whispered, "I love you too. I never desired such a connection, but I am very glad we have found each other. I am complete with you, as if a part of me I didn't know was missing has been found and replaced, making me whole." She paused momentarily before her words rushed out, unbidden. "If I am to follow my mother's steps then so be it."

His arms held her tight, and he rested his forehead on hers. "Don't worry. We are our own people and will follow a new path. I will go soon, but remember that from tomorrow onwards you will never be without me."

* * *

For Eloise, the night before her wedding was a magical affair. Her aunt had organised a gathering of family and close friends. A genteel evening of jovial conversations and light refreshments whilst those closest to the betrothed couple could take time to wish them well before the next day's crowded society wedding. Benedict's mother and sisters had arrived from the country and were effusive in their welcome of her to their family, and his mother seemed relieved that her son was to marry and she herself could pass on the reins of looking after the not-inconsiderable households of his estates.

Eloise needed a moment alone to settle her thoughts and relish in these new-found emotions. Benedict was in danger of becoming her life, and she found she did not mind this at all.

They were safe now. Gooding was undoubtedly dead, although his body had not been found.

As Eloise mused, she walked along the balustrade of the terrace, the scent of roses delicately fragrancing the night air. Tomorrow she would be the Countess of Rothsea; more importantly, she would be Benedict's wife. A shiver of anticipation ran through her, and she pulled her light wrap tighter round her shoulders.

As she neared the far end of the terrace, she saw Bellingham coming towards her up the shallow stairs that led into the garden and the streets beyond. She stopped in surprise, and it took her a moment to find her voice. "Good evening, my lord. I did not see you inside earlier and did not know you were invited."

He climbed another step towards her. "I am afraid that

His Grace did not see fit to invite me. That, however, will not be the situation in the future. Yes, I rather think my stock is going to rise with Westbury—and Parliament—when I am part of your family."

He was talking gibberish. The surrounding town houses cast dense shadows. and as Bellingham slowly climbed the shallow steps, darkness swept across his face, making it almost impossible to read his expression. Almost, but not quite. The hairs on her arm raised and her skin puckered and tingled, like a prescient warning, and suddenly she did not feel comfortable in the slightest. She was overcome with a compulsion to draw back, to flee.

Bellingham must have sensed her imminent flight, for a dramatic change came over him; his posture straightened, his stance hardened. Suddenly, there was an air of menace as he advanced towards her.

Eloise's eyes widened in fear; she was sure he meant to harm her. She turned, and ran toward the house. She took no more than two steps before a large hand grabbed her wrist and swung her around. As she opened her mouth to let loose a scream, her hair was pulled roughly from behind and a cloth placed firmly across her mouth and tied tight. She instinctively kicked back against her assailant, but her flimsy evening slippers were no match for her attacker. Her heart pounded, the beat erratic as she struggled to escape. Her head was spinning, she could no longer think clearly, as nausea rose and light-headedness blurred her vision and took her senses. The last she heard was "Quick, man, grab her feet and help me carry her" before oblivion came and she knew no more.

* * *

Benedict was in the drawing room, surrounded by existing and soon-to-be relatives and involved in a discussion with Westbury on the plans for the wedding trip. "I have arranged to take Eloise to a small estate I own in the north. The house sits atop a cliff and has views over the coast. It will, I hope, provide a relaxed start to our life together.

Westbury looked around at the guests and, seemingly satisfied that they would not be overheard, murmured, "I have heard no gossip surrounding Gooding, so the powers that be must have kept a lid on the situation. It is only right. His family should not suffer for his wrongs."

"I agree. Gooding's father has agreed to settle a generous sum of money on Jones' widow, so at least she will be in a position to maintain her lifestyle."

"The weasel knew you were investigating Jones' death and shot at you on my land. He was a cunning devil."

"Not cunning enough."

Before either man could speak further, Higgins appeared at their side and proffered a silver salver. On it lay a folded note with "Rothsea" inscribed across the front in a bold, black scrawl.

Higgins bent closer and whispered, "Said it was of the utmost urgency, my lord." Blood drained from Benedict's face as he read the note.

Join me outside. Eloise has been abducted. Hurry. Strathleven.

The words blurred in front of his eyes as an icy fist clutched at his heart. "Damnation, this cannot be. Come; we must hurry."

He passed the note to Westbury and headed into the hallway. He knew without looking that Westbury would follow him.

"What is this about?" His friend's voice was strained.

"I arranged for some of my grooms and footmen to keep an eye on the house. I wanted the wedding to go smoothly and thought it best to take precautions."

The huge double doors were open, and Strathleven was already seated atop his horse and held in his hands the reins to Benedict's black stallion.

"What the hell has happened? Where is Eloise? And how are you involved?" As he spoke, Benedict took the reins and mounted his horse.

"I had just arrived at Westbury's stables when I heard a commotion. Two men bundled a woman into a coach, and it immediately took off. I caught a glimpse of her. It was Eloise. Several of your men were agitated, and said you'd put them on alert in case something untoward happened. Two of them followed the coach and asked that I update you. They had readied your horse."

"Who took her?" The words tumbled over each other. He had no time to waste.

"I saw him clearly. It was Bellingham."

Benedict reared back. "I had no idea he was enamoured of Eloise, certainly not to the extent that he would take such drastic steps."

Westbury's face was ashen as he slowly shook his head. "He came to me two days ago. Said he had high regard for Eloise and that he had hoped his suit would have found favour with me at Huntley. Said that," here he flicked a quick glance at Benedict, "should Eloise's marriage not take place for some reason, then he hoped I would consider his standing offer for Eloise's hand. He was affable, and I found nothing untoward in his comments. The wedding is set, so he could have had no expectations. However, I did not want Bellingham to have false hopes, so I told him, clearly, that I did not think he and Eloise would suit, so my approval would not be forthcoming."

Realisation dawned on all three faces, and Benedict was the first to speak. "He knew all hope was gone, and his only option was to abduct Eloise."

At that, pounding footsteps rounded the corner, and Benedict recognised the breathless boy as one of his servants. "M'lord, we heard him. The gent told the coachman to follow the Great North Road."

"Thank you, Sam." In a flash, Benedict had turned his horse around and addressed Westbury.

"I shall bring Eloise back. Can you keep things quiet here?"

"Of course. I shall say you have gone to ensure all is in order with the travel arrangements for tomorrow and that Eloise is fatigued and has quietly retired for the evening." His voice cracked. "Bring her home to us."

Their pained eyes met, and a solemn oath was sworn—Benedict would bring her back, but not for Westbury. For himself. He could not find it in him to live without Eloise by his side.

CHAPTER TWENTY-SEVEN

The jolting motion of the ancient travel carriage roused Eloise from her deep, black sleep. She awakened with a jolt as the wheels unerringly found each and every rut in the road.

It took a moment for total recollection to slam into her, and her breath quickened as she realised her predicament. Her head was thick, heavy. Had she fainted? There was no time to waste in trying to remember how she had got here. She had to take stock of her situation. She lay on her side, the threadbare velvet seat cushions rough against her cheeks. Her hands, which were resting to the front of her, were tied with a coarse rope, looped tightly around her wrists. A sturdy cloth covered her mouth and, tied tight, rendered her mute.

Her feet, still shod in her evening slippers, were laid upon the seat, her ankles tied together with the same rough twine.

"Ah, you're awake. Excellent. Stop the coach, Briggs."

Bellingham, still astride his horse, peered in through the carriage window. The coach slowly drew to a halt as Bellingham dismounted and tied his horse to the carriage. Opening the door, he climbed inside. Grabbing her by the arms, he raised her to a sitting position, before removing the gag from her mouth. She instinctively drew back, shrugging his hands away with a jerk of her shoulder. She coughed and spluttered before licking her parched lips. Bellingham sat opposite her. He leaned back against the squabs, legs nonchalantly stretched in front of him, his smile not reaching his eyes. His knuckles rapped the roof of the coach, and it slowly moved on.

"Pardon my indelicacy, but I trust you are none the worse for your little fainting episode, my dear. We are on our way and will soon leave London far behind us."

"Where are you taking me?" Her tone was haughty, and her disgust of him was unhidden in her direct gaze.

"Why, I am taking my affianced bride to Gretna Green, where we shall be married, and from that moment on I shall be welcomed into Westbury's family."

"You are insane. My uncle and Rothsea will come after me."

Bellingham seemed to consider her words.

"Westbury? Perhaps, but I doubt it. He will know you are ruined as you've been alone in my company without adequate chaperonage. Your uncle will simply want the situation righted and scandal averted."

As Eloise looked on in horror, Bellingham continued, "As for Rothsea, well, he won't want a countess with a ruined reputation—God only knows he doesn't need your money. No, my dear, I am your only salvation, the saviour of your uncle's spotless reputation, and Rothsea, well, Rothsea gets to live. I tried hard enough to kill him, but the damned man is charmed."

"You, you monster—you tried to kill Benedict? Why would you attempt such a thing?"

Bellingham's smile was not quite human and a little feral as he grinned. "I have the potential to be the greatest prime minister this country has even known. However, what I do not have is sufficient money. And money is what it takes to buy votes, to soothe egos and to gain—and maintain—the highest position in this land. I have made some unfortunate financial errors and do not have enough funds for what I want to achieve. And that is where you come into the equation. Well-connected, beautiful and refined, you would have made an ideal politician's wife. But those aren't your main attractions, are they, my dear? No, I am afraid the attraction of your beauty pales in comparison to the lure of your fortune. And it is that fortune that I need to make all my dreams come true."

Eloise was aghast. "You, my lord, are mad, completely and utterly mad. You would stoop to kill a man, for money, solely to help you achieve your own pathetic ambitions. You disgust me."

Bellingham laughed. "I am afraid that bothers me not, my dear girl. Once we are married, your fortune will be mine, and I could not care less what you do after that. Well, I suppose I do care that you do not embarrass me and my reputation. Perhaps an unfortunate accident will befall you." His gaze insolently raked her from head to toe. "I shall, of course, insist on an heir, but, as we discussed previously, I would rather wait to see if Rothsea has already planted your belly."

Eloise recoiled at his base comment.

His laugh was more a snort. "Don't play the innocent. Rothsea acts like a randy dog when around you, and you flush like a bitch in heat."

Before Eloise could retaliate, there was a loud thud at the back of the coach and the sound of heavy scrambling across the roof. Grabbing a pistol from the deep pocket of his cape, Bellingham moved across the carriage to sit beside Eloise, the barrel pointed at her temple. "I fear I may have been wrong, my dear. I have a dreadful feeling that someone has indeed come to try and rescue you."

His voice was calm and perfectly civil, and that chilled her all the more.

The crack of pistols discharging caught their attention. The neighing of horses was accompanied by heavy thuds.

Bellingham smirked. "Those outriders were worth every penny. It was their shooting, and not their riding, that I paid for."

A muffled scream came from the front of the coach, its source becoming apparent as a heavy body tumbled past the carriage window.

"Briggs!" shouted Bellingham, a look of startled horror on his face as the coachman disappeared from sight. A voice shouted, "Whoa!" and the coach ground to a halt.

A deep, familiar voice broke the silence. "Well, whatever you paid these men, it was a damned sight too much."

"Benedict." Eloise's eyes filled with tears of joy. He had come for her. Benedict opened the carriage door, his relief evident. She answered the unspoken question in his steady gaze. "I am unhurt, my lord."

Bellingham laughed, a mocking sound. "That's as may be, but I've travelled in this coach with dear Eloise, alone, since we left Mayfair. She is ruined in society's eyes."

Benedict snorted. "We've had you followed since the off. You've ridden outside all the way and only got in the coach mere minutes before we apprehended you." Benedict raised his voice and called, "Strathleven, contain those men and make sure I am not disturbed."

Bellingham seemed distracted by this comment, and Eloise took the opportunity to warn Benedict. "It was Bellingham who tried to kill you. He admitted it."

Benedict tilted his head to one side. "Now why would you do that? I was shot at before I even arrived at Huntley, certainly long before you could see me as a rival."

Eloise gasped as all the pieces fell together, and she knew from Benedict's widened eyes that they made the connection at the same time. It hadn't been Gooding. Bellingham's crimes were far greater than kidnap. He was the murderer.

* * *

Benedict cocked his pistol before a heartbeat had passed. "It has to be you who killed Bartholomew Jones. You found out I was on my way to Huntley and looking into his murder, so you tried to get rid of me. Why? Why would you take someone's life? And Sarah and John? What was worth their dying?"

"This one, of course." He pulled Eloise across the

front of his body, his pistol still tight against her head.

Eloise's eyes widened and her mouth dropped open. She snapped it shut as the fire of fury replaced shock. "You utter swine. Don't lay your nefarious deeds at my door. Explain yourself."

Bellingham smirked, and Benedict wanted to punch the smile right off his face. "Yes, explain yourself. Gooding was a weasel who drove men to suicide, but you are a murderer."

Bellingham snarled. "A murderer of what? A low-life moneylender, a man who had the education to gain a respectable occupation but sought to earn coin from the misfortune and bad luck of others? A slatternly country girl? And the old fool who sought to make capital from seeing us together? Christ, she was deluded enough to believe I'd set her up, even make it a permanent arrangement. Gooding introduced me to Sarah. I am sure he would eventually have sought to blackmail me about my involvement with her. He was the one who put me onto Bartholomew Jones. I'd overindulged and was bemoaning my lack of available cash. It all goes back to Gooding."

"Yet you are the one to blame." Benedict flicked his eyes to the pistol held at Eloise's head. His palms were moist and his senses on overdrive. He had to ensure she wasn't harmed.

"Let her go. This is between us. Let us deal with this as gentlemen."

Bellingham's look of mock regret was accompanied by honeyed words. "Oh, I am so very sorry, but Eloise stays here. We are to be married, and I am sure Westbury will want any of my, shall we say . . . peccadillos . . . kept quiet. I hear he is a man who dislikes scandal."

"What did you hope to achieve? If it was, as I suspect, to get your hands on Eloise's fortune, it wouldn't have worked. You'd have got nothing."

"She's an heiress. I would have been her husband; ergo I would have controlled her fortune." Bellingham spoke slowly, as if Benedict were dull-witted.

Benedict let a long, slow smile cross his face. "Eloise is not yet twenty-one. If you had made it to Gretna, you would have married Eloise immediately. Yes?"

Bellingham furrowed his brow. "Yes, of course."

"So you'd have married Eloise when she was still twenty. Yes?"

Bellingham was patently losing patience. "I said yes, you fool."

"You may be interested to know that the late Viscount Barchester's will stated that Eloise's guardian, the Duke of Westbury, could control who she married until she was twenty-one. If she married before that age, without Westbury's prior written permission, then her entire fortune, apart from a small but respectable annual stipend, would automatically pass to her younger brother. So you'd have a wife, but no fortune."

If the situation weren't so dire, for Eloise still had a gun pressed against her head, Benedict would have laughed at the look of sheer horror dawning on Bellingham's face.

Face reddened with rage, Bellingham swung the pistol butt against Eloise's head. Her agonised cry ripped at Benedict's core, and he leapt on top of Bellingham, pushing Eloise off the seat and towards the open carriage door. "Go! Get out."

He heard her stumble as she fell out of the carriage, her feet tied together. She would be safe with Strathleven and his grooms. He was atop Bellingham, his arm muscles bunched and corded as he strained to hold Bellingham's pistol arm trapped against the squabs. Bellingham pushed against him, rendering his pistol ineffective as his own arm flailed. Bellingham drew back his head and, in a base and unexpected move, launched forward, smashing his forehead against Benedict's skull. He released his hold on Bellingham and fell to the floor, momentarily blinded by pain. His ribs already ached from his encounter with Gooding, and it took him a moment to gain his senses, which was a shade too late.

Bellingham was on top of him, crushing him. Benedict pushed back with all his strength, forcing Bellingham's pistol arm away from him. Where was his own pistol? He looked from side to side and saw the glint of the metallic barrel under the seat to his right. He reached out, wasn't close enough; he was a fingertip away from touching it. He rocked his body from side to side; all the while Bellingham held fast, his face purple, veins popping as he struggled to keep a tight grip. Benedict was inching closer, closer, and made a herculean effort to stretch until he feared his shoulder would dislocate. He touched it and flicked the pistol closer with his fingertips. Before he could grab it, Bellingham kicked out, and the pistol flew back into the corner. His manic laugh seemed to echo in the confined space. "Nice try, but not good enough. I tire of you."

"You idiot. Strathleven is outside, and he will see you hang for this."

"I think not. We still have the matter of Miss Eloise to deal with. Consider the scandal. Kidnapped and two suitors dead. No, all will be well. But I need you out of my way. Eloise will have no one to turn to with you gone and her uncle anxious to avoid any taint on his family name."

Bellingham moved closer still, his pistol pressed tight against Benedict's chest. A deathly click accompanied the hammer being cocked. Benedict's mouth was dry as he looked into Bellingham's crazed eyes. The man was surely unstable. He had to make one last try.

* * *

Eloise had fallen onto the ground in a heap. She quickly looked around and saw several men were lying face down under a tree, Strathleven's pistol pointed at them. Two other men, presumably grooms, stood over them, keeping watch. A third groom rushed towards her and drew a sharp blade that he used to slice open the cords that bound her wrists and ankles. With the aid of the groom's arm she rose to her feet, wincing. Her head ached with a pulsating, red-hot pain. Strathleven kept his eyes on the men but called out to her. "Retreat to that fallen tree stump and sit, please. You'll be away from the carriage but still in my line of vision."

She picked up her skirts and did as she was bidden. Her heart thundered as fear pulsed through her entire being. *Please, God, let Benedict be all right. Please.*

Her gaze was fixed on the carriage as it shook and shuddered. Suddenly, they heard a sharp report from inside the carriage, the smell of gunpowder heavy in the air.

She rose, clutched a shaking hand to her chest and held her breath for what seemed like an age, but it was mere seconds before the tall figure of Benedict emerged. He was dishevelled but seemed unhurt.

"Bellingham's pistol went off, which was unfortunate, for it was pointing towards his heart at the time. We shall say he was attacked by brigands on the road."

Eloise barely heard the words as, elated, she ran towards him. Benedict opened his arms wide and caught her as she leapt into his embrace, into a new life.

* * *

Benedict pulled her flush against his body, uncaring of Strathleven and the grooms. He breathed in the scent of her hair, cradling her in his arms and softly stroking the skin at the nape of her neck.

"Eloise." Her name came out as a sigh, Benedict's voice husky with emotion as his breath hitched. "I thought I had lost you. I couldn't bear it." He pulled back and held her away from him so she could see the truth in his eyes. "I don't want a comfortable wife, Eloise. I want passion and desire and, most of all, I want love—and all of that is what I have found with you. I adore you and love you, and I will never have enough of telling you so."

Eloise's eyes filled with tears. "I love you so very, very much."

Benedict bent his head and, cupping Eloise's face with his hands, covered her mouth with his in a long, slow kiss. True, passion was always there—at this moment it was lying beneath the surface—but that was not what this kiss was all about, for it was all about love.

CHAPTER TWENTY-EIGHT

The next day dawned bright with the welcome promise of summer sun. Eloise had tumbled into bed as soon as Benedict had delivered her to her anxious family, and her eyes had closed in blessed relief.

Her heart thudded in time to the organ music as she took her uncle's arm and slowly walked down the aisle towards her groom who waited for her at the altar, Strathleven by his side. Benedict had turned as the first notes filled the air, and Eloise smiled in joy at the look of appreciation on his face. The dressmaker had outdone herself, and Eloise shimmered in her silvered dress, her shoulders covered with a pale blue half-cape as she walked towards her future.

When they arrived at the altar, her uncle released her arm and passed her hand to Benedict, who wrapped both his hands around hers and squeezed gently, his eyes fixed on her. Her uncle bent, kissed her on the cheek and whispered, "Be happy, my darling."

"Dearly beloved . . ." The minister's words floated over, above and around her as she recited the words of promise instinctively, binding her to Benedict for their lifetime together. She was caught in Benedict's gaze and stared into the loving eyes of the man to whom she was giving herself and her future.

"I now declare you man and wife."

* * *

The wedding breakfast sped past in a flurry of congratulations as Eloise and Benedict moved amongst their guests. Not an hour had passed before Benedict bent and whispered, "If we don't leave now, they will keep us talking forever, and I, for one, am anxious to begin our life together. Let us go home."

She was happy to agree. Her belongings had been moved to Benedict's town house earlier that morning, and it was strange to know that tonight she would sleep in a new bedroom with her new husband by her side. She shivered, the excitement mixed with trepidation.

She bathed in scented water, and Anna brushed out her hair with long, soothing strokes. Neither of which settled her emotions or nerves, which ricocheted from excitement to dread and back again. She ran a hand across the front of her nightgown, a fiery blush burning her cheeks. The pink-tinged aureoles of her breasts were visible through the translucent material, and when she moved the split skirt flashed the length of her legs and showed them to advantage. The flimsy gown and sheer peignoir had been laid out on her bed with a note that proclaimed them a present from her husband. Would he like what he saw? Would she have the courage to enter wholeheartedly into this marriage?

She heard a clicking sound behind her and quickly turned. A door she hadn't noticed was set into the far wall, and Benedict filled the frame. A startled Anna scurried out as he advanced into the room. Her breath caught in her throat as time slowed. He wore a dark red silk dressing gown and, dear God, probably little else. His calves were bare, as were his feet. She stared at the light sprinkling of hairs visible where his robe crossed over his chest. Her heart flipped and her stomach lurched.

"Have you seen your fill?" His voice was a deep rumble, his face serious and his gaze intent.

She took a deep breath. "No, I don't believe I have."

He smiled. "I have the remedy for that. Come here." He reached out and enclosed her hand with his, and a tremor shot through her as she willingly moved into his arms, where she belonged. She was home, in more ways than one.

Epilogue
6 weeks later

Eloise, Countess of Rothsea, blinked sleepily as she sat up in bed and stretched luxuriously, her raised arms drawing her sheer lawn nightdress taut over her breasts, much to the delight of her husband who had just walked into their suite.

Benedict lifted one eyebrow in appreciation as he bent to place a soft kiss on the top of his bride's head. "Well, my dear, that is a fine sight to greet me. I look forward to more of this, every day for the rest of my life."

He was already dressed for the day and wearing a loose white shirt tucked into perfectly tailored beige riding breeches. A carelessly tied cravat completed the look. "You are going riding?"

"Yes. I waited to see if you would care to join me."

Benedict absently nodded as he sorted through their mail, and stopped as he came upon an embossed envelope. "This is in my mother's hand. Look."

The usually elegant penmanship looked careless and, surprisingly, the words "most, most urgent" were scrawled all along the top. "Benedict, my love. What is the matter?"

Benedict slowly shook his head, as he walked to the desk and used the paperknife to open the letter. Eloise watched in alarm as Benedict's eyes quickly scanned the one page letter, which he re-read and sank onto the edge of the bed. Eloise pushed the covers back and scrambled towards him. "What is it?"

"My mother. She writes that we must come home as soon as possible. Her words are garbled and I can barely make sense of them but it seems that Beth has caused a rumpus, Maddie is to blame and – Dear God."

"What?"

"and – Your Uncle – Westbury – is embroiled in a scandal to top all scandals."

THE END

<<<<>>>>

ABOUT THE AUTHOR

Julia Hardy is my pen-name for my romance novels. In my other life I am crime thriller writer Kelly Clayton.

I live in the Channel Island of Jersey with my husband and several cats.

An avid storyteller, I've been writing for over twenty years. This is my debut romantic historical fiction.

If you have enjoyed reading Fortune's Hostage, please consider leaving a review on Amazon. It really helps other readers discover authors, who may be new to them.

I would be immensely grateful for your taking the time to do so.

You can find me at www.kellyclaytonbooks.com for information on my books, writing and my reading blog.

Printed in Great Britain
by Amazon

39978430R00170